AND
THE
TREES
CREPT
IN

AND THE TREES CREPT IN

DAWN KURTAGICH

(L)(B)

Little, Brown and Company

New York   Boston

Little, Brown and Company

Hachette Book Group
1290 Avenue of the Americas, New York, NY 10104
Visit us at lb-teens.com

Little, Brown and Company is a division of Hachette Book Group, Inc.
The Little, Brown name and logo are trademarks of Hachette Book Group, Inc.

First Edition: September 2016

A terrifying horror novel about two sisters trapped in a cursed manor, with a man with no eyes and woods that are creeping closer.

Library of Congress Cataloging-in-Publication Data

Names: Kurtagich, Dawn, author.
Title: And the trees crept in / by Dawn Kurtagich.
Description: First edition. | New York ; Boston : Little, Brown and Company, 2016. | Summary: Sisters Silla, seventeen, and Nori, four, are trapped in their aunt's cursed manor and can only escape with the help of a mysterious boy.
Identifiers: LCCN 2015049762| ISBN 9780316298704 (hardback) | ISBN 9780316298698 (ebook) | ISBN 9780316298735 (library edition ebook)
Subjects: | CYAC: Blessing and cursing—Fiction. | Supernatural—Fiction. | Sisters—Fiction. | Aunts—Fiction. | Mutism—Fiction. | Horror stories. | BISAC: JUVENILE FICTION / Family / Siblings. | JUVENILE FICTION / Family / Orphans & Foster Homes. | JUVENILE FICTION / Horror & Ghost Stories. | JUVENILE FICTION / Social Issues / Depression & Mental Illness.
Classification: LCC PZ7.1.K877 And 2016 | DDC [Fic]—dc23
LC record available at https://lccn.loc.gov/2015049762

10 9 8 7 6 5 4 3 2 1

RRD-C

Printed in the United States of America

414B

∞

This is the way the world ends.
Not with a bang but a whimper.

—T. S. ELIOT

There
Is a
Reason
For
Everything

Three Little Girls
in the Wood

1980: Catherine, the tallest and wisest of the girls, had the idea first, but that fact would soon be forgotten. Because the idea was a little like a drop of ink in water, it spread quickly, dissipating into each of the little girls in turn, until none of them could say for certain who had thought it up in the first place.

Anne, the youngest, was the keenest of the three, desperate for their idea to take shape and be made real.

Pamela was a little scared, and didn't want to go into the woods at all, but she would never say so. She followed the eldest and the youngest, like she always did, and was a buffer between the two. She really ought to have stopped the whole palaver, but she was swept along with the tide, a pebble skidding along the bottom of the riverbed.

The three little girls gathered in the wood, knelt down in front of the biggest alder tree, and pulled from their baskets the things they would need to make a protector:

1. The basic materials for a rag doll. Really, it was just a stuffed head and a flap of material for the body. Genderless and featureless. (Anne was easily distracted.)

2. Twine

3. A needle

4. Strips of cloth (The only color left in Mother's old store of material was black, so there was a lot of shadow in the basket.)

5. Buttons (for eyes)

6. Clay

7. Candles and a box of matches

It was Anne who took the lead, even though she was the youngest. She gripped her rag doll between her fingers and then lit the candle very carefully. She lifted the open body of the thing and stuffed it full of clay.

"God made Adam out of clay," she said. "So this will give our protector life."

It was messy work, but Catherine and Pammy were nodding their approval, so she kept stuffing and pushing until the doll was full. Then she sewed him up—rather clumsily, for she really did get bored very quickly in her sewing lessons—and put him down next to the candle. She had managed to sew him two *very* long, thin legs.

"Now his eyes," Catherine said. "Give him eyes." This seemed important.

Anne groaned, so easily bored of her own project. "I'm sick of sewing. Can't we play hide-and-seek?"

"You have to put clothes on him, at least," Pammy complained. "Otherwise he'll be naked."

"Fine, then. Clothes—quickly—but afterward I'm playing. This is dumb, anyway."

Cath sighed. "You wanted to do it in the first place!"

Anne shrugged, and as she worked, Pammy said, "We summon a protector out of Python Wood. We summon thee! Let him be fiercely terrifying to any who try to harm us. Let him be tall, taller than the tallest tree. We summon thee! We—"

"Oh, shush!" Catherine said, scowling.

Anne gave their protector clothes of a kind, made from strips of black, kissed his head, then dropped him heedlessly in the mud, and dashed off, back to La Baume. Pammy followed.

Catherine was left to gather up the remnants of their half-finished ritual. When she picked up the doll, she was very disturbed, very disturbed indeed, to see that he had no eyes. And also that Anne's clumsy needlework had made him look like he was scowling, and draped all in shadows. She pulled off the excess cloth, leaving only the clumsy black suit behind, but some-how that was even worse!

She peered closer, looking at his legs. His two long, gnarly legs...

They looked like *roots*.

BOOK 1:
Sanguinem Terrae

Two little girls ran away
from the dark and stormy city.
they happened upon a manor one day
and the lady inside took pity.
in they flew and perched quite fine
and ate all but one juicy berry.
the little girls slept and sang and smiled
and the memories: they vowed to bury.

THREE

PRETTY LITTLE TRAP

Nori keeps asking me where I'm going, what I'm doing, where Mam is.

It's so dark, Silla.

Do you have a biscuit, Silla?

Where are we, Silla?

Why are you crying, Silla?

I want to tell her to shut that trap hole, but what bloody good would that do? Her words are in her hands and I can't silence those.

I lift my hands and tell her. *Quiet like a mouse, remember?*

I wasn't crying, I think.

She grins. *Mousy, mousy, mouse. Squeak!*

We trudge on.

Ω

After a while, she gets tired. I lift her onto my back. Her good arm strangles me, trying to hold tight. I grit my teeth and trudge on.

Ω

My feet will rot. Clean away, they will. The days of mud have started to waterlog the flesh, swelling it to twice the size it should be, cracking, soggy, raw.

My foot skin will flop off soon.

I can feel it.

I trudge on.

Ω

The manor is the color of *blood*.

I drag Nori by the arm, through the mud, the last few feet. The rain has started hard, but at least we are cleaner. I drop her hand, thinking, *I hope you're not dead,* and stare up at the manor. It's the kind of big that makes you smell cakes and tea, see sugar lumps and silver tongs to lift them with. But the door is old. Paint flaking and peeling off like pencil shavings, the wood swollen by years of hard winters. The shabbiness of it gives me the backbone to lift the cast-iron knocker.

KNOCK. KNOCK. KNOCK.

It echoes beyond the door.

Seems like a bad idea at first; I want to run away. Hear Mam's voice telling me that Auntie Cath is *circling the loom, Silla darling.* Only Nori is lying in the mud, rain pounding down with her completely oblivious, so I set my teeth and I pound again.

Let. *Bang.*

Me. *Bang.*

In. *Bang.*

The door opens a crack. A thin, weathered face with large, sunken eyes peers out.

"No thank you. I don't buy anything—"

Funny how she seems to freeze when she realizes. When she sees.

"Presilla?"

I nod, once.

The door widens then, like a book opening on the first chapter, and there she is, standing in the gap to a warm, dry place, stunned like she just saw a giraffe doing backflips in a tutu. I can see her wanting to ask all kinds of questions, but her brain short-circuits with all of them rushing at her, and all that comes out is:

"Oh my God. Oh, you poor thing. Why...why are you here?"

I turn away to get Nori and she must think I'm leaving 'cause she reaches out a hand and says, "Wait!" like *she's* the one desperate for us to come muddying up her carpet and not the other way around. "I didn't mean..." She trails off when she spots the lump that is Nori, in the mud, dead asleep.

"Oh my God! Is that—is it—"

I haul my little sister up and stagger a little. The woman—Cath—gapes at me but lets me pass. I drag Nori through and dump her on the floor just inside. The dark beams of wood that run the length of the entrance hall look older than Cath herself.

Cath shuts the door, leaning her head against it for a good half minute before she turns around. I get that. Needing a moment to gather strength. Though, when she *does* turn and see us, it's all too much, and she slides down the door onto her bum and stares at us completely bewildered.

"Presilla...Eleanor..."

"It's Silla now," I tell her. "And Nori, she's called."

"Silla, yes. Nori. Okay."

"Hello, Aunt. We've come to live with you."

Ω

1

la baume

Welcome home,
warm and whole
to open arms
and healing balms
welcome child,
welcome, child.

Cath wore a blue-and-yellow kimono-style dressing gown, wild hair hovering around her shoulders like a mane. She stared at me with horror when Nori's head thumped on the lip of the door as I dragged her inside. She flinched and reached forward like she wanted to lift Nori up into her arms. She didn't, instead standing back, hand over her mouth.

"My goodness, oh dear." She took a breath and straightened her shoulders. "I'll get a blanket." She turned away, and then hurried back. "Oh, dear. She can't come into the house dripping like that." Cath leaned forward and lifted Nori's shirt up to pull it over her head.

I pushed her away. "Leave it."

She blinked at me.

I forced a smile. "I can do it."

"Okay. I'll bring two blankets and we can get you both cleaned up and warm."

She hurried off, her footsteps echoing through a house draped in shadow. I sat down beside Nori and turned her over, resting her head in my lap. She was fast asleep, so I leaned down and kissed the top of her head.

"We found it. We found the jewel."

I stared around me, taking in the entrance hall. So dark. So empty. Safe. We were safe at last.

Ω

The tea was good, but that was about it. It was a touch snooty, maybe, with weird flavors and all—no Tetley here—but that was expected in a place like this. A *manor* like this. That's where my amazement stopped.

This wasn't so much a manor as a skeleton.

Where were all the baroque antiques? The oil paintings of stern, proud old men, and the string of ancestors in suits of armor? Wasn't there supposed to be a plethora of finery and riches? I looked around with a sinking feeling in the pit of my stomach and took another sip of fancy tea.

I was still wondering about the bloody color of the manor, to be honest. Made Mam's voice pop into my head uninvited. *Crazy Cath. Circling the loom.*

Nori was dead noisy when she ate, for someone who couldn't talk to save her life.

"Shut your mouth, would you?" I muttered.

Sweary word, mouth's a turd. She made quick work of the signs, despite the jam gooing up her fingers.

"Yeah, yeah, yeah."

I no longer saw questions in her eyes, which was nice. The quiet was nice. But she trusted me when I didn't have a clue or a plan, and that really wasn't.

"So," said Cath, coming into the room with a new pot of tea. "What's happened?"

I shrugged.

(Crazy) Aunt Cath poured more tea. "Take it from the beginning. Because, I have to tell you, the Pamela I knew wouldn't have let you come here. Not in a million years. And I would never have..." She laughed like it was a joke, a little game between her and her sister. But I could tell the laugh was covering up something else entirely. "I sent letters asking how you were. We both agreed never to let you...Well. Here you are." She laughed again, shaking her head, and I noticed that her hair, though long and quite wild, was the warm color of wheat at sunset. Just like Nori's. Just like Mam's before it faded into a pale gray. But her face was off somehow. A little too old.

I got my looks from my father (lucky me), which meant I was like the sunspot after you looked too closely at the sun. Black hair, black eyes, too-white skin. A walking cliché.

Cath sat down at the table, her face stilling when she spotted our bag dripping in the corner. "I see. Well. Well, yes. You weren't joking about staying."

"He got bad," I said, and it's all I intended to say.

It was enough. Cath's expression soured, then she nodded. "I'm glad you're here, anyway. I'll have to make arrangements, I suppose. School, clothing..." For a moment, she seemed overwhelmed.

"Leave it to me," I said, even though I wanted to let the silence draw out to infinity so I could see when it imploded.

The lights flickered at the same moment I saw the relief on her face; she didn't know me yet. Nori didn't go to school, and I didn't plan on going back either.

"Nori and I can share a room, too," I added.

"Nonsense! That's one thing I'm *not* worried about. Have you seen the size of La Baume?"

I frowned.

"The manor," she explained. "That's what it's called. Did Pamela never say?"

I took a sip of tea.

"Hm." Cath put her hands into her lap. "I don't suppose I'm surprised that Pamela didn't tell you what it was called. Neither of us much liked it here growing up."

Now that *was* a surprise. Mam always said Cath was born to stay in the "blood manor." And now I knew what she meant by blood. I suddenly felt like there was a lot I didn't know. I wasn't sure I really wanted to. Not then.

Cath looked into her tea and frowned. "Why did you come here? He'll never let you leave."

"What?"

But Cath drank all the steaming tea in her cup and smiled at Nori, who had stopped eating and was watching my face closely. I forced a smile and signed, Not *hungry, little bug? I'll have it, then!* And I reached for her food.

Her mouth opened gruesomely wide, revealing the gaps in her teeth where Dad had knocked them out, and she grabbed the scone and jam with her good arm. The twisted one, too small, too bent, jiggled rigidly at her side.

Cath and I both watched Nori stuffing jam scones and biscuits into her mouth. With that smile on her face, Cath didn't seem to half mind.

I, on the other hand, thought I might vomit.

He'll never let you leave.

I thought I knew what she meant. My bones shook with the

idea of my father staking out the woods, ready to drag us back to the prison he called home.

Ω

When Aunt Cath said she would get us cleaned up and warm, she meant it. We entered the only room she had made up, and it smelled of sweet vanilla and roses.

It's so big! Nori signed, rushing up and down to look at one object and then another.

"Yeah, right," I said, lugging our bag onto the bed. "A big fat disappointment."

Nori stuck her tongue out at me and continued her exploration. I busied myself pulling out the remnants of our life:

Three shirts each

One pair of ratty jeans each

Six dresses for Nori

Three dresses for me

Underwear

A hairbrush

A hair dryer

My paper

My pen

I carried our clothes, which now seemed meager and pitiful, to the chest of drawers in the corner and reached down to open the top drawer. It was stuck, so I tried the next, and the next, and the *next*.

"Oh for heaven's sake!"

The last, however, gave signs of movement. Putting the clothes on top of the chest, I bent down and tugged on the last drawer, gritting my teeth and muttering my entire range of vehement expletives.

"Come on, you son of a—"

It gave way by three inches, revealing a drawer jam-packed with bric-a-brac. I squinted into the gap and saw feathers, fossils, and Crayola pens, items that had no place in a bedroom.

God almighty.

I kicked the drawer shut with my foot—a little too hard. "Crap! Damn it!"

Nori tugged on my dress.

"Sorry, bug. Just stubbed my toe."

There's something under my bed.

I forced myself not to roll my eyes. Not the monster-waiting-to-get-me bit again. We had played this one out to death.

You're too old for this, I thought. "Let me look," I said.

I bent down and lifted the bed skirt. And there it was. A dusty, flowery chamber pot.

"You have *got* to be kidding me."

What is it?

"You pee in it."

Nori's nose wrinkled.

"My thoughts exactly."

Let's see! I want to see!

I heaved the pot out from under the bed, and we both jumped back. The entire bowl was a dusty network of tunneled cobwebs, so thick we couldn't see the bottom.

"Hell no," I muttered, pushing the thing away from us with my foot into the corner of the room.

I ran to my side of the bed and found another just like it.

Also covered in cobweb tunnels, only mine had torn, revealing the husk of a giant house spider, long dead.

"Bloody hell."

My chamber pot joined Nori's far, far away from us.

I can't sleep if there are spiders in the bed.

"They're gone. Just climb in and sleep, okay? It was a long walk."

I don't remember.

Of course she bloody didn't. She had been sleeping without a care in the world for most of it. I, on the other hand, had felt her full weight, and my body was screaming for rest. Added now to my burning feet: a throbbing toe.

"Go to bed," I muttered, climbing in beside her.

Before I even fell asleep, she was drooling on my chest.

Ω

I snapped awake.

I needed to pee.

Damn. I *really* needed to pee.

Nori had rolled over to her side of the bed. Dead to the world. She would sleep through a tsunami if allowed to.

I squeezed my legs together and shoved my hand in between.

Nonononooooooo—

I was too comfy to get out of bed. The air on my face was an arctic blast, and the idea of pulling my duvet back was cringeworthy. But my bladder constricted, threatening me, and I didn't dare call its bluff.

I left the bedroom on the balls of my feet, leaving the light off for Nori's comfort, but as soon as I was in the hall, my body greeting a glacial wall of frosty air, I felt up and down the walls for a light switch. Nothing.

"Bugger, bugger, *bugger*."

It was *freezing*. Even the floor felt like rough ice under my toes.

I knew that the bathroom was at the end of the hall, but there was no toilet in that room. I had no idea if there even was a toilet here. To say the idea of having to go squat outside was both ridiculous and unappealing at this point was an understatement.

I felt the darkness with my hand; it was as thick as blood pudding. Managing to get to the staircase and down without breaking my neck, I wandered blindly, taking slow and tentative steps, more convinced now than ever that I would just have to go in the middle of the floor in some random part of the house. All around me, the manor creaked and expanded, groaned and sighed.

"You and me both," I muttered.

And then a lantern appeared, and Cath's face behind it.

"Oh, Silla! What are you doing up at a time like this?"

"I...I needed to go to the bathroom. Couldn't find it."

Cath laughed. "Oh, dear, you poor girl! I didn't even think— come, let me show you."

And she chuckled the whole way there. We went into the kitchen, to a room off to the side. A *tiny* room, the size of a wash-closet, with a sink outside on the left-hand wall, oval shaped and more like a small fountain than a faucet.

"Here you go," Cath said, smiling. She left me with the lantern and closed the door.

The room was big enough for the toilet and nothing else. The wallpaper gave me chills: a repeated pattern of a boy drawing water out of a well in a sunny pasture. He was like a cherub with a lamb in his arms—and he looked like he was going to glance up at me and grin at any moment.

I was on the toilet, midstream, when I felt movement in the bowl. At first, I ignored it, but then I felt smoothness, tickling between my legs. I jolted with fright and looked down.

And screamed.

Scales, shining under the lamp, two territorial eyes—cold-blooded and cunning—and a forked tongue, darting out from between my legs.

I screamed and screamed, launching myself off the toilet and slipping in my own urine, which was *still coming,* and scuttling back on my butt like a terrified spider.

The snake just sat there on the rim of the bowl, its head resting. Tongue tasting the air. Eyes watching me. It looked bored.

"What is it?" Cath cried, pulling the door open onto the scene. "Oh, my goodness!" She breathed heavily for a moment, and then smiled. "Look at that! My mother used to tell stories about snakes in the toilets in this place. I never believed her." She laughed and took up the lantern. "Maybe we could keep him, huh? Name him Henry—or Peek-a-Boo!" She chortled some more. "We could let him live in this toilet, and have him as a party joke for guests." Her laugh was intense—*hawhawhawhaw*!—while I lay in pee and stared at the thing and then at her.

"Oh, Silla—are you all right?"

I nodded, unable to speak, for the adrenaline draining from my body.

"He's gone," she said, and he was. "Here," she added, and kicked the lid down. "You finish up."

"I...I'm done."

"All right." She stared at the toilet and shook her head. "Incredible. Do you think we dreamed him up?"

"I hope so," I muttered.

"Well, don't forget to flush." And she turned to leave.

I couldn't find the cistern or the flusher. "I don't..."

Cath popped her head back in. "Oopsy! I forgot." She climbed onto the toilet seat and reached up to the cistern mounted near the ceiling. "It's an old one. Have to flush by pulling the chain."

"What chain?"

"This one." And she grasped a single link in what used to be a full length of chain and pulled down on it. "The only one left," she added with a smile.

As the water drained from the bowl, I could hear the entire house grumbling with the plumbing. It sounded like the manor was eating my waste.

"Time for bed," Cath said, pushing me gently on my lower back, not saying a word about how I was soaking wet—or about the smell.

"Here," she said, holding out the blanket that had been wrapped around her own shoulders. "This is no time to be awake. Straight to bed."

I nodded vaguely, flinching back when she leaned forward. She kept coming, until she had planted a little kiss on my cheek.

"It's so wonderful," she whispered, "to have you here."

She wiped away the kiss in a caress and then turned toward the parlor.

"Good night," she called over her shoulder.

I still had her lantern.

I went up to bed and crawled straight in, not caring for a second that I was sleeping in my own pee or that the lantern was still burning. It was dark, I was freezing, there were snakes, and I didn't feel safe.

But the ghost of her kiss lingered on my cheek, and I closed my eyes with a smile.

Ω

In the morning, Aunt Cath came upstairs with toothbrushes, toothpaste, pads (which she handed to me discreetly, and which I took with a burning face), one of her dresses (for me), and one of her shirts (for Nori). Plus a sash from some other garment for a belt.

"Do you want me to cut it?" Cath asked later, when she saw me in the bathroom, looking in the mirror and tugging on my matted hair.

I looked at her through the reflection and nodded. Somehow, I felt like we had gone through *something* together last night. Something *weird,* but something, together.

"How short?" she asked.

I indicated a line by the side of my cheek.

"Lovely." She gave me a warm smile. "You would look lovely like that. Just like Clara Bow."

"I love her," I said, without thinking.

Cath smiled. "Me too." She heaved a sigh and lifted up the majority of the dreadlock my hair had become over the years. "They don't make actresses like that anymore."

"I liked her in *Wings* and *It.*"

"Two of her best."

She raised the scissors so I could see them in the reflection. "Ready?"

"Very."

When she was done, my hair was cut into a very short bob, the way I had always wanted—à la Clara Bow—and Nori's tangle of curls actually *looked* like curls, rather than a bird's nest.

"Come down when you like," Cath said, putting my dreadlocked hair into her pocket. "I'll have some breakfast ready."

I wiped Nori's face, trying to clear some of the more hard-worn dirt and marker stains, and then turned to look at myself again.

Who is this?

I looked like a girl. I hadn't looked like much of anything in so long.

Ω

Cath had just put three teacups onto the kitchen table, along with warm tea cakes, jam, and butter, when we came in. When she turned to us, her face lit up. "Oh, my dears! Oh, my goodness. You look just like her," she said to Nori, cupping her smile in her hands. She looked at me. "Presilla..."

"Silla now."

She nodded. "Silla, of course. You look—"

"Like him. I know."

"—beautiful. Better than Clara."

I smiled and looked away. I did look like my father. But he was *not* a beautiful person. Black hair. Black eyes. Pasty skin. We were *not* beautiful. That was an impossibility. I felt flawed. But Nori...Nori was perfect. Almost. Her teeth were... bad. And that was *his* fault, too.

Still...Clara Bow. Inside, I glowed.

Cath noticed my stare leveled at the table. Probably noticed my scowl, too. That was my most recognizable feature, and in my opinion, my best. "Yes, come now—eat something. Have tea. You look starved half to death. And, Silla, tell me everything."

I sat down at the table and grabbed a tea cake for Nori. "Eat," I told my sister, and then turned back to Aunt Cath. "Like I said last night: Nothing to tell. He got bad. We had no choice. Mum said this was a safe place."

Aunt Cath's gaze changed. Not for long, but I saw it. It was sharper. "Really?"

I shrugged. "Yeah."

"I'll have to phone her," she muttered, her gaze drifting to the side, her fidgeting hand coming back up to squeeze her bottom lip.

"No! You can't. She's...she's busy." I swallowed. "I mean, he might...get angry."

Cath nodded. "That's true. It's impossible anyway. I cut the phone lines years ago. Couldn't stand all the sales calls. If it's really very important, they'll write or visit. No, I'll simply have to use your cellular phone."

"No phone," I said, glad that this, at least, was true, and took the biggest bite of the tea cake I could manage.

No phone. No one home.

Ω

We were given separate rooms that night—our "forever" rooms, as Cath said with a smile. Mine was too big, too cold, and too empty—not to mention the floor was slanted and crooked in parts.

I had spent years imagining this manor, this magical place where nothing could hurt or upset us. A place of plenty, of light, of riches and luxury. And yet...this place was barren. The wallpaper hung loose, old and peeling, the furniture skeletal. Almost everything I had seen so far was either repaired with tape and glue, or broken entirely. And everything was older and shabbier than could be called elegant or antique. Even the wall sconces flickered unsteadily.

Still. All this space, all this room, and all I could do was stare at the ceiling.

Is this what safety feels like? I wondered, because I was still afraid and I was still alone. Nothing had changed, except now I had more area to move in. An actual bed. Clean hair and clothes.

But it was the same.

● ● ● ●   ● ●

Knocking at my door. *Knock, knock, knock, knock;* pause. *Knock, knock.*

━━ ━━ ━━   ●

Scratch, scratch, knock.

hi. me.

For a four-year-old, Nori was gifted. I hated that she would never say the letters she knew so well. Despite my sadness, I was thrilled she had come. I knocked on the side of my bed frame.

━━ ━━ ━━ ━━   ━━ ● ━━

OK.

My door creaked open and Nori slipped inside, dashing over the cold floorboards, hopping onto the bed and under my open duvet. She was a freezing little bundle, so I hugged her into me and rubbed her arms until she stopped shivering. The moon lit our room like silver.

It's big, she signed.

I nodded.

There are funny noises.

"It's just the wind," I said. "Or maybe just the house cooling down."

Nori pursed her lips, uncertain. *Sounds like this,* she signed, and then reached down and scratched at the bed so that it sounded like mice scuttling.

"Mice," I told her. "Maybe we can make a pet of one."

She snuggled closer into me. *Don't like my room.*

"It's bigger than you're used to. But, trust me. When you get older you'll be complaining that you have no space, just like we all do."

The thought comforted me.

Her sleepy hands had more questions. *What do you think Mama's doing?*

"Go to sleep."

Silla?

"Mm?"

Are we safe?

The same question again.

"Yes," I told her.

Are we? I thought.

Ω

2

under the table

Lookie here, why don't you
you family all around
plenty of things to do
dangers lurk and abound!

Despite our fears, La Baume *did* become a haven. We went outside most mornings with Cath, into her prized garden. We'd watch her mow the lawn with an old-fashioned mechanical cutter, and then help her gather up the piles of grass. Nori would jump into them half the time, but Cath didn't seem to mind. After a while, I loosened up and found myself laughing.

Picking the gooseberries, rhubarb, and mustard greens was my favorite. Digging in the earth and planting new seeds, even better. But Cath was the only one who cooked.

Days passed. A week. Three months.

"Lasagna tonight!" she'd announce on the days we were kept outside until evening, and then we'd eat until we couldn't stuff in a single forkful more. And dessert, *always* a dessert. My favorite was milk tart.

It was paradise. It was almost a home.

Ω

One night, after a long day tilling the soil, we sat in the library together, Nori curled up on Cath's right, asleep with her head on Cath's lap, and I on the other side, sitting close, but not touching. I stared into the fire and felt my muscles begin to loosen. I was dozing comfortably when the lights died with a *thwack!*

I sat up, startled. Nori slept on.

"Don't worry," Cath said, her voice sleepy and warm. Lit only by the fire, she reminded me of my mother. The way she used to be before Nori came. Before Dad got bad. "It's only the generator. I'll see to it in the morning."

"You run the power with a generator?" I whispered.

"The wiring here is old. Too old to be useful or safe."

"I noticed my hair dryer cord didn't fit in any of the plugs in my room."

Cath smiled. "Sorry."

We fell into a companionable silence.

After a while, she turned to me with warm eyes.

"I'm so glad you came, Silla." The fire was reflected in her eyes. Mam's eyes. I looked away. It was torture. I didn't want to think of her, or Dad, or London—none of it.

She took my hand, and the touch jolted me. So warm. So foreign. "I really am," she said. "Things must have been … awful."

I nodded stiffly. What an understatement.

"I want you to know, I'm your family, too. And family isn't always such a higgledy-piggledy." I stared at her, mouth open. Hearing the words *higgledy-piggledy* coming from her mouth— *anyone's* mouth—surprised a bubble of laughter out of me. It rose without warning and escaped before I could pop it.

"I like that," Cath said, grinning down at me. "Your laugh is sweet. Did you know, I used to run an orphanage here, a while ago?" She stared deep into the fire. "You remind me of those children, Silla. So lost. Always afraid to laugh." She looked down at me again. "Please don't be afraid to be happy."

"I'm...not."

But she knew I was lying.

The bubble came again, but this time it was a sob. I couldn't stop it any more than I could stop the laugh. Before I knew it, she was hugging me, and the tears were coming too fast, and I didn't want to wake Nori, but her hug was so warm, and I hadn't been hugged in so long, and I dissolved into something between the child Silla and the broken Silla, and all the while, Cath kept kissing the top of my head, rubbing my back, and saying, "I'm here. I'm here, Silla. I'm not going anywhere."

Ω

We built forts in the dining room on a Tuesday morning. There was nothing particularly unusual about the day. Cath had mowed the lawn with her manual cutter, and I had stacked the grass into tall piles. Nori had jumped into half of them before I was done. Cath had laughed at the spectacle: Nori running back and forth in her white dress, and coming inside an hour later streaked with green, the leaves of grass poking through her curly hair.

Then Cath had decided that a magical day of grass-fort invasion deserved a special kind of lunch. We stood at the kitchen counter and watched her prepare a large silver platter with raspberries, strawberries, gooseberries, and small tomatoes (all from the garden), as well as cured meats—chorizo, *jamón* Serrano, and turkey slices that she got at the village store. After adding some hot green peppers, sweet morello cherries, and two spoonfuls of soft *sobrasada* that she had ordered in from Spain, we followed her into the dining room.

Only, she didn't sit down.

Instead, she pulled out her chair, got down onto her knees, and crawled underneath the table, one-handed.

I stared at Nori. "*Okay...*"

Nori threw her hand over her mouth and began to giggle silently. I raised my eyebrows—*This is not okay* was the meaning supposed to be conveyed, but Nori just carried on laughing.

"Where are my princesses?" Cath called from underneath us.

I rolled my eyes. "Fine."

Underneath the plush tablecloth, which Cath had washed and placed the day after we arrived, we were in another world. Nori's face glowed pink in the light from the lamps in the room above us, and we ate the food with our hands.

"Barbarians," Cath said, laughing. "Today we are barbarians!" A long red stain of cherry juice ran from the corner of her mouth to her chin. She wiped it away and then burst out laughing again, looking at the juice on her inner wrist.

"My father would *kill* me right now if he could see this!"

"Do you want me to get some paper towels or napkins?"

"Rubbish!" Cath said, dismissing my offer with a flick of her wrist. "I can do whatever I want! La Baume is ours now."

She grinned at me like a child with a new toy, and I laughed in return.

"In that case," I said, popping the single cherry I was holding delicately between two fingers into my mouth and grabbing a fistful of *sobrasada* instead, "I'm going to take advantage!" I smeared the soft chorizo spread over some baguette and took the biggest bite I could manage.

"Well, *finally*!" Cath declared, throwing up her hands, adding to Nori, "She gets it! She finally gets it!"

Nori nodded furiously, grinning from ear to ear, her cheeks stuffed with one of each item on the tray combined.

"We do *not* follow social conventions here," Cath said. "All that formality? Ugh! Sickening." She threw up her pinkie finger. "La-di-da!"

I snorted through the *sobrasada* and bread and Nori rolled around laughing soundlessly.

Not for the first time in my life, I wished I could hear what that would sound like.

Ω

The fire was burning low now, and we sat around it on the sheepskin rugs, curled up in fleece blankets while it stormed outside. The skylight above us was the deep black of nothing, but now and again a flash of lightning revealed the raging rains and whiplash winds.

Nori, wrapped up in Cath's lap, sat staring at the night sky, flinching with every rumble of thunder.

"It's just God up there," Cath said. "He's moving his furniture around. Nothing to be scared of. It just sounds loud because we live underneath him."

Nori's eyes widened, and she looked up again.

A flash of lightning.

"He's taking photos of you!" Cath cried. "How wonderful! He must think you're beautiful."

Nori grinned. She fumbled to get out of the blanket and then ran to stand beneath the skylight, posing and smiling and spinning as "God" took "photos" of her.

I grinned at Cath, embracing the warmth in my chest and wondering if this was what love felt like.

"Time for a story," Cath said later, when we were all snuggled close and sleepy. I had retreated to the armchair closest to the fire, my legs dangling over the arm.

"I want to tell you a story about those woods out there. A true story."

I glanced up from my sleepy haze.

"You must never, *never* go into Python Wood," she whispered, making sure she had Nori's full attention. "Python Wood is a bad, bad place. Long ago, something bad came out of it. A man, of sorts."

I frowned. This wasn't exactly my idea of a soothing bed-time fable.

"He was more of a . . . monster."

"Auntie Cath—I don't think—"

"Ssh!" Her head snapped in my direction. "Let me finish. You need to hear this as well, Silla. A monster of sorts. He did terrible things. And then he returned to the woods. He's still in there, waiting for young girls to go wandering so he can capture them. So he can tear them up and eat their flesh from their—"

"Cath!"

She looked at me with dagger eyes. And then she relaxed and smiled, turning back to Nori. "Well"—she tapped Nori's nose gently—"the Creeper Man won't get you if you just *stay away* from the woods."

Nori was staring up at Cath's chin. Then she looked at me. *But we came through the woods.*

Cath sensed the movement. "No need to be afraid."

"We came in through the woods," I said, winking at Nori.

"Oh yes," Cath said, smiling. "Of course you did. Well, he wanted you here, didn't he? But now . . . now that you are . . ."

"He won't let us leave?" I offered, remembering her words.

Cath stared at me. "Exactly."

I was relieved. Boogeymen I could handle. My father coming after us, I couldn't.

Beneath Cath, Nori's eyes had filled with tears and she was sniffling quietly.

"Oh, bug, come here. It's all right." I held out my arms for her and she crawled over to the foot of my chair, where I lifted her into my lap and wrapped my own blanket tightly around her. "It's only a story," I said. "Isn't it, Cath?"

Cath smiled, a little too long. "Oh. Oh, yes. It's just a story, Eleanor, nothing to be scared of."

"See?" I said, and kissed her head.

"So long as you stay away from the woods," Cath added quietly.

I kept kissing Nori's head and staring into the fire.

Just a story.

Just a freaking *weird* story.

Ω

I like it here.

Sometimes I see Silla looking out the window feeling bad.

But she shouldn't feel bad because I like it here.

It's nice.

Auntie Catherine is nice.

I like the food.

Silla shouldn't feel bad.

She really, really shouldn't.

I miss them, too, but I like not being scared and I'm not sore anymore.

And the bad man is locked in the woods.

So that's why Silla shouldn't feel bad.

Ω

3

birthday cake

Things can stay safe for long
they can pretend to fit
but then you hear Discord's song
and things crack bit by bit.

"Nori!"

By the time Cath screamed, Nori was almost at the bound-ary to the woods. I startled and looked back at my aunt. She was standing in the kitchen doorway, staring out at Nori with wide eyes, her mouth twisted into an almost-cavern, flashing with teeth and tongue.

She screamed again. *"NORI!"*

"What is it?" I yelled, my heart thudding like it hadn't in months.

"Get her away from the woods! Get her away! Get her, Silla, *get her*!"

But she was already running. I followed on her heels, winc-ing every time Cath screamed Nori's name. Nori was already standing in front of the trees.

I overtook Cath and when I reached Nori, I yanked her behind me and turned to face Cath.

Cath was there a moment later. *"Did she cross? Is she okay?"*

"Calm down—"

"*DID SHE CROSS?*"

"What do you—"

"The woods!" Cath screamed, and bent down to grab Nori by her small arms. "*Did you go into the woods?*" she yelled, the force of her shake bringing Nori to tears.

I shoved Cath away, and she fell onto her back, sliding a little down the hill. "Don't touch her!" I yelled, old rage and old memories rising like a tsunami. "*Don't you touch her!*"

Nori clung to my dress, looking up at me for guidance. "It's okay," I said, the anger draining from my body like sickness out of my veins.

I couldn't bring myself to turn around, to look at Aunt Cath lying in the grass, her dress ridden up to her hips, to hear her soft sobbing.

"We…we should go back," I said meekly, and glanced behind me.

Cath's shoulders shook, and I noticed how thin her legs were, covered with varicose veins. I turned away, a horror at myself—and at *her*—rising within me.

"We could tend to the garden."

She raised her head and, after a brief glance at the woods, nodded. I helped her to her feet and we walked to the house, Cath leaning on my arm all the way. Nori took Aunt Cath's hand before we were halfway back to La Baume, and I hung back. The sun was setting, and they looked quite beautiful in the red light.

I couldn't believe my reaction. Why had I shoved Cath away? Why had Cath acted so fiercely about keeping Nori from the woods? The story about the Creeper Man was just that. A story. A stupid child's warning.

By the time we got back into the house, Cath was laughing,

waving me inside, and Nori was smiling. Nori's tears had stopped, as had Cath's, and the oncoming night had dissolved my rage.

Something in the house had changed, though, before the night was over.

Ω

The garden sparkled in orange hues of sunset, the old wooden table draped with a pale cloth and sprinkled with bundles of dusty-pink roses from the garden. I smiled at them, even though I wished Cath had just left them on the plant.

So pretty.

Cath made a cake. I took a slice from her offering hand, noting that her nail polish matched the roses. Her smile was so wide that a jolt of pleasure jumped through me.

Until I saw that it didn't reach her eyes. And that the nail polish was actually textured and lumpy, slopped on over her cuticles. There was a drop of it in her hair.

And then I noticed something else. She was still smiling, but she wasn't looking at me. Not directly. She was staring at the tip of my left ear. Or something over my shoulder.

"Enjoy!" she proclaimed, wiping her hands on the floral apron.

I took my plate into the garden, away from the light of the kitchen, which licked the grass with a paraffin tongue, and sat by the hedges, alone. It was moist cake, and I had three pieces.

The breeze brushed my cheek, and I laughed.

I was *happy*, I realized. I'd never felt so happy, despite Cath's strange smile. Amazing that a cake could do that. Or maybe it was more about the acknowledgment. Acknowledgment that I was born fifteen years ago, and that I was here and it was worth celebrating. Maybe.

Nori skipped over, carrying a paper plate. She put it down and showed me what she was holding. Something dangled from her fist, the one attached to the bad arm, so it shook a little with the strain of lifting it up to show me. Her mouth was covered in pink icing. More pink.

Look, she signed, one-handed. Look!

The thing swung like a fatty bit of raw bacon covered in cake.

Worms! She laughed, digging into the piece of cake to find more.

Everything s l o w e d down around me.

Wrong. This is wrong.

Cath stood in the kitchen doorway, the light pooling around her. She was laughing, tears running down her cheek.

I felt cold bite my hands.

The next day Cathy went up to the attic.

And never came down.

Fifteen passed.

Sixteen, too.

Seventeen arrived, and so did he.

Ω

BOOK 2:
Earthen Sky

The man in the trees
came in the night
to steal the girl
and give her a fright.
the little girl blocked
her ears and eyes
but the Creeper Man wears
many a disguise.

OLD MAN IN HIS CHAIR

In a faraway place, an old man sits in his armchair.

Next to him, on the table, there is tea.

It went cold a while ago.

He's been staring at the picture in the frame—it also sits on the table. Beside the cup of tea.

He ponders it, unblinking.

Thinking of all the things that were, that are, that will not be.

The picture is old now. The face no longer real. Only to him.

The days have grown long, and longer. The dusk droops languidly over gray skies that seem as aged as he is. As wrinkled, too.

And the nights: endless, as they have always been. Too many memories. Too many nightmares.

Too many *nights*.

He is tired.

A life, too long, has made him so.

He reaches for his tea at last, but it seems his wait is over.

His eyes are closed now, his jaw slack.

His nightmares are done. And so are his nights.

Ω

1

beautiful disposition

A silly girl did silly play
with dolls and mud and thread
the tall blind man who watched her game
did send her round the bend.

BROKEN BOOK ENTRY

I was **born** on a moldy mattress in a bad **part** of London. Sometimes I think that's why I'm **crazy**. But (crazy) Aunt Cath doesn't like to talk about **all** that. She doesn't want to think about the grimy windowsills or the **dirty** ceiling, or the fact that her sister, Pamela, had to live that life. She hates it when **I** talk about how all Mam **had** to wear was a blue nightdress—silk and faded. I didn't even have shoes. It was an emergency—**a** *real* emergency—that forced my father to buy clothes.

No less. He thought all humans should remain **beautiful** and naked, which he was most of the time. I don't know if he was a nudist or just extreme. It was simply his strange and sometimes sinister **disposition**. Auntie Cath thought he was trash. By the end, I thought so, too.

There was **fear** in Mam's eyes when she **held** Nori sometimes. I know she felt it. **Everyone** thought she was weak, but I thought she was strong. Until the end. Nori would think her weak, too, if she'd been old enough. It was no secret that **we were all afraid**.

She didn't have many **words** to use by the end. He beat them out of her, with his words, with his hands. They **were** knocked clean out or crooked, like some of Nori's teeth. But, see, Mam wasn't crazy. Or maybe she was. We were all a bit **gone** living with him.

We snuck onto the train at 10:03, me and Nori alone, and we watched the gray of London **fading** away into green and yellow fields, and then **into** gray mountains. It was a long trip, and a big woman served food from a trolley in each compartment. But we had **nothing** to spend.

People get precious about money, funny thing that, it being paper and ink. Nori tugged on my hand and pointed to her belly **and** I shrugged because what could I do? But there were **tears** on her cheeks, smudging the dirt, so I pulled off my button– the only one left–and gave it to her to suck, and she fell asleep, wrapped up in the good blanket.

When the train stopped it was **dark**; I couldn't see anything, **and** I could feel that something was different. There were tall trees outside, black in the throes of midnight, and I felt the **absence** of the London smog and buildings fiercely. Then **came** the storm and a walk longer than I have ever done and I nearly lost my foot skin. What a joke, all that effort to end up *here*.

La Baume is a big, sprawling manor. **I** could tell that even in the dark. I **felt** it. A big, **empty** place, half falling down, **and** it was all for Cath. It must have been lonely all by herself in that house the color of blood. She must have been **afraid** to be alone.

But we've come to her **now**, to the place where **there's** space and food and joy and light. The place where Mam grew up, too. **Only**

nothing lasts forever, does it? Which is the only perfect truth.

We liked it at first, but then **the thing in the woods** came, the people left, **and** now we are alone in **a ghost** town.

Ω

Nori sees him first.

By the time I look up from the ashy soil, she's almost at the boundary with Python Wood.

"*NORI!*"

My screams should echo across the field, but they don't. Nothing has buoyancy anymore, not even my terror.

"*Nori, stop! STOP!*"

Her hand signs reach across the distance. *I'm playing!*

"Come back here right now!"

But she's already turned away, skipping toward trees that loom before her like sentinels.

Nonononononono. I don't know if Cath is right about the thing in the woods or not, but I remember her terror before she went mad, and I have felt...*something* about Python. And I can't risk losing Nori, too.

"Nori, damn it, *stop right now, I mean it*!"

She doesn't stop, and I run. I'm faster, but not by much, and when I reach across the distance that separates us to grab at her shoulder, her dress, her hair—anything to get her to stop—we are right at the boundary. I feel the coldness of the wood like a fridge door just opened. A breath. A puff. So eerie.

I shake her roughly, and the crooked bone of her right arm shocks me, even now. It's so weak, thin, warped. Her mouth opens in an O that should have sound, but never has.

"You stop when I call you, *do you understand me?*"

She begins to cry. It occurs to me that I'm still holding her arms tightly, so I force my grip to soften, and then let go completely.

She signs: *But the boy is hiding and I have to find him.*

"What boy?"

He's going to win!

I should ignore her. Take her hand and march her back inside. But something stops me. It's always the same, so close to the wood. A feeling of being seen. Not just watched, but *really* looked at. I still remember, three years ago, when Cath screamed like that...her terror at the idea of Nori going into the woods. Maybe her fear is infecting me, too. Now that she's not really here anymore.

Staring out at the ancient boughs, all of them dripping moss, I whisper, "Nori, tell me right now. *What boy?*" My skin is crawling.

She wears a pout, unaware that a certain sense of darkness is growing up behind her, deep within the trees. It's as though the day is somehow later in the wood than it is out in the field. Impossible.

Look! Her hands yell. *There he is! I told you!*

And someone *is* coming. I maneuver Nori behind me and wait, muscles tense and ready to fire. What can I do? Run? With Nori? I look around for a weapon, but the only thing of use is a fallen branch, and I don't want to touch any part of Python Wood. I'm not even sure I know why.

Don't be like Cath, I berate myself. But I still don't touch the branch.

The figure gets closer, and I step back, pulling Nori with me. But then I see it's just a boy, stalking out from between the trees, hands in his pockets. Dark hair, dark eyes. Like me.

"I didn't mean to frighten you," he says. He crosses into the field like it's nothing. Like he's *not* the first person we've seen in months. "We were playing hide-and-seek. I think I was losing." He winks at Nori, but stops smiling when he looks back at me. "Or maybe I've already lost."

"Who are you?" My voice is gravel. "What kind of perv are you? Trying to get my sister to go into the woods. She's *seven*!"

"That's not...I'm—I think you have the wrong..." The boy half smiles, then thinks better of it. "My name's Gowan. I was just...I used to live here, ages ago, when it was an orphanage? I took care of the garden." He nods down to the house.

Some vague memory of Cath running an orphanage pricks the edges of my mind. Must have been ten years ago at least. Did she ask him to come back because of what's been happening with the garden? Possible, but improbable. There's no phone. The postman hasn't been in ages. So, unless Cath left the attic at night, in secret, and crossed Python to get a letter to town, then this boy—this Gowan—is lying to me.

"Where did you come from?"

He laughs, then frowns. "I live on the other side of the woods. About three miles from town."

"There is no town," I say. "Not anymore."

"How do you know?"

"I went to look...once. There's nothing. Everything is still, empty and falling down."

I don't want to remember. I don't want to think about this.

The boy shifts on his feet and glances over his shoulder. "I, um, well...I've obviously said or done something wrong. I'm sorry for that." He hesitates. "I'll go."

He turns to leave, to go back into the woods—the *woods*!—but I cry out a wordless plea, my arm reaching forward before I'm aware I've done it. He turns toward me.

I don't understand myself.

His eyes question me.

"What are you looking at?" I growl, folding my arms over my chest.

"I—you looked like you wanted to ask me something."

Nori stares up at me, sucking on the hem of her dress. Damn.

I clear my throat. "Do you...do you have food? Some pears? Or radishes? Anything?"

He laughs. *"Radishes?"*

"We don't have much. The land is...off."

"What do you mean?"

"Are you blind?" I snap, though I regret it when he steps away from me. "Look around you. The garden's dying. Everything is dead. The threat of war..."

"Threat of war?"

"World War Three, some say. They were saying that when we left."

"Left?"

"London."

"Oh."

The boy, Gowan, looks down at Nori, who is staring up at him, still munching on the hem of her dress. "I have to go now. I'm sorry."

I hesitate, wanting him to stay, wanting him to leave—regretting my abrasive nature, my stony heart. I hate my need, my loneliness. I stand silent as the first visitor in so long leaves us behind.

Idiot.

I retreat from the edge of Python Wood as the boy vanishes from view, once again certain that the trees have been watching the exchange. Now, though only minutes have passed, the woods look like they are greeting an early dusk. Weird stuff like this is enough to give Cath's warning more weight.

I scowl at them. "Piss off."

You ruined the game! Nori signs, then she stomps away from me, back to La Baume, which sits eerie and alone, a large ruby in the center of three rings. Wood, field, garden: the blood manor.

I scan the trees again, the eerie stillness of it so *wrong,* but I don't see the boy anymore. Maybe he was a hopeless wish. Or a desperate delusion.

I scowl, staring for long minutes into the murk.

For a moment, I'm frozen where I stand, acutely aware that I'm alone at the boundary with *Python.* Python damned Wood.

"You let me think this was paradise," I whisper at my mother. "You let me believe this…this lie."

At last, I turn away. I've seen too much to let *trees* scare me. I walk back to the manor, which sits under a dank midday sky, while the woods behind me greet a rising moon.

Ω

Mam used to write down the things that scared her, or the things she wished for. Fear. Hope. Two edges of the same knife if you ask me. I would see her scribbling on tiny pieces of paper or the margins of books. She'd tear them off and then burn them in the candle, locked forever as a perfect truth.

This is mine: We are alone. I am alone. La Baume is wrong and Python Wood is watching. A boy came today, but I scared him away. He might have been my only chance. But I know what cause and effect are. Cause: Python delivers a boy. Effect: A girl stays away. I'm going to burn you now, tiny, perfect truth.

Ω

Creak. Creak. Creak.
I grind my jaw.

Creak.

Creak.

Creeeeeeaaak.

Always the same. Never ends. The floorboards squeak and move above us as (crazy) Aunt Cath paces. Cause, effect, step, *squeak.*

Hungry, Nori signs. *Is there jam?*

Creak. Creak. Thump.

I flinch with the sound, but Nori doesn't seem to mind it, and she dances around the filthy kitchen, utterly unaware. It is an agonizing symphony that I alone must endure.

No bread left in the cupboard. No jam. Tins, oats, some peanuts; that will do. I shake peanuts out into the mortar and grind them into a dusty paste with the pestle. Add sugar, a little butter. Grind some more. I'm almost manic with stirring before I feel Nori tug on my sleeve.

I hand the bowl over. *Eat.*

Nori doesn't complain, but the mess is gone in under three seconds. It isn't enough. It has to be enough. Need to save the rest—make it last as long as I can.

How different things are now. I still remember when we first came to La Baume. Fully stocked pantry with bread, jams, and more. We had potatoes, turnips, and squash grown in the garden; it was a place of hope even with rumors about another war. There was a tomato plant and a cucumber plant and Auntie Cath would sing while she baked, and there seemed to be endless sunshine.

Whatever: I'm probably exaggerating the memory. Curse of hard times, I suppose. The only thing streaming through the window now is a vaguely foggy gray. I've come to hate October.

I glance through the glass.

The trees are closer.

The thought manifests without warning.

I resist. *No. No, they aren't.*

They are. The trees are *closer* than they were yesterday.

Impossible.

Yes, look. And you found that root in the garden this morning, like an old crone's finger, pointing right at you, remember? It was sticking out of the ashen soil—accusing. A root in a garden that has no trees. Face it, doll.

I shut my eyes. *Shut up.*

Go into the garden, I sign at Nori, pushing away useless memories and crazy theories. *Go and look for strawberries.* I hide behind sign language because my voice can't crack and give me away when the words come from my hands. Nori looks at me, the corner of her mouth bunched up. *Go on,* I sign again, and then give in. "Strawberries."

Maybe. Just maybe there'll be some left. Some life in the ashes. Please. Oh, please...

Who am I asking?

Nori goes outside, carrying the bell she will ring if she gets into any trouble. It's tied to the ribbon around her waist; I breathe easier hearing the sweet tinkling of metal on metal as she skips away.

I make more of the peanut paste and walk through the kitchen, the lower hallway, the entrance hall, up the first, second, and third flights of stairs, and pause in front of the attic staircase, thin, narrow, and menacing in the near-darkness of this part of the house.

"Catherine?" I call up.

As usual, she has no reply for me.

"Auntie Cath. I have some food for you down here. Okay? Catherine, okay?"

Nothing.

I place the bowl at the bottom of the ancient staircase and hurry away, trying not to rush like someone is behind me, but failing.

A beat more of silence, and then (crazy) Aunt Cath resumes her pacing in the attic:

up

and   up.

down   and

down

It never ends.

Ω

That night, the creaking still filters down to my bedroom, grinding through my head and bones like a tiny drill.

Nori sleeps through it, and I vow to protect that innocence. The innocence of complete and utter, stupid ignorance. I hear music in the night. Endless creaking, on and on. I no longer sleep very much. The bedsprings poke the flesh of my back. The shadows seem to move. I sigh. I stir.

Creak.

I clench my jaw as the night sings on.

Creak.

I wish the horrible percussion away.

Creeeeaaaaak.

The walls begin ticking. La Baume is old. The noises from the attic—(crazy) Aunt Cath pacing back and forth, up

and

down

—are inevitable in a place like this. There's too much wood in this house. Were the walls built from Python trees? I wrap my arms around my torso; the idea of being inside a box of Python planks is horrifying. Cursed planks.

Creak.

La Baume is cursed.

Creak.

I didn't expect to think it, but that's kind of what it feels like.

Creeeeeaaaaak.

CURSED.

I force the thought of screaming trees away. Trees don't scream. Trees don't sing.

Yeah, right. Trees also don't move.

I meander to the window on the balls of my feet, peering out through the strangling vines at the trees. They thrash and moan through the lightning and thunder like inmates in an asylum.

Creak.

It is going to drive me mad.

Creak...

I am going to lose my mind.

Ω

SILLA DANIELS'S GUIDE TO LOSING YOUR MIND

1. Notice things.

2. Notice the things that no one else does.

3. Notice everything. Too much. All the time.

4. Sense the wrongness in things.

5. But don't feel them.

6. Feel alone.

7. But never <u>be</u> alone.

2

crazy is just a word

A bit of dirt and soil and bone
and blood pricked from a thumb
the Creeper Man so little known
is come, oh yes! He's come.

Silla is very upset today, so I sit in the corner
very quiet and I wait. Maybe if I am very, very
still, she will notice that I am not moving. Maybe
she will stop long enough to hear my tummy
rrrrraaawwwwrrrrrr like a monster. I know what
it means—it means Feed me—but Silla doesn't
always know that.

It is dark today, darker than yesterday, and I
think maybe a storm is coming. Maybe it will blow
a path for us to follow to a big garden full of
strawberries and gooseberries and potatoes! They
can't all have died? They might just be deep, deep
down or far, far away.

I like that boy. That boy, Gowan. He was nice
and he played with me when Silla was angry, and
I forgot about the monster in my tummy for

a bit. But the monster is back now and Silla _still_ hasn't noticed.

Hungry, I sign.

She doesn't see me. I tug on her sleeve.

Hungry.

There is a flash of a different monster in her eyes and I shrink back. I don't like it when she looks like Daddy. I look over at the tall, smiling man in the corner, but Silla doesn't seem to mind him staring at us, even though he has no eyes, so I just go back to being very, very still.

Ω

He's nice, Nori signs.

I know she means that boy from yesterday. "I don't trust him. Why was he here?"

He's come to look after the garden! Said he used to live here.

"With Cathy?" I force my nature down and think. "She'd remember him, then, I suppose, back from her younger days. Maybe I should try to ask her."

Nori, at seven, looks doubtful. _Okay…_

"She could have told me she asked someone to come. I didn't even see her leave the attic."

Nori shrugs.

She might have bloody well brought back some food.

I shake my head and continue to fold the laundry, which is still damp, though it has hung outside all day. Nothing ever dries anymore in this damn climate. Our clothes are all slightly moist, and they have the smell of it, too—of mold, of wet, of rotting material. Even my skin smells mildewy.

God, I need a proper shower. Hot, running water. Stupid bloody generator. It broke a few months ago. I fixed it, and it works...some of the time. But the water pressure sucks the farther up the house you go. And the shower is on the third floor—in the abandoned hallway.

I can't get my thoughts off that boy. Gowan. If he really did live here once, why come back? There's nothing left. It's so isolated—not a single neighbor now for thirteen or fourteen miles. Unless you count him. Three miles from town. Three miles from us. But this land is poisoned, infected, dying, and I doubt he can fix *that*. I doubt anyone can. So why come? What's the point?

"Have you seen him before?"

No.

"He seemed familiar."

He's fun. We should go visit him.

"No!" I spin, grab my sister's tiny shoulders, and give them a shake. "We are *never* entering the woods, do you understand me?"

Nori blinks at me and then begins to cry. She tries to wriggle free from my hands, her bad arm bent and useless.

"Nori, I'm serious. He could be a spy or a hobo or some kind of terrorist! He could be looking for a place to set up some kind of military base—"

Stupid! Nori yells with her hands. I have to admit, I do feel kind of idiotic.

"It's possible," I insist. "Remember what they were saying on the news before we left? We could be the only ones left for all we know."

She tugs away from me again. *Go away, go away, go away!*

"Nori, *promise me you won't go into the woods! They're coming closer!*"

I don't mean to say it. It slips out. There is a pause, and then Nori jerks hard, manages to get free, and rushes from the room. At the doorway, she turns back, her face red and wet. *Too late! The woods are coming! And he's already here!*

$$\Omega$$

THE KIND MADE FROM LOVE

"Auntie?"

I am getting older now and creaking in all my bones. I turn; my eyes fall on the girl who stands at the bottom of the stairs. I know she'll come no closer, so I linger in the doorway, looking down. How much the girl has changed. . . . She is not a child any longer; she is a younger version of me. Of little Pammy. Except for that dark hair.

When first the two children came, there was life in this house. Not much, but I managed to hold the dark at bay. *He* was confined to the woods. The children, my nieces, were innocent—or at least the young one was. The eldest, though—Silla, who stands before me now an almost-woman—had seen a sliver of darkness already. Still, she was innocent in that she was untouched by the madness that infects this house.

But that is gone now, too.

"He's out there," I say, turning back to the window. "Always watching. Getting stronger."

The girl steps hesitantly onto the bottom step, eyes darting up and away like a skittish cat, and stands awkwardly on the very edge. "Who is?"

I sigh and curl my legs underneath me as I sit on the floor, shifting so that my back is now to the window and I am facing the girl looking up at me.

I don't want to do this again.

"When I was a little girl, your mother and I used to love it here."

The girl looks skeptical, and I expect no less.

"Back then the house was blue. It's tradition that every new family head paints La Baume a different color, did you know that? Father started to paint it blue the day he married Momma. He never was very good at finishing anything. When I was four and Pammy was still a little baby, Father got it into his head that those few bits of green paint showing through were bad luck. We spent a whole summer running around the house, filling in the gaps. When we were finished, the house looked like the sky." I smile and wrap thin arms around myself. They were good days. Good memories. "The soil was rich and fertile."

"What happened?"

"I did." I choke back a sob. "I came. I grew up, Father died, then Mother, Anne...and then Pammy moved away with that awful, hard man." The man who is your father. I don't say it, but I know the girl heard it. "I could see the stone in him clear as day...but your mother has an airy nature and was too flighty to see. Soon you were there with them, too, a little pebble yourself, and my hopes of having her back were dashed upon the rocks." I pause, my lungs fighting to find purchase in the air.

I feel spite deep inside me as I watch the almost-woman, Silla, who is my niece and to blame. It is a curling thing I can't suppress. "The day you were born, I began to paint the manor red. The new color for my rule. Red was blood and rage and passion." I smile wanly. "It seemed fitting at the time."

"I'm sorry."

I laugh, cackles bounding along the walls. The girl is *sorry*.

"Ten years. Waiting. And still I hoped that Pammy would come home. I bought so much yellow paint, hoping against hope that she would join me and we could remake this house again. A giant sunflower, full of light and joy..." Oh, it was such a glorious dream! Such grand ideas! Such wonder in the darkness! "And then Eleanor came. Little Nori, so *precious*. Precious enough to tie your mother to *him* for longer. Little Nori, full of water, fluid—an easy survivor. She couldn't be tainted by your father the way—"

"Say it."

I look away.

"The way *I* am," Silla finishes. "The way I have been."

I nod. *You have stone in your heart.* I look on Silla. "When you came, things went bad again."

"You're blaming this on me? The townspeople leaving, the land dying, the woods—you're blaming me?"

I shake my head. *No.* But I mean *YES.*

"Who is he?"

Does the girl know? Has she seen him? She doesn't look afraid. . . .

"When I was a girl, I had stone in my heart, too; it was my fault. Or maybe it was Pammy. So hard to remember. Pammy was like water back then, before she evaporated for your father. For *Stan*." My lips curl around the name with distaste. "She was like Nori." I swallow. No. That's wrong. It was always Anne. But things are so muddy now, and I can't quite remember, and there is nothing left.

Too many secrets. Too much danger. Nothing to hold on to.

"Catherine." The girl is standing now, her hands clenched like the rocks they are. She is so very *hard*. Granite, through and through.

The hardness I see there resolves me. Absolves me. After all, why should I care?

"He's watching you," I say. "He comes from the woods, lives in them. He's drawn here, and when he comes, the land dies. People sense it and leave. It's happened before." I suck in a shudder of a breath. "The Creeper Man. He's not a protector at all...."

The girl seems warmer. Like fire coals, burning inside. "What are you on about, you crazy old witch? That was just a story."

"This place is cursed."

I can tell that the girl already knows this.

"Why didn't you tell me? Why did you let us stay?" The girl is yelling now. "Why not warn us or send us away!"

"Because I was alone!"

Silence rings loudly. Clarity. Air. Truth. *Truth-truthtruthtruthtruth:* something true at last.

"I was alone," I whisper now. "I didn't know what was real. I didn't know if I was..." Crazy. "And then there you both were...so young. Nori looks so like Pamela, those little golden-red curls." My voice hardens. "I couldn't let her go." A pause. "Besides. Once you came through, there was never any leaving."

"So. What? We're trapped here?" the girl spits, a speck of saliva landing on my lip. Water from fire buried under stone. "With *you*?"

Ω

At least with my father, the danger was out in the open. I knew what to expect. But Auntie Cath is a different kind of dark altogether.

The worst kind.

The kind made from love.

Ω

3

he's already here

The Creeper Man is watching you
while you think you rest
he sows discord between the two
who love each other best.

The boy is there when I hang the laundry, leaning against the garden fence with his arms crossed.

"You were right," he says. "It's a ghost town."

"There *is* no town. Not anymore. You didn't believe me?"

He shakes his head slowly. A piece of dark hair falls into darker eyes. "It seemed…impossible. It's crazy. What happened?"

I wipe the dust from my hands, though I'll never be clean. "Everybody left?"

"Yeah, but why?"

"The land died. Everything's gone. This is a poor place." My voice fades away. "Nothing like London." I blink. "No one comes here. Not ever. Why would you go to the saddest place on earth?"

"And they say the countryside is so rich in resources," Gowan says. There's a smile in his voice. "I can help with the garden. I'm good with earth."

"Threat of war makes everything die." I don't mention the ashes in the garden.

"There's no war. Not even out there, yet. Just a bunch of people scared and ignorant." I feel as though he is lying to me. "Why don't you come and see me. I have apples and pears *and* radishes. Come and see."

He offers me his hand, which is so clean it hurts, but the woods loom behind him, and I feel like he's laughing at me.

"I can't," I say, and turn back to my digging.

"Please."

"Why?"

"Because this place looks fed up." His eyes scatter over La Baume behind me like marbles. "It's not how I remember it."

I stop again, and throw down my tiny spade. "Who *are* you?"

He grins, and then settles next to me, heedless of the gray that filters into his trousers, his fingers, his skin. I almost want to pull his hand out of the soil, but I stop myself.

It's infecting you.

"Gowan," he says unhelpfully. Then he gestures to the manor. "Are you here alone?" In this light, the blood-paint looks like a fresh scab.

Maybe he's a robber or a rapist. "My aunt is here. She"—*is crazy*—"takes care of us."

"And school?"

I shrug. "Done with all of that, I guess. Like everyone is. We have a gun, you know. So you better not try anything," I add.

He laughs at me. It's like a jingle from a TV commercial.

"What?"

He shrugs, but the gesture is awkward on him and I know he is copying me. "There's a library in there. In the manor. I remember it. You can keep teaching yourself. Don't need school for that."

I'm surprised that he knows about the library, but then I remember he used to live here. I guess he was telling the truth.

"You were one of Cath's orphans." I state it. It's the truth.

He nods, but makes no further comment. My gaze slides away.

"You're preoccupied," he says.

"You don't know me well enough to think that."

"Sure I do. You're distracted. Your eyes keep jumping from the ground to the trees, to the sky...and you've been digging a hole in the same spot since before I sat down."

I can't stop the slow smile. I feel it cracking my granite. He is the first person I've had a normal conversation with in three years, two months, and sixteen days.

"So? What is it?"

"I just wish I had news. From my family in London. From my old friends. I'm beginning to feel completely cut off from everything and everyone I used to know. I keep waiting, even though it's been months since anyone wrote to us. And the postman used to come at least once a week, but he came less and less until one day he just stopped. They closed the post office, I guess. He left, with everyone else. It's weird not having him come by every few days. It's weird not having the corner shop in the village open every night, all night, or having the sounds of people at all hours like back in London." I look at Gowan. "First-world problems," I add casually.

"Those are pretty big problems," Gowan says. "Are you lonely?"

"A TV would be nice."

"No TV?"

I shrug. "Cath isn't big on technology. No TV, no phone, no computer. The radio barely works and is this giant piece of furniture all on its own."

He smiles fondly, gaze turning inward. "I remember."

I sigh and rub at my arms. "Is there even a world out there anymore? Have we blown ourselves to bits yet?"

"There's a world. Just beyond the trees. Not half a day's walk. And it's beautiful, full of beautiful things, even if they're scary."

Bullshit. I don't say it. I wish I hadn't said anything.

Instead, I say, "I don't remember there being so many trees when we first came here. Nori was only four. They're assholes."

"They're just trees."

I look up, not at him, but beyond him, at the trees. I know they're watching us, laughing at my distress.

I clench my jaw. "There are so many . . . they go on forever."

"Don't be afraid."

"I'm not!" I retort. "But there's so much work to be done. I have to look after"—*Cath*—"Nori."

I gather up my spade and garden fork, shaking loose the fine gray sand. "Go away."

I get up, turning my back on him, and head toward the manor, the scorching-red manor, and I hear his retreating footsteps. I turn, want to say *I'm sorry, please stay* but instead I watch him leave. Alarm bells ring inside me: DANGER. DANGER. Can't he see the dark, the curse, in those trees? Can't he feel the *wrongness* when he crosses into those shadows?

He's already here.

I don't think Nori was talking about Gowan.

Ω

I'm digging in the garden, looking for potatoes or turnips or carrots or *worms*, when I find another root. It can't be the same root . . . but this is the same spot I found the other one. Only this one is three times bigger. And I pulled the other root out completely.

No. "This is not happening. It's *impossible*."

I look up

and scream.

The woods are closer. They are definitely closer. Every time I look away and then back, they seem to have moved, the trunks looming ever taller. I keep wiping my hands on my dress—*get it off me, get it off*—when I feel it.

Another root.

Sticking out of the dirt like *another* broken finger. Pointing, accusing. *I know,* it seems to say. *I know, Silla Daniels.*

The woods are coming. *He's here.* I shake my head. *No. No, this is not happening. Stop it. Stop it now.* But I know that this land is cursed more than I know that Cath is mad. It has to be cursed. What else is there? I have felt it for a while now. First the town left, then (crazy) Aunt Cath went mad, and now the woods are closer and the garden is dying…

And I am not crazy.

I'm not like Cath.

I get to my feet, never taking my eyes off the trees for paranoid fear that they will be closer once again if I look away even for a moment. I step backward, toward the house, my feet finding their way, and when I'm through the doorway, I slam it shut and pray that the woods will not be right outside when I open it again tomorrow.

Ω

I hate the mirrors in this place. As if it isn't big or creepy enough already, the largest mirror just makes the corridors longer, repeating ever onward to infinity. It's warped in its age, and doesn't reflect the truth. The edges are all blacked out and mottled like an old crone's hand. The head on my first reflection is distorted: too narrow, eyes too dark. The next, her head is normal, but her neck is too long and thin. Each one not quite me. I am looking at hundreds of little almost-me's, decreasing in size down an endless corridor until I can't see the last at all. There is no last.

I lift a hand and wave at the me's. They wave back, and when I laugh, they all sneer.

As I turn away, something about the reflection strikes me as not right, in a way I can't put into words. Is the reflection out of time with me? Is it too dark at the very back there? The very last tiny me, waving? I rub my eyes and turn away, but then jolt at the idea that I've turned my back on hundreds of little versions of myself, all watching me. I glance back and they all do, too. But they are wrong. Somehow.

"Stupid," I tell myself, and walk farther away.

I'm trying, even now, after three long years, to get a handle on this manor. There are still rooms I haven't explored, and the idea of not knowing every inch of this place is suddenly very wrong. I need to know La Baume inside and out.

Besides. We're now running dangerously low on food, and I need to try again to get Cath to tell me if she has any hidden supplies. And she's not about to tell me.

And I'm not about to go up *there* and see her.

A creak behind me startles my thoughts away. I turn to look back down the hall, but see nothing. Not even the little me's are big enough to make an appearance in the mirrors now.

But something is wrong.

"Nori, if you're spying, then stop it."

I wait for her to jump out, but there is nothing. Only a stillness that is too still.

I need to be firm with myself, so I turn away.

An old manor, at night. Who wouldn't get the creeps?

Except I hear the *creak* again. Barely there. Like a shifting of weight on the floorboards.

"Cath?" I call.

The stillness becomes deeper.

And then I hear Cath upstairs, pacing above me.

Creeeeeeaaaaak. Creeeeaaaaaaak. Crrreeeeeeaaaaak.

And I know that whatever is at the end of the hall is not Cath.

So I run.

I don't think about anything except the movement of my legs, and where I'm headed: the library.

I rush in and shut the door firmly behind me, ignoring the mocking voice inside telling me I'm a child for being so afraid of what is probably nothing. Probably.

The library is a monolith. Central to La Baume in the way the heart is to a human body. It's a semicircular room, three floors high—a cylinder cut right through the middle of the manor. Standing in the center, you can look right up through each floor and the skylight to see the sky. It's a sanctuary, but even here, the oppression of the house is all around, trying to press in.

I'm determined to keep the door to this room locked at all times.

And I have no reason to think this, but I *know* this room is still uninfected.

I don't even really know what I mean. Only...that La Baume is somehow sick. Like it caught a nasty bug, and the library is the last defense of its immune system.

I came here looking for...the past. Some feeling of how things used to be. When Cath, Nori, and I would sit here for hours, reading or talking or playing. When Cath stroked my hair and told me everything would be all right, when she cuddled Nori close, like she was her own daughter. If I could catch even a breath of that, I would feel okay.

I wander up and down the rows of books, some of which sit neatly in the bookcases, others stacked in haphazard, leaning towers. While I walk, I sing: *"Nobody likes me, everybody hates me, I think I'll go eat worms…"*

I touch the books as I pass, reading the spines.

"Big ones, little ones, fat ones, juicy ones, itsy-bitsy, fuzzy wuzzy worms…"

Some of the titles are the most peculiar things I have ever seen. I'm not sure if they unnerve or delight me.

"Bite their heads off, mmm, they're juicy, throw the tails away…"

I pick up one and stare at the spine; the title is half-erased by the passage of long years. *Bulgarian Thimbles: A History.*

"Nobody knows how big I'll grow eating worms three times a day."

I decide to make a mental note of my favorites.

A Gentleman's Guide to Coffin-Making

An Argument Against Tea Cozies (eight hundred pages)

Bulgarian Thimbles: A History

A Typology of Bed Fleas

Weaving with Dog Hair

A Practical Guide to Embalming

Despite myself, I grin. But I'm looking for something specific. I touch many of the tomes, hoping that somehow I will know which one to open. Which to explore. There has to be an answer in here. A history of La Baume, maybe. Or of the town. Something that will suggest what could be happening in this manor.

If nothing else, this is a distraction from the roots in the earth and the trees creeping toward us.

A distraction from the fact that I am almost convinced I'm being haunted. From the fact that Cath is mad, in the attic, pacing up and down, that the garden is dying, that we're running out of food, and that something is terribly, terribly *wrong* here.

Circling the loom, Silla darling. You're circling the loom.

Ω

4

too stupid to see

Mash it up and add some spice
put it in, keep it down
rumbling is a childish vice
hunger is the dark's device.

BROKEN BOOK ENTRY

These are my **dreams**. Someone will **walk** from the trees, and the sky will be **bleak** above him. **And** then he smiles, waves. He is **gray**-faced. He begins to jog **across** the green toward me, smiling, and **my** heart swells into the universe, which cracks open, revealing an infinity. It's almost like a **memory**, but of course it is just the night visions. **Nightmares**. There are **too** many of them these days. I **have** them almost every night. Most people have nightmares about **their** past, but not me. I have them about my present. He reaches me. He takes **hold** of me and pulls me closer. His head **on** my shoulder. He wants **me**. He pulls back to **look** at me but his face is gone. In **its** place an **eyeless** thing watches; **I scream**…

And **I wake**.

Ω

Light flickers and flashes through the skyline of the library. The trees are dancing in the storm out there. They *creeeeeeak* and moan through the night. Or is that Cath pace-pace-*pacing* in the attic? Nori was asleep in her bed when it got bad, so I left her there, but now I regret it.

It's just so…*quiet*…in the library. So still. There is no thunder. I've riffled through so many books that my eyes are itching from the dust. There are no answers here.

hopeless.

Such a pretty word.

The floorboards complain in the hallway beyond the door and I freeze, waiting. Too heavy for Nori. Cath wouldn't leave the attic, surely?

"Silla?"

"Gowan?"

"Yeah, it's me. Open up, would you? It's bloody freezing out here."

I crack the door open a little and see his face pressed to the gap. "Let me in," he says, his breath fogging.

I step back, more out of surprise than anything else, and a

waft of freezing air follows him. I slam the door shut and lock it compulsively.

"*What are you doing here?*" I whisper. "It's the middle of the night!"

He heads for the fireplace and sits down on the sheepskin rug, shivering. "It's freezing in this house. I forgot that."

"*Gowan!*"

"What?"

"What are you *doing* here? How did you even get inside?"

"I fancied a visit," he says. "I used to live here, you know. It's kind of a memory. I could still get into this house if you locked every door."

"Yeah, but in the middle of the night?" Part of me wants to call him stupid, idiotic, pathetic—pervert. I swallow my anger, unsure where it is coming from, and allow myself to feel the relief that is flooding through me. *Someone is here. I'm not alone.*

He shrugs. "Couldn't sleep."

"Wait—did you walk through *Python* in the middle of the night?"

"I know the way."

You are insane. My urge to yell at him becomes an urge to push him, hit him, bite—stop it. Again, I force away my anger. Stop this. Relief rises again.

He laughs at me, as though he can hear what I'm thinking.

"Do I get a hug?"

I step back. "Excuse me?"

He grins. "For warmth purposes only."

"Uh-huh." I go to the sofa and throw my blanket at him, a little too hard maybe.

He catches it deftly, grinning. "Thanks." Wrapped around him, it looks much more pleasant. He's so...tall. I blink and look away.

"What are you reading?" he asks, coming over, a bulk of fleecy white.

I shake my head, dropping the old text on the sofa by the door. "Nothing in particular."

"I used to come here every night," he tells me. "I'd sit for hours, reading. Sometimes just looking. Half of the books are in French, but they are beautiful and I could get lost in the look of the words. Tiny, endless words filling pages upon pages. I used to tell myself I'd fill a whole giant book with words one day, in gothic letters, pressed tightly together. Didn't really mind what they said. Just seeing the text building up, like a collection, was enough."

"Mm. Fascinating," I drawl. But in fact, I am intrigued. By him, by his voice. There's something so warm and appealing about him. But anger rises again, unbidden.

"This is ridiculous," I mutter.

He ignores my comment. "I brought you an apple." He reaches into his pocket and pulls free an apple that is mostly green, but with a blush of red on the side. I take it.

There is a lengthy silence.

"I can see we're not going to spend much time talking."

I don't bother with a reply.

"Do you love anything?" he asks me suddenly. Unexpectedly. "Anything at all?"

He waits for a long time. Patience must be his forte.

"Humor me," he says at last. "It's a simple question, and a long night. But it has to be honest."

I glance at the old clock and see that it's only ten p.m. I sigh and sit down beside him on the rug, and consider the question. Irritability rises steadily until, finally, at exactly twenty to eleven, I have a truthful answer.

"I love my sister. That's all."

Ω

Once upon a time, when I was three, Mam told a whispered bedtime story about a manor lost in the woods, where a crazy old lady lived in an enchanted place. A place that was full of magic, surrounded by enchanted woodland, and where things out of the ordinary happened.

Her weak moment became my dream.

I was four when I started begging for a sketch.

And ten when she finally complied.

A ring of woods, denser and blacker than her sketch revealed, and inside it: a ring of fields sloping downward. Inside that, a tiny fence slung around a ring of garden, and there, at the center like a jewel, La Baume. Paradise. Perfect. A secret. How magical it all seemed. I watched Mam's hands as she sketched, but I should have paid more attention to her face.

I was fourteen when I dragged Nori by the arm to La Baume's front door. Fifteen when Cath baked me a birthday cake with two tiers, big raspberries and cream decorating the edges. I had eaten three huge pieces before I noticed she had put worms in the batter.

Looking back, I know that's when things started to change. An endless procession of years leading to this.

I was just too stupid to see.

Ω

The man is in the corner again. His head touches the ceiling, and he still has to bend! Even though it is very dark, I see him because he's darker. It's much less lonely now that he's come to play. Oh, the games we play! But we have to play at night, in the dark. But that's okay because I'm not scared anymore. He told me the secret. But I'm scared of making Silla angry.

I push back the bedcovers late at night when the man calls. He calls with his long index finger, smiling wide—oh, how fun! I giggle. <u>Quick, quick!</u>

Silla paces in her room.

Auntie Cathy paces <u>hiiiiigh</u> up in the roof.

I run on my toes to the corridor and then I go down, down, down into the basement.

My friend follows.

And we play.

Ω

5

edge of reason

Children made him
and children call
children play
like flies on the wall.

BROKEN BOOK ENTRY

Most **people** will tell you that he doesn't exist.
Might be a bad feeling, or a trick of the light.
Most people will **say** that he's a scary bedtime
story to terrify the little children. They say that
he is an urban legend or folktale, or a shadow on
the wall. And if you believe in him, well, **ain't**
you just the peach? But I know in my bones he's
real because of what I saw that day. Some of it's
fuzzy **because** of the crazy crowding out **the**
truth. But I know he **is** real. I know it because

I've seen him at **the edge** of Python Wood, watching, bent and gnarly, tall as a tree, thin as a reed. **Of** course he watches. The **reason** is so simple, so primal, so necessary. **He** wants us all, and that **is** something I have to live with. I'm the only one who knows. Or maybe she does, too. He's **hungry**, and we're the only ones left. He's getting **desperate**. I wonder how long it will be before he leaves his cover of trees and slithers closer.... He is **watching me right now**, waiting for the day when I am stupid enough to go wandering again, **wanting** it more than anything. And **me**? I just sit and watch. Because why would I go? Do I want to end up **dead**?

Ω

It's a tree.

I tell myself this for the first hour.

Just a tree.

A boring, stupid tree.

I've got cabin fever, and it's making me imagine strange things. *[JUST LIKE THAT ONE TIME IN THE WOODS.]*

A tree, thrashing out there in the wind, far back in the wood. Or it's a splash of rain on the windowpane. A bat flying past—

It is not what it looks like.

After a second hour, I have convinced myself of all of this. Dawn is almost here, and my feet are aching. I might sit down. I might just...stop looking.

After all, it's just a tree.

Mam would howl with laughter if she could see me now. But then, she would have laughed when I went into the woods that one time. I can hear her laughing, all the way from London.

I close my eyes for a moment, half falling asleep. And when I open them, I realize: it's not a tree, not a trick of the light, not the rain on the windowpane, not a bat flying past.

A tree. It's a tree. I convince myself of this, almost fully. Until the thing steps forward, his head turning a fraction in my direction. I can almost hear the tiny *creeeeeeeeeeeeeeak* as his head rotates. It is a tall, long-limbed, bulbous-headed shadow.

I blink again.

Closer.

And again.

Closer.

Closer each time. Like the trees. Tall, thin. Eerily still. Still and *watchful*. A man. Something like a man.

But he has no eyes.

I notice that right away. He has no face. *Wait...is that...is it—* There's a mouth.

A long gash of a mouth, thin and smiling. A jagged line. Until it falls open, revealing teeth and an endless blackness.

Grinnnnnnnnnning.

And then it falls forward on all fours, long and thin and *impossible*, scuttling back into the woods, head cocked up to me, until he is nothing but tree and shadow and I don't know if I've seen it at all.

The Creeper Man.

Of all the things that thing could have been, a *man* is not it.

Cath's voice gurgles up out of my head. *"The Creeper Man. He's not a protector at all...."*

Crazy old witch.

The Creeper Man is here, dearie, says a voice inside.

She doesn't know what she's talking about.

It's too late.

No. That's not true.

You've seen him now.

It was a tree.

He's seen you see.

If I end up like Cath, remind me to kill myself.

I rest my heart in anger to keep away my fear.

Ω

SILLA DANIELS'S GUIDE TO KEEPING SANE

1. Don't believe the things you see.

2. Trust that your mind is lying.

3. Ignore, ignore, ignore.

4. Sleep.

5. Accept, with a rational mind, that sanity is a rock. And rocks can be eroded.

6. Don't let yourself believe that the thing you saw in the woods was a man. Don't let yourself believe that he was watching you.

Ω

I watch Nori play in the garden from behind the pane of glass as I dry the dishes. There is no food. I must find some food. The garden is dying—no. Dead. The garden is dead. The only things that grow now are the roots. Impossible roots from trees too far away.

[THE TREES ARE COMING CLOSER.]

Yes.

I'm certain now. They are closer. They *are*. By several yards. And they may be taller...I can't tell. They watch me. Their gaze is a touch on my back. Physical.

Something I can't explain sets my teeth on edge. Nori is running for the trees. Again. The plate in my hand shatters on the floor, shards scattering like milk teeth.

"For *God's* sake, Eleanor."

By the time I reach her, she's standing in front of Gowan at the very edge of Python Wood. I'm out of breath, startled and annoyed. But mostly, I'm...relieved. It's so *good* to see him. To see anyone.

He looks up from where he kneels. "Hello."

I nod, feeling the frosty air behind him.

"I brought some apples."

And I can see them, bulging in his pockets. They are the green of neon, rich with color I haven't seen in so long. A bag of garden tools dangles from his other hand. He really *is* going to work in the garden. *Good luck*.

Nori bounces on the balls of her feet, her hand making quick work of the signs. *Can I have an apple?*

"He doesn't understand," I tell her. "She's asking for an apple," I explain.

Gowan grins, and roots in his pocket for the biggest, juiciest-looking one, and then throws it high up into the sky. Nori opens her mouth in a hideous gaping grin, turning from doll to gargoyle as she runs back and forth, trying to see where it will land.

Gowan doesn't flinch at the sight of her mouth, wide open and rotten. He *smiles,* and I stare at him. He didn't flinch. He's *smiling*...I smile a tiny smile in return and turn back to Nori.

The apple falls a few feet away from her reaching hands, and she runs to get it, laughing silent laughs.

"It's good to see you," Gowan says, watching Nori.

[LIAR.]

I want to believe him. He's still laughing, throwing apples for Nori to run and catch. He isn't paying attention to me. In that moment, I wish I could be like them. I wish I could ignore what's happening at La Baume and Python Wood and the dead garden. But this house, this land, is just...*wrong.* Not in any small way either, but in the very makeup of it. It's like the garden is dying because the manor has a kind of scar or cancer or something. I should have known it the second it got Aunt Cath. I want to be able to talk to her about it, but those days are gone. Besides, I tried and look what happened. Crazy talk and a lifetime of hate. Even if she talked to me again, why would I be stupid enough to think that she would make any more sense than she did last time?

hopeless.

Such a pretty word, for what it means.

h o p e l e s s n e s s.

I let the word drift in my mind, like an unmanned canoe on a slow-running river.

[LEAVE THEM TO THEIR PLAY,] the cynical me thinks. [USELESS, POINTLESS PLAY.]

I come to my senses as Gowan throws an apple for me. I miss, my hands slow and languid, and it falls into the dead-ash dirt.

"Never mind," Gowan says, picking it up and dusting it off before handing it to me. "For you."

Cursed. Tainted. Spoiled. Ruined. Defective. Wrong. No.

I take the apple, but the cavity in my tooth beats in painful little pulses. I don't want to put anything in my mouth. Don't want to mention the cavity because what can they do except drag me kicking and screaming through the woods and to a dentist?

No. I'll knock the thing out myself if I have to. After what I saw...*think* I saw...

Nori skips over. *Try it! Oh, Silla, try it! It's so good, so sweet, I love apples!*

I raise the thing to my lips—*No, I Don't Want To*—and open my mouth. The apple hovers there in front of my teeth, and Nori claps her hands. I get the strongest notion that this is a Snow White kind of moment, life-and-death curse and all, and I let the apple drop.

[HUNGRY. I AM SO HUNGRY.]

Poison. Sleep. Death. Curse. Wrong. Stop.

"Not hungry," I say, smiling so that the horrible expression of confusion will just get off Gowan's face and he'll go back to focusing on Nori.

He shrugs. "No problem. More for us!"

Nori squeals silently. He can't tell, but I can, and for once I'm glad of her silence, but her hands blare joy and I shudder.

Then I despise myself.

Ω

UNNOTICED BY ALL

The floorboards *crack* and splinter. I hear them from high up here in the attic, through the planks of wood under my feet. I stop my pacing to listen. They break and fracture, bending down and inward. Tiny screams as the fibers shatter. A plank bends inward, and then another, splitting and falling away.

I can't hear its impact, and I know it is back. This house...this evil old house.

A small, insignificant hole appears in the entrance hall.

It goes unnoticed by all, except for me.

And I don't say a word.

Ω

Silla Daniels. Presilla Mae Daniels. This is my name. It is real, and so am I.

Silla Mae Daniels? Present!

I don't say La Baume.

What's the point?

La Baume is a shadow, a cage, a sketch, a lie.

I tear the piece of paper off and burn it in the candle. Then I catch my reflection in the mirror.

"What are *you* looking at?"

Ω

6

i had loved her

One, two, three, four
will you open up the door?
five, six, seven, eight
he wants you to feed your hate.

It's wrong that Gowan isn't baking in the sun. Instead, the misty gray of the day settles around us as he tills the ash with a long garden fork and I watch him do it.

"You were right about the garden," he comments, wiping nonexistent sweat from his brow. "It's not been cared for in a while."

I bite back a retort, since *I've* been *trying* to tend to it for months. He'll see soon enough. *Idiot.*

"Soil's dry," he adds. "Not been much rain, I suppose."

I shake my head.

He stares at me all the time. Ever since he started coming every day. It's like having a constant flame at my back. His eyes are full of impossible context, and I keep thinking: *You don't know me.* And then I think: *You are beautiful. So achingly beautiful. It hurts to look at you.*

"You seem to have pixies," he says wryly, and when I turn to look where he's indicating, I see Nori skipping around at the other end of the garden, two twigs behind her ears, her body hunched over and her hands clawed. She has lifted up the back of her dress to hook over the twigs and she is doing a weird kind of hopping dance. For once, her arm suits her.

I snort, the laughter bursting out of me unexpectedly. I blink with surprise, and test out my smile again. It still works.

Gowan's smile is bright and wide and his eyes turn from glass to crystal.

I grin at him, but then the horrible feeling comes, like it always does, and I turn away, frowning.

He looks surprised. "It's okay to laugh, you know. Come on, Silla," he adds when I don't look at him, but move farther away. "It's okay," he says, and then I hear his spade slicing the earth.

I don't say anything because he's got fire inside him for sure, and fire burns.

Ω

Later, when we are gathered in the kitchen—me making the last of the oats for Nori (though she prefers the apples), and Gowan washing off the ash-soil with tight lips—the light begins to fade quickly.

Gowan looks out the window and bows his head over the towel he's drying his hands with. "I should go."

Nori signs, *Let him stay, Silla! Let him stay!*

I sigh, and Gowan turns to me with a frown. "Everything okay?"

Nori whips her head between us, her eyes as wide and manic as her smile.

I sigh and pinch the bridge of my nose. "Nori wants you to stay," I say. "For dinner," I add quickly.

He smiles at her and puts the tea towel back on the rack without looking. "Is that right? Well, I'd have to get permission from the lady of the house, wouldn't I?"

Nori grins at me, and then nods enthusiastically at him.

I fold my arms. "That would be Cath, then, wouldn't it?"

"Well, she's infirm. I'd say that leaves . . . you." He nods at Nori in a two-person conspiracy against me. "Right?"

She grins. Mutiny, more like.

"Fine. Then stay. We have"—I check the remaining apples—"two apples and some god-awful oats that expired months ago. Gourmet meals, here."

He reacts to the hardness in my eyes with a sheepish smile, but Nori doesn't notice.

I'm full, she signs. *Can I go play?*

I nod stiffly at her, and she runs off, grinning back at me. Gowan watches her go.

"Was it something I said?"

"She said she's full and she wants to go play."

"More for us, then. How about it? An apple each, stale oats, and some water?"

I sigh. "Does anything dampen your spirits?"

He shrugs. "Not really, no."

Ω

I roll the apple around in my hand, listening to Gowan chew his. His oats are still waiting, and I don't see how any of this is appetizing to him.

"So, how long have you been here?" he asks around a cheek full of apple.

"Around three years." It feels much longer.

"I never found out what 'La Baume' means," he muses.

"It's an old word. It means something like 'the grotto.' Appropriate. It's pretty grotty all right."

"So...what happened to Cath? She was, well, normal last time I checked."

I don't bother to answer the question. Talking is tiring, and the subject is depressing.

"I should go up to see her." Surprisingly, he seems more alarmed by the prospect than I am. Is it because he remembers her one way—matronly, or motherly?—and doesn't want to see how she's changed? He must assume she has, given that she won't leave the attic, and I've told him she's lost it completely.

"You should leave," he says suddenly, putting his half-eaten apple down and breaking into my thoughts. "You should take Nori and just leave."

"That's your professional gardening advice, is it?"

"Silla, anyone could see you'll starve unless you go. There's no shop in town anymore. We could go to London—"

"Never."

"Or north? Anywhere else."

"I don't think so."

"Think of Nori."

"I do," I snap, scraping my chair back as I stand. "I think of her every day. And we're not leaving."

He sighs. "Just...think about it, Silla. I don't understand what's stopping you."

He doesn't have to. How could he possibly believe what I barely believe? That this place is *wrong* somehow, and that... *something* is in those woods? The tall, thin—*thing* waiting for us to come? *All* he needs to know is that I am *not* going into those woods. Not ever again.

Ω

THAT ONE TIME
IN THE WOODS

I take nothing but my coat, and hurry out while Nori is sleeping. She won't even know I was gone.

I run down the field and into the woods, pausing for a moment to look back at the manor. The light is fading, but it'll be okay if I do this quickly. It's light enough to find my way, if I'm fast.

"Please be safe," I whisper. "Safe until I get back."

I push away the image of Cath stalking slowly downstairs and cornering Nori, cornering her to scream at her or strangle her or—

"Please be safe," I say again, and then I run.

The trees fly past at first; I duck and weave through the ancient woodland, skirting fungus-grown trunks and moss-hung branches, until the land begins to change. Rains have created soft mud out of the rotting leaves and earth, and I slip—almost fall—then catch myself on the trunk of a tree. I go slower after that, as the mud gets looser.

The farther I travel through Python, the trees of which thrash and move around me in the wind like dancing voodoo priests, the deeper the mud gets.

Ankle.

Midcalf.

Knee.

Before I know it, I'm wading through icy mud that clings and sticks and squelches as I go. Glancing behind me, I consider turning back, but I can't even see the manor anymore, and I think I'm nearer to the village than not.

I can't turn around. We need help. I can't fail.

The weather is only going to get worse the closer winter comes. It's now or never.

I begin to notice things. Things moving in the dusky dimness of early evening. A twitch here. A buzz there.

I feel the mud seeping through my jeans and into my socks, and when I glance ahead of me, I realize that I have no idea how deep the mud will go. Maybe I'll walk and walk, and then suddenly step off the edge of a ravine and be plunged into inky-black mud, miles deep, struggling to return to light and air—forever. I grip the tree beside me, hanging on to one of the low branches, trying to steady my mind and calm my heart.

They're just trees.

Get a move on.

Then movement again: the buzzing sound. The sound of something small, *many* things small: Crawling. Scattering. Squelching. Slithering. Something runs over my hand and I flinch away. A beetle. Or an ant. I squint at the tree, which seems to buzz like the static on an old TV. I step closer, trying to make sense of what I'm seeing. And then I do. Hundreds of thousands of crawling things all over the tree. Ants, beetles, borers, cankerworms—some I can't identify. I move away—as far as I can—unable to take my eyes off them. Their rhythmical, random movement congealing into something disgustingly tantalizing, and I revolt against the sight, but I can't look away.

At my knees, the mud bubbles and moves, like the depth hides some swimming creature down there, curling and coiling in the mud.

I hesitate.

I run.

As fast as the mud allows me, until I *do* go over the edge of some tiny precipice and find myself trapped, the mud pooling around my upper thighs like cold, clammy pudding. Like hands clasping.

"One step," I say, taking one forward. "Another step," I chant, stepping again. "One step...another step. One step..."

On and on I walk, and the light fades to a dark gray that turns Python into a maze of tall, thin walls and obstacles I can't quite make out. The buzzing, hissing, creaking sound of the bugs grows louder as the light dies.

I can see the village now—a few more rows of trees, and I'm there. Except...something is wrong.

Where are the lights? Where are the signs? Where are the people who should be in the pub drinking their beer and watching the game? Where is the sound of their laughter, the cackling beneath the pump of music and the white noise of chatter?

Where is the *life*?

I squint, leaning closer, my thighs squelching in the mud, and spot the corner store.

Boarded up.

Along the lane, the post office—boarded up.

Farther still, the pub—no lights. Doors chained.

Dear God...Everyone's left. The *whole* village has just... left.

Left us here alone.

We're alone.

I'm alone.

The terror is like a foghorn in the darkness. Like a spotlight pointed at me, notifying the monsters of the world exactly where I am: exposed, armorless.

How could they leave us behind?

Very suddenly I don't want to be in Python anymore. I want to be on the pavement of the lane. I want to find someone—*anyone*—who might still be here. It can't be just us. It can't. I have no money, we have no phone, there is no postman—and the nearest town is more than seventy miles away.

There has to be someone.

I have to find *someone*.

In desperation, I claw my way up the bank, out of the woods, and roll onto the grass by the town lane. I lie there for a moment, ridding myself of the sensation of moving mud around, ignoring the dark sentinel trees waiting for me to return.

Wandering down the lane confirms what I saw from the woods: Pub, locked. Post office, boarded up. Corner shop, too. I walk down Prairie Street—the houses are all dark and empty, some boarded up, others left wide open, doors swinging on their hinges. I go inside some of them—take the two cans I find. Apricots in syrup. Corned beef.

I walk the half mile to the train station, and when I get there it is dark. No trains. No lights. No nothing. No sun in the sky.

I stand at the ticket office, waiting. Hoping. Useless.

"Hello?" I call.

I wait.

"Hello! Please! PLEASE!"

The returning silence is louder once my echoes have faded.

On the way back, heart hammering now that my shock is wearing off, I pass the village school. Drawings hang in sad, dark windows, and the school gates swing with high-pitched screams as I pass, the wind blowing through me.

For the first time in my entire life, I feel truly, utterly, and completely alone on the planet. And I realize: No one is coming. No one is going to help us.

Cathy's medieval way of living means it's likely that no one even knows we're here.

Oh God.

What are we going to do?

Nori.

I left her with Cath. Crazy Cath in the attic. Nori won't understand why I'm gone. She'll panic. Maybe try to come after me. Get lost.

She can't cry out. She can't scream.

I'll lose her.

I sprint down Prairie Street, along the village lane, and back into Python. I'd give anything to have a way around the woods, or a path through; there is nothing but the waiting mud.

I slip down the rise and jump into what looks like a black stretch of nothing, with dark figures floating in it, impossibly tall.

Trees.

I take a last look at the village, a shiver of dread dripping down my spine and lower, and then I turn my back on it forever.

The mud is thicker now, and I've gone no more than five paces before I am panting, using the branches of the bug-infested trees to pull myself along. The mud is sucking down on my legs, pulling with a force I didn't know mud could have. I lose my shoes, they are sucked off my feet like a giant tongue has whipped them away. I try to find them, my feet freezing now in the mud, feeling the texture of whatever the mud conceals, but they are gone.

I pull myself along, five more paces, my toes feeling every rocky or slimy spot, and then I see the dog. I see it because of the eyes. They glint in the moonlight, shocks of white in the dark. The moon is rising fast now, and I have no trouble seeing that the poor thing is dead. Teeth bared, eyes open. Staring.

If I were to say anything about it at all, it would be that the dog—a cocker spaniel—looks as terrified as I feel. So odd. I'm *sure* the thing died in fear.

"Poor pup," I say, looking down at the corpse. "Did you get lost? Left behind? Me too."

And then the mud bubbles around him. I see other glints then. On eyes, on teeth. And lumps in the mud as far as I can see in the moonlight. The things stirring in the mud are rising.

Oh no...no...it can't be.

Dogs.

Cats.

Pets.

All the village pets—*all* of them—are here in Python. And all of them are dead. Dozens of corpses, all of them staring, mouths open in a final growl, a final shriek, fur clogging with black mud, and all of them

s t a r i n g

a t

m e

I shake my head. Back and forth. No. No, this is wrong. I suddenly wonder what the hell I'm standing on.

The village empty...and all the pets dead in Python Wood. Wrong. THIS IS WRONG.

I back away, but they follow. The suction of the mud means that the faster I move, the faster they come, eyes open and mouths begging.

"Go away," I whisper, choking on the words. But they keep coming.

I turn and I heave myself through the mud, pulling on tree trunks and trying to beat my exhaustion, but I feel them chasing me, all of them pulled by the vacuum I leave in my wake. Or are they swimming?

The tree trunks give the sudden impression of coal, rather than wood, and beyond them—or in between them—I spot a flash of movement some way off from me. Low down. A long, dark thing.

Boar?

Deer?

Something else entirely.

There—again. A shadow, scuttling as though *on top* of the mud. Long-limbed and fast. Impossibly fast.

I wade and wade, pulling against the suction with every last desperate ounce of energy I have left, chanting, "One step, another step," all the way. I break out in sweat; it runs down my face and neck, my body exhausted to the bone, until at last I can see the faint, flickering light of La Baume in the distance, up on the hill.

The thing in the woods is no longer long. It is *tall*. A torso. Long arms. A bulbous head.

Maybe not so alone after all, something inside me thinks.

The thought doesn't comfort me.

I pull myself, fighting against the mud, which tugs like something trying to keep me. I fall forward, reaching for the grass beyond the tree line, and I heave myself, gasping and grunting out of the mud, which *still* tries to drag me back like hands tugging on my jeans.

I claw my way out, collapsing on the grass, and crawling on my exhausted legs, panting and sweating, yearning to run back to La Baume, but unable to get to my feet.

The woods seem taller, looming above like they are getting ready to chase me, and I dig my nails into the earth and haul myself farther away. Eventually, I manage to get to my knees, crawling, then half standing—stumbling, and falling all the way back, shedding Python mud in my wake, leaving behind dozens of animal corpses with their pleading eyes, and the tall, thin shadow of something I will ignore until I have no choice.

Ω

I push the memory of that night away. Later, when I'm sure Gowan is with Nori and not spying on me, I put the old root I found in the garden into the grass no more than ten paces from the boundary to Python. I tie a length of Cath's red ribbon to it.

Then I walk back inside, convincing myself that the trees are *not* laughing at me.

Ω

Creeeeeeeeaaaaak.

Aunt Cath's pacing is endless. I miss her. I miss the way she used to be. It hurts to remember....

Ω

Can I have some cream? Nori had signed.

Cath, who had been sitting with Nori and me every day to learn the signs herself, had smiled.

"You like cream, little slug. But too much will make you a maggot! How about some big, juicy raspberries from the garden instead and maybe you'll be a butterfly?"

Nori had squealed silently, clapping her hands.

Cath had winked at me over the top of Nori's bobbing head, and I had smiled.

And I had loved her.

Ω

October 17, 1980: Three little girls played by the lake. It had been drying up for years, and Papa said that within their lifetimes it would be nothing but a muddy patch no one would look twice at. The water, he said, was going, dying, *vanishing*. It was being reclaimed by the sky.

The girls believed there were still fish in the lake, small and putrescent as it was, and they ran the circumference with their nets, trying to catch one for supper. Only one of the three persisted for long.

One sister, the eldest, sat neatly on the grass, watching while she sewed a new skirt for her doll, Nancy.

Another sister, the middle one, stood in the mud, letting it squelch between her toes. She was watching the last sister, the littlest of all, run round and round, dipping her net into the water and squealing. But there were never any fish, only tadpoles.

They had tried to keep one last summer, thoughts of a pet frog to play with tumbling around their young minds. It had died in its bucket. Anne, the littlest, had sobbed for days and carried out a funeral, which even Papa was forced to attend.

They were sisters three in a house the color of the sky.

Anne. Youngest. Most precious.

Pamela. The middle sister. Wildest.

Catherine. Eldest. Most sensible.

The Jewel.
The Adventurer.
The Protector.

Three little girls did a very bad thing.

Ω

7

chew chew chew

Choo, choo, train!
chew, chew, brain.
bite, bite, swallow,
I am hollow!
night, night, man,
dream, I can
cry, cry, cry!
bye, bye! Die.

La Baume is a mammoth. Three stories, not including the attic. The third floor is derelict—everything from the wallpaper to some of the floorboards stripped away by the soldiers or refugees or something during World War II. I'm hazy on the details.

I have a habit of wandering the third floor by myself. It always feels eerily cold, empty enough to feel slightly sentient. It's a barrier between Cath and the rest of us, though it doesn't do much to filter out the creaking of her pacing. It has textured wallpaper. Mostly it's peeling away, or gone entirely in patches, and it smells like abandoned bees' nests, the floors of the rooms at the far end littered with the shells of wasps and hornets. A carpet of decay. I closed those doors a long time ago, but every now and then I poke my head inside. Those floors are what my insides look like. Hundreds—thousands—of dead husks of what used to be wasps. These walks are an indulgence.

Pull yourself together, I tell myself.

When I go to check on Nori, she is sitting in her room, staring at the corner again and grinning like an idiot. I might be bold and take one of Cath's old dolls. It's not healthy for a seven-year-old to be alone so much. The fact that she finds *walls* so interesting is proof enough.

Ω

We are so alone here. We're beginning to feel it. I don't know if Nori does. But I do. All the time. What's happening? Is there a quarantine? Did the war start, like they said? Did they bomb away the world? Are we all that's left? Why doesn't Mam write to us? We are her only daughters, who she let go, and nothing. Did she forget about us as soon as we left? Did she try to visit us already? Have the trees trapped her? Has he got her? My mind can't stop turning. This can't go on forever.

Ω

Gowan brings apples again. Nori is at the boundary to the woods before he even clears the trees. I'm too slow to stop her from running off, but when I get there, I pull her back and wrap my arms around her. She holds on to my arms and waits.

We both wait.

I scan the ground for the root that I stuck into the ground yesterday. I tied a ribbon around it to make sure I could find it again. But it's gone. Maybe the wind, the storm, maybe the trees themselves—

And then I spot it. Twenty paces deep into the woods.

They *are* moving.

Oh, God. They are.

"A welcoming committee!" Gowan calls when he sees us.

Nori calls his name with her hands, and he grins at her and winks. Then he puts down a sack of apples. There have to be twenty in there at least. My stomach roils but I force a smile anyway.

The woods are moving.

Gowan leaves Nori with the fruit and then wanders over to me.

He folds his hands behind his back. "Hello."

"Hello."

"Would you like an apple, Miss Daniels?" he says, presenting one to me, deftly produced from his pocket.

"Maybe later," I offer, a little weakly, eyes flickering to the woods and back. My stomach is doing backflips and I really would rather *not* vomit on Gowan if I can help it. "Want to go inside? Looks like rain."

He stares at the sky for a few moments, briefly closes his eyes, and then looks back down at me. A nod. I try to see what he saw up there, but it's just another overcast day. It always looks like rain will come. None ever does. The sky is as ashen as the dirt, and once again I wonder about London and the government—their wars and their bombs and their threats— and whether there's anyone left at all.

Gowan grabs the bag of apples, lifts Nori onto his back, and we head to the manor.

"You know, I never see you eat," Gowan says when we're inside.

I send Nori off to drop three apples at the foot of Cathy's stairs, and then I sit down at the kitchen table and watch as Gowan stacks the green balls of fruit flesh in the center.

"So? Just because you don't see me do it doesn't mean I don't."

My stomach answers for me, a rumbling growl to rival Nori's.

"Point proven," Gowan says, the edges of his eyebrows hiked up with satisfaction.

"I have to feed her first. There isn't much, and it's my job to make sure she gets food."

"Well, I've brought food. So take some. Please, Silla. You're wasting away."

I reach for an apple. Poison. Dirt. Disgusting. Toxic. Snow White. Sleeping Beauty. Sleep. Die. Don't. No.

I lift it to my lips. Open them. I shiver as I bite down, the sound a *crack* and a *creak* as I chew.

Chew. Chew. Chew.

Swallow.

Swallow.

Silla, my brain commands. *Swallow.*

I can't.

I swallow. It scrapes its way down my esophagus like paper, no pleasure at all, and lands like lead in my stomach. It is a stone in the cavity, and I want to get it out.

"It's wonderful," I lie. "Thank you."

He looks so proud of me. For this one, stupid thing. But then that look fades as he watches me get up and put the rest of it down on a plate to save for Nori later.

"Will you come and visit me?"

"Not that again."

"Please, Silla." And he takes my hand.

His flesh on mine.

Someone touching me.

No one has touched me, except Nori, in months. Maybe years.

I'm so distracted by it that I just stare at our hands, missing half of what Gowan is saying.

"...and you might be right. It might be too late. But gardens can lie barren for years and recover. Humans can't. You and Nori and Cath have to leave. It's not healthy here. It's..." He looks around. "Not what I remember."

And I suddenly wonder what he *does* remember. How does he see La Baume? Is it very different from what it was then? In what ways? So many curiosities, but that's the trick, isn't it? That's how it happens. An investment. An intrigue. And then a trap. Friendship is a trap. Family is a trap.

Love is a trap.

And it's all lies, anyway.

I decide to tell him a truth, which is far more brutal than a lie. Because he should know what he is trying to get himself into. With me. And with this place.

"The trees are moving."

That stops him short. "What?"

"The trees are moving. Coming closer."

He plays with my fingers. He does it absentmindedly, without thought, without reason. *Sensation*—real, present, oh, so *real*— and I haven't felt that since...when? Have I ever really felt it?

"What are you thinking about?" I ask. *My skin? My bones? My bones under the skin? The trees, inching closer, even as we sit here?*

He smiles as he looks at me. "My mind is as empty as air."

"Liar. Tell me."

A hesitation. "You won't like it."

"Wanting us to go with you again?"

"Yes. And if what you say about the trees is true, and they really are—"

"Moving."

"Yes...moving. Getting closer—"

"They are. I measured them with a root."

"—then maybe that's all the more reason to go. Get away from here. This house...it's not good for you."

It is W R O N G.

I glance back at La Baume. In the early-evening light it looks even more like blood.

"It's home."

"Home can be unhealthy."

I know this too well.

"And Nori?" I ask.

"She'll come, too."

"And Cath? She won't leave."

Gowan hesitates, then opens his mouth to reply.

I cut him off. "I'm not leaving her behind. Besides...I told you before. Those trees are wrong. I won't go back in there."

"They let you in the first time; they'll let you leave. You just have to be strong. Small and strong and...beautiful."

Beautiful. Broken. Cracked. Decaying. Wrong. You are wrong.

"Why would we go with you anyway? We hardly know you."

I could have spat on him he looks so surprised. Then he nods, with a terse smile.

"Anyway," I add, "going through the woods was different then. Everything was different then. They let us in. They won't let us leave."

"You just have to have faith."

"In *what*?" I don't mean to sound so bitter. "Tell me other things, Gowan. Tell me stories of the sky and the sea. Open places full of magic. Tell me tales of places where music dances on breezes and girls go twirling through the sand. Tell me, Gowan."

Tell me pleasant lies, and I will believe them before I throw them away.

Ω

We spend our days like this. Me, sitting close by, my head cocked, or lying in the patchy, dead grass, crunchy beneath me. Gowan, weaving strands of longer grasses into plaits and telling tale after tale, while Nori plays in the ash-dirt of the garden or dances around us. Sometimes she stretches herself on the ground beside me, too enthralled by the tales he weaves to do anything else but listen.

I watch him closely.

And swallow my beating heart.

And push away my burning stomach.

And remind myself that he is a stranger.

I know nothing about him. I shouldn't trust him. You can't love what you don't know.

But he's so familiar.

But that, too, might be a trick.

Ω

"Come for a walk with me."

Gowan holds out his hand.

"No."

"Why not?"

I fold my arms. "I have to look after Nori."

Gowan grins. "She's in the library sleeping on the rug. I checked on her before I asked."

"Doesn't matter. She'll wake. Get scared." *[YOU ARE AFRAID TO LEAVE HER. YOU NEED HER.]*

Gowan's hand is still waiting, open and ready. "We'll bring her, too."

"You want to go walking with me...*and* my little sister."

"If it gets you to come with me."

I consider him, reading his every muscle, his every blink, twitch, and smile.

And I take his hand. It closes around me like a warm bath, comfort and safety—

[DON'T GET COMPLACENT.]

We walk the perimeter of the garden; he never lets go of my hand. When we arrive at the gate, I pull free. He looks back at me.

"You're like water slipping through my fingers."

I shake my head. I don't understand him.

He opens the garden gate and walks out, into the field, leaving it open behind him so that I can follow, if I want.

I follow when he is thirty paces in front of me, panting with the effort of walking uphill, my calves burning.

"Look at this." There is wonder in Gowan's voice, and it calls to me. He is crouching down some way ahead of me, and I hurry over, breathing hard.

"I can't believe it..." Gowan murmurs.

A yellow flower, small—minute—has pushed itself from the earth. It's not three paces from the woods. I haven't seen a flower in weeks. Longer. Not since the end of summer, which feels too long ago now.

"I can't believe it," he says again. "It's strong. Small, but strong. Like you." He looks at me. "It's beautiful."

"Asshole," I whisper, though my chest is filled with a rushing warmth, like a river in a growing storm. "It's a weed. Useless."

"Beautiful like you," he persists, grinning now.

I nudge him. "*Shh*. Nori might hear."

And then something horrifying occurs to me. Before I know what I'm doing, I pluck the flower from the earth, fragile and delicate roots dangling from my fist, crush it in my hand, and throw it into the woods.

"It's a trick," I say, shrugging away the look on Gowan's face and the awful way I feel inside. "The trees are trying to trick me."

Gowan swallows. "I have to go."

Ω

Later, when I go and look, hoping to use a stick to pull the flower back to me, it's no longer among the trees. *[THE CREEPER MAN TOOK IT.]* I swallow my guilt, and the shock I feel at myself—

His face.

Oh, God. Why do I even care? He's nothing. And yet, I can't stand the hurt I saw there.

—and I vomit into the earth.

Ω

I should have told him. I should have told him the horrifying thing that might be happening.

When I walked to him today—it was uphill. Slightly. Ever so slightly.

But when we arrived at La Baume, the house was at the top of a hill, not in the dip of a valley.

God help us.

I think the house is sinking.

Ω

8

food infiltration

Rotting in your skin
rotting in your mind
you are rotting in this house
in this house you'll die.

I frown down at my dress. The pale material is spotted with green. It puts me in mind of a rash, or an infection. A spreading bacteria in a petri dish.

I peer closer.

It can't be...

Impossible...

It's...fungus. Or mold. Suddenly repelled, I brush it off. *Try* to. I want it as far away from me as possible. It does nothing but smudge, turning my white dress into a blotchy green mess.

I rip it off and fling it away across the floor. It lands and sits like a curled snake. I'm shaking as I pull on the yellow dress instead. The clean cloth soothes me, even if it is a little damp, and I loose a half-hysterical giggle into the silent room.

"Enough of this," I tell myself, my voice grounding out the unreality of the moment. "Get Nori up. Now."

Her room is closest to the stairs, so I head for them, resisting the urge to look down at the ground floor, imagining I will see something or someone looking up at me. Nope. "Getting Nori up," I sing in a half whisper, "so we can start this crappy day."

I pause at her door, force a smile, and breeze in. "Wake up, lazy bug," I say, but then I stop beside her bed. A horrible, chilly feeling dances along my spine in unpleasant tingles.

Little patches of green—like tiny verdant freckles—are scattered upon her unblemished little cheek.

With a rising sense of horror, I raise my hand and wipe my own cheek, then look down. My fingertips are green.

Mold. Or moss. Or fungus.

It's growing on us.

Ω

Cath paces.
Creak. Creak. Creak.
Apple is masticated.
Creak. Creak. Creak.
The wind is agitated.
Creak. Creak. Creak.
My heart's full of hatred.
Creak. Creak. Creak.

Ω

The whole house is rotting. I can smell it. Rising damp, maybe. Mildew and wood rot everywhere. Even on us, now. Even the damn *air* looks a little green.

I watch Nori eat, seeing how the apple falls apart piece by piece, how Nori chews—*squish, squish, squish*—and swallows—*slosh!*—I am

revolted.

"All right?" Gowan asks.

I nod, though I'm queasy. "Why are you here?"

Gowan blinks. "You...you asked me to watch Nori so you could take a look at the walls inside, remember? Find the rising damp?" Trying to cozy up and be my friend.

I did? I...maybe I did. I can't remember.

"Right," I say. Here to look after Nori. But he's wrong if he thought I was trying to make him a friend. I swallow any pinch of embarrassment I might feel, get up, and walk away.

I feel half in a dream. I wander without thought. Anything to be away from Nori's apple mastication. The *creeeeak*ing of her little rotten teeth and the *slurp*ing of her saliva. I'll feel better when I'm alone. When it's quiet.

Only, when I *am* alone, I feel far from okay.

Ω

Hunger

so intense

it's like

there's a fence

between my urge

my need

my desperation

and the body that

seeks

food infiltration.

Can't swallow.

So hollow.

Could I borrow

your tomorrow?

I can't eat.

Can't swallow.

Why am I so hollow?

Ω

9

daddy

Where are you going?
won't you play here?
storm winds are blowing,
bringing me near.
I've waited so long,
for you to see.
if you must go on,
then go on with me.

LEAVE THIS HOUSE

AND YOU WILL DIE.

I wake up with his sylvan, rootlike voice rattling my skull.

LEAVE THIS HOUSE

AND YOU WILL DIE

AND SHE'LL BE MINE.

I shut my eyes, and then open them again, straining my ears so that the silence hurts. A dream. Just a dream. Branches moving, clawing roots twisting around my legs. The Creeper Man grinning, his mouth opening, Nori screaming—

Just a dream.

I lie back down, letting my heart settle, trying to ignore the incessant creaking, which seems to have crawled beneath my very skin. Even with this smallest sleep tonight, I heard the *croaking*. I have just closed my eyes once more, when—

Silla.

A voice. An impossible voice.

Presilla, daughter. Come to me.

My lungs won't inflate. "D-Dad?" I choke the word out on a strangled whisper, searching my shadowy room for him. "Dad?"

I slip out of bed. The hallway is still and empty. He can't be here, he can't be.

Silla.

I follow his call

Silla, come.

down the stairs

Daughter mine.

and to the entrance hall.

To a hole.

No bigger than my foot.

Presilla.

And his voice

Come on, girl.

is coming

Come to me.

from

Give in.

the darkness below.

Ω

He comes again the next night. It begins with a whisper I can almost ignore. More like the suggestion of breath on my shoulder. By midnight, the breath has become a touch. Every now and then, not enough to know for *sure* that I'm not alone, the sensation of a finger bruising my collarbone. Or a tug at the edge of my nightdress, too sharp to be nothing, gone too quickly to be something.

I sit up in bed and wrap my arms around my legs.

I wait.

And it comes again.

The hole in the entrance hall.

Presilla. Daughter.

I want to answer. I no longer know why I don't.

I know you like no other.

The door to my room stands wider than when I went to bed, the black beyond it deepening farther along the corridor until I see nothing. Nothing at all.

Come and talk to me. I understand you.

No, you don't, I think. No one understands this. *[I WISH GOWAN WAS HERE.]* The thought is unexpected, but *urgent. Gowan, I need you.*

The door is wider.

The black outside it is pregnant with presence, and I can't tear my eyes away. Something is watching me.

And I left my door open.

An invitation.

LEAVE THIS HOUSE,

AND YOU WILL DIE.

AND SHE'LL BE MINE.

Paralyzed, I stare at the space beyond the door, waiting. How is it possible to know—know with *absolute* certainty—that I am not alone? Know without knowing why, that the thing outside my door is still, too. Not still like me, but still like a predator. Something that had eyes *fixed* on me, pupils dilated. I remember the way the creature out there in the woods fell forward onto all fours and stared at me with cocked head. I remember the animals sinking into the quagmire, their terror, their demise.

I hear the bugs from that day, feasting on the pets' carcasses, only the sound is *real*, here, right now. A quiet chewing, wriggling, smooshing sound. The sound of thousands of worms wriggling together, over and under and through one another. The sound of exoskeletons beating with paper wings, the crunching sound of mandibles eating the rotting wood around me.

My body bolts out of bed before my mind can catch up, running for the door. I feel the thing in the corridor bolt, too, a fraction of a second later.

But I shut the door, heart T - H - U - D - D - I - N - G in my chest, and then

nothing.

I hear my father laughing at me from downstairs.

Stupid girl! Kill yourself and get it over with!

I have to get out of here. I pull my blanket off the bed, wrapping it around myself before tiptoeing back to the door. I feel frail in my own skin—it feels like a membrane, about to tear should something blow hard enough. It isn't enough protection.

I take a tentative peek into the corridor; it stretches away into gloom like a death-row march. I kick myself for being so damn foolish and hug my blanket closer. The library has only one entrance, and it's downstairs. The upper floors are all reached from within the cocoon. Which means I have to walk along the corridor, left along the hall, down the stairs, past the whispering hole, through the entrance hall, past the basement door, and then, finally, to the library. It's a lot of floor to cover. A lot of dark.

A lot of—

Stop. Stop. Just go.

I hesitate for only a moment, but it's enough for the spearing ice of dread to puncture my chest. Enough for me to regret stepping beyond the confinement of my bedroom. Enough to make me trip over my own feet, or my blanket, and stumble into the wall. I ignore the chill of it, the way it seems almost soft, as though it weren't the stone beside me, but something more like flesh.

My heart thuds in my ears so loudly I can't even hear my footsteps. I hear my breath, jagged, because I caught movement from the corner of my eye as I righted myself and pushed off the flesh—the wall.

Something is behind me.

I break into another run, passing Nori's room and noting the silence with relief, before flying down the stairs. I yank the blanket closer to me when it snags on the banister—

it was the banister

it *was*

—and pulls me back. It tears but I ignore it and hurry on.

Past the hole. Past the basement door—

WHICH IS AJAR

—and into the library.

I slam the door behind me and gasp into the wood, keening animal sounds leaving me in terrible wheezes.

The basement door was open.

And something was behind me.

And the wall was flesh.

And my blanket *didn't* get caught on the banister. It got caught on something else. Because when I checked—it was torn. Ragged as if claws *[OR BRANCHES]* had ripped the corner to shreds.

Circling, circling, circling the loom…

"Stop it. Please…stop it."

From beyond the door, I hear a faint

shufffffling

like something dragging itself closer. I hear the

thumping

of something meaty and heavy, like the sound of an object

rolling

and

falling

down the stairs. One at a time.

Closer.

The sound changes.

Stops.

And then I hear a giggle.

I turn the lock on the door to the library, even though I know that means Nori is locked out, but this is crazy and I am terrified and she is safely asleep and so is (crazy) Aunt Cath.

It is only me, alone in the night, who needs this protection.

I don't need it against the imaginary thing out there.

I need it against myself. Because, surely, this can't be real. Please, please, don't let this be real.

I turn, squaring my shoulders, and stride into the library. I am safe in here. Nothing can get through that door.

Just to be sure, I look over my shoulder.

And find the door wide open, a black, endless corridor yawning at me in greeting.

Ω

10

liar liar liar

Hold your breath,
close your eyes
you are in
for a big surprise!

BROKEN BOOK ENTRY

What is Cath doing up there in the attic? The creaking—her pacing—is so constant. Is **she** just walking up and down? **Is** she even eating the food I bring on the trays? I picture her **doing** all kinds of gross things with it—painting the walls, throwing it at the ceiling. She never comes down; **nothing** will make her. It must reek of her waste. Maybe she eats that, too. I want to go **up** and talk to her, I want to make her see reason. But **there** is nothing of the old Cath left. She is as mad as Mam always said she was.

Ω

Remember, I sign at Nori in the kitchen. *Remember that game we used to play? You would go and hide and then I'd come looking. You'd make little sounds—clap your hands, close a door, give a whistle—to give me clues?*

Nori nods, a wide grin breaking the softness of her face.

"You would cheat," I say. "Move around. I always thought it was so funny...." I shut my eyes for a moment, and then open them. "Remember?"

We should play! Nori signs, hands so fast in her excitement that I almost don't see. I shake my head no.

Please! We can play upstairs! Please, Silla, please!

"You're too old. And so am I. No more games."

Nori's smile dies and I hate myself.

No more games.

There's danger in it.

Ω

My eyes take in the straight line of his jaw, the suggestion of stubble as we sit in the library. The flecks of brown in his eyes and the way his hair falls just so. I linger over the curve of his shoulders, and I inhale his scent. So heady, so wonderful. I'm careful not to let my infatuation show on my face, but I can't deny it. He is like a shining beacon in this place. Everything is slightly damp, slightly moldy, slightly pale. But he is beautiful and bright and, well, handsome. You notice him.

Gowan.

Something stirs in the stone of my insides. Something warm. Vital. Totally dangerous.

Despite the danger, I'm grateful, for the first time since the day he stepped out of Python Wood, that he's here.

I am careful to school my face.

But Gowan senses my regard and looks up, smiling. "Hi."

A slow smile touches my cheeks. "Hey."

"See something interesting?"

"As a matter of fact." I nod at the book in his hands. "Looks interesting to me."

He actually looks disappointed, and a pebble of remorse drops into my stomach. And a little bit of satisfaction, too.

"It's an old copy of *Amadís de Gaula*."

"You read Latin?"

"Spanish, and yes. '*Gran locura es la vuestra en hacer enojo a quien tan bien vengarse puede,*'" he quotes. "The author's talking about anger, madness, and revenge."

"Charming."

"I think you'd like it, actually."

I close my eyes, but I can't seem to do that for long. I look around us, at all Cath's books. Books that have been in my family for generations. "I wish we didn't have to leave this room."

Gowan makes a face. "Are you sure?"

"It's a haven."

"Only because the manor is so worn out." I know what he wants to say, what he wants to ask me. I brace myself for it, waiting for the *Please leave this house, Silla*, but it never comes. Instead, he looks at me for slightly too long, even after I have looked away.

When I look back, the only thing that's changed is his jaw, which clenches and unclenches, over and over in a rhythm of frustration.

Something like regret bleeds through me. *I'm sorry. Why do you keep coming here? Why do you like me?*

And then the voice from my dream is there in my head.

LEAVE THIS HOUSE

AND YOU WILL DIE

AND SHE'LL BE MINE.

Never.

Something of my thoughts must reflect on my face because Gowan, now observing me again, sighs, his mouth pinched, and goes back to his book. I watch him for a while, but he's not seeing the pages. He's lost somewhere else, probably in a fantasyland where I'm not myself and I take his hand and follow him stupidly into Python, singing and dancing, both of us draped in sunlight.

I have to admit, it sounds appealing. Not being me. Being... I don't know. Warm, or something. It sounds sort of perfect.

And very naïve.

Ω

THEY COME

I don't move as much anymore—or maybe I move more. I know this space very well. So well. And I know what to expect, even though they think I am *craaaaaayyyyzzz-zeeeeeee*. I know, oh yes I do.

"This is all your *fault*!" I spit, my saliva, white and drying, hitting the glass. "This is all your *fault*!"

I look out the window, past the creeping ivy.

Here they come.

Here they come.

"Oh, dear. oh, dear, oh, dear."

Here they come again.

Ω

I wake to the sound of clapping. Little claps somewhere in the house. Distant, at first. I climb out of bed and open the door.

"Nori, would you quit—"

The corridor is dark and empty, but I still hear the claps. They are coming from down the hall, too far down the hall, and in the opposite direction from where I am looking.

"N...Nori?"

I stand frozen as the claps draw closer. Grow louder. Until I am sure someone has to be standing not three feet from me, watching me.

Clap, clap, clap.

And then the clapping stops. And it is infinitely, infinitely worse. The silence. Loud, awful silence.

And then *creak*.

Upstairs, in the attic.

Creak...

From (crazy) Aunt Cath.

Creeeeaaaakkkk.

I hold my breath, my mind so full I worry it might burst with fear and—

Stop it.

Stop it now.

But as I close my bedroom door, the clapping starts again. Slow. Mocking. Exulting.

CLAP. CLAP. CLAP.

Ω

Hide-and-seek is our favorite game to play. He is reeeeeeally tall, but he's very good at it! There are a lot of places to hide away in the basement—it's my new favorite place! I cover my eyes and count, "One...two...three!" And then when I look, he's gone! When I find him, I giggle, but I try not to be very loud because Silla will get angry.

Silla doesn't sleep anymore. And we hardly eat anything and the monster in my tummy gets loud. I think her tummy monster is even bigger. And she gets upset. Sometimes I see that Gowan looks at her funny. He looks at the pointy bits on her hips and then his mouth gets all hard and he looks away quickly. I think he thinks something is bad inside Silla. Maybe Silla is sick.

I want to tell her about the tall man and my game very, very much because I hate Silla being upset. But there is the game and I'm not allowed to spoil it. There are rules.

And if you break the rules, then bad things will happen.

So the game will carry on and I won't say a word.

Ω

I can't stop watching the trees.
I can't let Nori go into them.
If it's true, even only a little,
then we will never leave this house.
Remember what Cath said
when we arrived? "Poor thing."
That's what she said.
I thought she meant the state of me. Of Nori.
But she meant something else.
"He'll never let you leave."
She knew we were stuck here.
From the moment we crossed
through those dark woods.
I thought it was just a story.
It makes so much sense now.
And now there's the other thing.
My suspicion.
We might be sinking.
Which means I might have no choice.
I might have to go into the woods.
But I believe what I heard.
I will die, if I try.
It makes sense why Mam never
wanted to talk of La Baume.
She wasn't hiding a paradise.
She was hiding a hell.

The next day, the trees are in the garden.

They *are* the garden.

And they are definitely taller than before. Or, we are lower. Lower in the earth, which is softening like out there in the woods that day...full of worms and mulch and dead animals and—

I realize, with dawning horror, that we might be at the head of a kind of funnel,

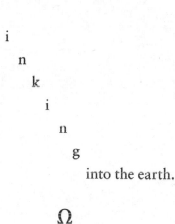

s
   i
     n
       k
        i
          n
            g

into the earth.

Ω

BOOK 3:

Sky Roots

The earth and the sky
will not obey time,
I bet you don't know
your life's on the line.
the earth and the sky
met in the wood,
decided to try
all that they could.

11

bloody creepo

Wear him down?
You could try!
But patience is
His one true vice.

BROKEN BOOK ENTRY

I found a book **lying** in the library, less molded than the others. Smells of mildew, still, but then everything does. It almost **fades** after a while. Picked up a pen—plenty of those—and began to write. **Nothing** very important at first. Who would **ever** read it? It **feels** old, and hard like stone; there is a long crack in the leather, calcified. A symbol in the center — from the Greek alphabet. Omega. I wrote nothing much, but then slowly, little truths. **Like** this one: I don't know if I'm more terrified of the woods, or of the fact that we are going to die here, and that is **the end of the story**. I'd like to write it all down first, if **I** may. If I **have** enough time. It seems like all I have is **time**. But I know it's only a matter of... Ha. Ha. TIME. And then there will be... I don't know. **So** I will pick up my pen. It's all **I** can do. And I **write**.

$$\Omega$$

His face is pale when I open the kitchen door. Behind him, the trees stand sentinel in the garden.

[THEY HAVE PASSED THE GATE.]

I give a panicked laugh, and step back to let Gowan in. In my hand, I clutch a broken book. He stops and stares at me, taking in my pale, thin face, my collarbones, which protrude beneath my dress, and my matted hair, and it's like something inside him snaps.

"We have to leave," he says right away, snatching up one of Cath's baskets and piling in the apples he has brought with him. "No more excuses. No more delays."

"I..." *In the garden. They are in the garden.* "I can't."

"For God's sake, Silla," he snaps, stuffing the last scraps of food in with the apples. "You have *got* to get out of here. This place is going to kill you!" He is almost hysterical. "Get Nori and we're going."

His panic calms me. It distills all around me like a warm cloak, and I feel my old anger returning. "No."

He freezes, turns to me, and his voice is barely controlled. "What are you *talking* about?"

"I am not leaving this house, Gowan. I told you that before. I'm not going into those woods—and they're the only way out. We're going to...we're just going to wait."

He puts the basket onto the counter very slowly; his hands are shaking from—what? Rage? Panic? Adrenaline?

"What do you think you're waiting for, *exactly*?"

Now it's my turn to walk away, but he grabs my elbow.

"What are you waiting for?" he yells.

"I don't know, *I don't know*!"

"You're lying—*tell me the truth*!"

I pull myself free. "Don't touch me!"

He turns and, with a speed I've never seen in him, he punches the wall. His fist goes right through the plaster, an explosion of white and gray, leaving a massive, dusty hole, and revealing the stone behind it. He yells at nothing, then puts his plaster-covered palms on either side of the destruction and tries to control his breathing.

"What the hell are you waiting for?" he asks, but he's not really asking me.

What *am* I waiting for? Waiting a bit longer to live? Waiting a bit longer to see what happens. Waiting to keep Nori safe, just a bit longer. Waiting to avoid a repeat of what I saw in the woods that day...what I felt.

Waiting to avoid his promise.

You will die and

she'll be mine

Gowan leaves me there in the kitchen and I follow him into the entrance hall. He stumbles over the hole there, and turns back to look at it with horror.

The hole is small, but definitely bigger than it was yesterday. And he knows it.

"When did this appear?"

I shrug. "A while ago. It's gotten bigger." *[DADDY'S VOICE COMES OUT OF THERE.]* "It's weird. I couldn't see anything down there. I mean—nothing at all. The flashlight just found more darkness. I checked the basement, but the entrance hall isn't above it. This is just—a hole."

[A SINKHOLE, WAITING TO GET US ALL.]

"I'll fix it," Gowan tells me. "I don't want this here. Do you have any unwanted wood? Crates?"

I shake my head; I can't look away from the place my father's voice comes from.

"Never mind. I'll cut back the trees. Use that wood. I saw an ax by the kitchen door."

He has my full attention now. "The trees? You're going to use the trees?"

"We have to get out of here, Silla. You have to see that. You can't ignore it."

"Yes, but—"

"So I'll cut us out. The trees are in the garden, and I can't explain it, but we have to cut through them to get out—"

"This place is weird. You sense it, right?"

"—so I'm going to take that ax—"

"It's haunted or something. . . ."

"—and I'm going to cut those damn trees, and I'm going to fix this hole." His eyes bore into mine. "And then you're coming with me."

As he leaves, I wonder why he's taking the time to fix the hole at all.

Ω

Tried to eat the apple.
Can't keep it down.
Think I have anorexia
or maybe a stomach bug.
Food feels disgusting.
Can't imagine putting it
inside my body.
Thought makes me squirm.
Another cavity
even though I knocked
out the other tooth.
What is wrong with me?
I think I'm getting sick.
But I can't help feeling
that it's La Baume
doing this to me.

Ω

It is another gray day, too still. Darker than yesterday, which was darker than the day before. It's barely noon, and already the day is at half-light. Maybe less. It feels like five in the afternoon, or six.

I slump over a cup of cold water and glance up at Gowan, sitting next to me. "What are you thinking?"

He looks at me pointedly. "I don't think you'll believe me."

I know it's probably true, but I want to hear it anyway. "Spill."

"Because I love you."

"You're right. I don't believe you. I asked for the truth. Don't lie to me, Gowan."

"It wasn't a lie." He takes my hand. "I *love* you, Silla Daniels. Please believe me. I love you."

"But how could you? You barely know me. And I'm..." *[A BLOODY MESS.]*

"I do, I know you. Maybe it's just instinctive. Like a scent that you smell, fresh like apples, and can't ignore. Maybe when you know, you just do. Maybe we knew each other in a past life. But I don't just feel this, Silla. I *know* this. It just...is."

I recoil from him. "I don't believe in that." I pause. "And I hate apples."

He laughs. "Since when?"

"Since you brought them."

His face falls. "Oh."

A moment of silence, and then he says, "I still love you, even if you hate my apples."

Flights of fancy, passion...*love*...What good do they do? They destroy people. Women. My mother.

But he won't listen. I can see it in the way he looks at me. Gazes at me. As though I hold all his hope.

But I'm the wrong person to hold so much. I'm clumsy with emotion. Rage is pure, eloquent, and I can weave it into a tool. Sadness, loneliness, anguish—none of them require a partner.

Love? Love is a crack in my armor.

I pull away.

"I wish you'd save yourself," he says. "So stubborn."

I almost smile at that.

I hear them talking in the kitchen. I stop just outside the door.

"In the woods. Across them. Would you like to see?"

I don't know what her reply is because I'm too angry to look around the corner.

"You want to go away from here, don't you?" Gowan says.

I do peek around the corner then, and I see her nod: *Yes*.

"We need to make Silla see. She won't listen to me, but maybe if you tell her, she will."

Nori looks doubtful. She reaches for the notepad and pencil, and she writes something I don't see.

"She might be angry for a little bit, but it's for her own good."

Nori looks uncomfortable, biting at her lip.

"If you go first," he says, kneeling down to her level, "then she'll come after you. We could find somewhere nicer than this horrible house. All you have to do is go into the woods."

Blood boiling

Traitor!

Bones cracking

Manipulator!

Feel my veins in my face

Liar!

Slowly, Nori nods—and that does it. I storm into the room and yank her away from him.

"Go to your room."

But I'm hungry.

"Go to your room!"

She runs from the kitchen and I round on Gowan. "How dare you."

"Silla—"

"How dare you use her to manipulate me? You thought you could use her as a weapon? Sending her out there *alone* to lure me in?"

"Silla, she asked me where I go. Where I come from. I told her. If she wants to come, that's how she feels."

My voice is venom. *"Don't lie to me."*

He throws up his hands. "I had to do *something*."

I look at him. Look at every line, every crease and bend of his face. Look at the textured brown of his eyes. Look at his lips, which almost quiver with emotion, and I wonder why he even cares.

Oh, right. He "loves" me.

"I already told you: *We are staying here.*"

"Goddamn it, Silla, what are you doing?"

"I'm keeping her safe!"

"You're not! You're hiding in this dying place because you're a coward!"

COWARD.

"Screw you..." I shove him away from me. *Liarliarliar* bastard liar! *"Screw* you! You're like a trampoline, bending under whoever's feet trample on you, and bouncing back into the same old shape!"

He nods, laughing derisively. "Yeah. You're right. I am. I'm a trampoline. And you're the bloody feet." He closes his eyes and takes a deep breath. When he opens them, his voice is lower. "If you do nothing, you'll die here."

"You don't know that. And you don't know us! You have nothing to do with us!"

"How can you say that after all this time?"

"What, the few weeks you've been toiling in my garden and hanging around like a bloody creepo, bringing apples like some pied piper or something?"

He takes a step away from me, all his fire gone. "Is that how you see me?"

"I see a manipulator, a traitor, and someone trying to force my hand. Just get out of our lives. I will *never* go into those woods with you! *Never!*"

He nods. "Okay." He shakes his head. "Okay."

He walks to the kitchen door and turns the handle, hesitating only a moment.

"It's been months," he says, his voice low. "Not weeks."

And then he leaves.

The sickness I feel when he walks out is enough to make me double over, breathless.

"No...no, no, no. Gowan..."

$$\Omega$$

This book is consuming me. I carry it everywhere.

It's broken, like me. It's hardened over time.

The once-leather is more like stone now.

Calcified. The pages crinkle, some tear.

There is a symbol on the front,

I remember it from school.

The Greek alphabet. It's called omega.

Omega means... I forget. The end?

Like alpha and omega.

Beginning and end?

It's like it was left for me to find.

It feels like a secret worth having.

I wonder who left it behind.

I burn the note.

Ω

12

the sane never come, the crazy always do

Hush little baby,
you're to blame
to give your heart
for lies and shame.

BROKEN BOOK ENTRY

I wish she would be **a** bit more coherent. She said this was a **curse**, her exact words, but **is** there or was there **a** point to telling me that stupid **story**? All that about the house, and the color...**is** it just to rile me up? **A** bit of fun for her? What? She is acting like a **ghost**. Like she's not even really here anymore. Is that how she **is** helping us? How she's loving us? I couldn't think of **a** better joke. She lied. She's a liar. She's the **lie**.

Ω

Tears, like the rain, have all dried up.

On the day Gowan didn't come, I felt it like a sickness. That day, Nori hid.

I spent hours searching room after room, calling and then yelling. And as the panic rose and the day wore on and the sickness grew: screaming.

Nori came out laughing, and I pulled her by the arm, yanking hard. Too hard.

"You can't hide!" I screamed into the little face. "We talked about this already! Don't you ever listen? You can't disappear, Nori! Not you! Can't you see that you couldn't cry for help if you fell? You couldn't call me if something crashed down on top of you! You would be trapped and you would suffocate and you would die screaming screams I couldn't hear!"

I tugged even harder and fell to my knees before her.

"Do you understand me?"

Nori nodded fiercely, too stunned to cry, and when I released her, she stood frozen.

Ω

LEAVE THIS HOUSE AND YOU WILL DIE.

HE WON'T LET YOU LEAVE.

THE CREEPER MAN IS WAITING.

COME AGAIN, OH PLEASE DO. YOU CAN COME STAY IN MY PETTING ZOO....

I saw him in the woods.

$$\Omega$$

I wander the house like a specter. Like a wraith. A shadow. Everything seems…empty. When did this happen? Was it the first night he snuck into the library? Was it his sunny greeting every day? Was it his stupid apples that I can't even eat? I only realized this morning, when I woke and came to the door, waiting, that I've become…*used* to him. He is the start to my every day.

It is incomprehensible.

It is impossible.

It is ridiculous.

But when he doesn't come, something inside me moves. Like a book falling off a table; it hits, deep down, with a low *thud*.

Nori, too, is silent. Her hands don't flap. There are no words on her fingers, no laughs in her smiles. There are question marks in her eyes, though.

There are accusations.

You sent him away.

He liked us but you made him angry.

This is your fault.

They are little blows and I have to look away. I *am* to blame. Why was I so resistant? When he comes back…*if* he comes back…then I will try. I will try to take Nori and Cath and I will try to go into the woods.

I catch my reflection in the window.

I will not be a coward and die in this house because of moving *trees*. [*BUT THERE'S MORE TO IT.*]

LEAVE THIS HOUSE AND YOU WILL DIE.

It was just a dream. [*YOU'RE FOOLING YOURSELF.*]

HE WON'T LET YOU LEAVE.

Cath is crazy. Why should I listen to her? *[SOMETHING IS WRONG WITH THIS PLACE.]*

If you leave the house, I will get you. And I will get her.

When *[IF]* Gowan comes back, I will go with him. I won't be afraid. *[YOU WILL DIE.]*

I will go anywhere with him, something inside me declares. *[HAHAHA!]*

"I don't know what to do!" I cry, and I hold my head until the thoughts all die.

Ω

SILLA DANIELS'S GUIDE TO DELUDING YOURSELF

1. Imagine you are a doll, sewn together with twine.

2. Fill yourself up with straw, crunchy and dry (no heart allowed).

3. Use lies mantras to get by (you will eventually believe them).

- Mantra, option 1: This is not real.

- Mantra, option 2: You are not circling the loom.

- Mantra, option 3: You do not feel anything.

Ω

The walls are no longer firm and hard. They sink and warp with moisture and even more mold. We're all damp now, all the time. The days are never quite days anymore, but rather a depressing half-light. It's like everything is winding down. More and more, it looks like five or six in the evening when the clocks read noon.

The only new food has been the apples. The cupboard holds only those damned peanuts, some butter, some sugar—and his apples. The trees are definitely taller and closer, but worse: the basement windows are covered almost to the top with soil.

There is no doubt about it now. We are sinking.

One gloomy day, I walk uphill in the garden and bring a box of sand-like ashes into the house, into which Nori climbs and stares out of the window. The trees cover a lot of the sky now.

She misses the light on her face, and the still air in her hair. So do I. But the window frames are rotten and warped and the glass no longer slides open. It's so musty in here.

Nori sits

and she stares.

Her bell doesn't tinkle.

Ω

The book's cover is a callus. A scab. With a crack *[SCAR]* running through the middle. As though someone slashed it with a knife right through the omega. It looks like it's smiling.

I open it slowly, and it *creaks,* the pages hard and dusty. The cover *thuds* against the table as it hits, the pages fanning out, dust flying in an upward arc. The impulse comes over me again. I pick up my pen and I begin to write.

I don't stop until the candle dies with a sigh, plunging the room into darkness. We don't even have the generator now.

It's only when I feel Nori tug on my skirt that I realize she's been with me the whole time.

Ω

I stare at the apple in my hand. I am hungry. I can do this.

I have lost three teeth now, but I am sure I can still bite. Can still chew. I scratch my scalp, and my fingernails come away full of dry white skin.

All around me, the books seem to cry out their encouragements.

You can do it, Silla!

Take a bite.

Nourish your body.

Don't be afraid.

In the bowels of the house, my father is laughing.

HA HA HA HA HA HA HA HA HA!

I close my eyes and try to remember the sweetness of apples. To recall wanting to feel the weight of food in my stomach. Before La Baume changed. Before the thing in the woods started watching. Before my father's voice floated up out of the hole in the entrance hall like a vile toxin.

I bite into the apple.

I chew, ignoring the *creaking*. Upstairs, Cath starts her pacing. *Creeeeeaaaak. Creeeeeeaaaak.* I chew in time to her rhythm. *Creeeeeaaaak.*

I swallow.

I am less hollow as I feel it slide down the insides of me. I feel it scratching me up in there as it falls, the skin of the fruit sharp as paper. Paper cuts on the inside. Skin cuts.

My stomach heaves. Once, twice.

I run to the fireplace just in time.

The apple skin cuts on the way up, too.

I sit down on the sheepskin rug and cry silently into my hands, while the masticated apple and saliva spits in the grate.

"Leave me alone," I beg the manor. "Please, just leave me alone. I didn't do anything to you."

I am partly talking to him, out there in the woods. "Please... go away. You can't be real. Please..."

The apple is nothing but ash in the grate now. It might never have been there at all.

Ω

It has been three days.

Gowan has not come.

The sickness has grown.

I am losing my hair.

Ω

SOON

I know that boy. That boy, down there, walking away through my garden. I know that boy, I do, I do. It's getting so hard to remember, though. All these higgledy-piggledy thoughts.

It's going to happen soon. Oh, dear, yes! It's going to happen soon!

Ω

It happens in the night of its own accord. The wood bends and splinters and falls away, disappearing into the nothing of the hole. Darkness rises and a voice begins to hum.

When I awake, I'm lying on the edge of a bottomless pit the size of a small chair.

I teeter for a moment, undecided, and then lazily roll away.

The thing in the hole bares its teeth and reaches, but I am already gone.

Ω

Maybe I'm just very, very sick.

I read about cancer patients once.

They hallucinate. The drugs or the sickness makes them see things that aren't really there. So maybe I'm just really, really sick.

Which begs the question: Was Gowan real? He came after the hallucinations of the man out there began.

The Creeper Man.

...

I went to ask Nori. She looked a little bit scared at first. I told her I was playing a game. She signed: <u>Yes. Gowan went away. He went away because of you.</u> So I guess that's real. Unless Nori is an illusion, too. So: illness.

That's only one of my theories about what the hell is going on.

It's the least bad of all of them.

Ω

13

long memory

Promises made like breath on the glass,
mean nothing to those who see the time pass
lingering on in a house made of blood
he's brought closer by Python Wood.

BROKEN BOOK ENTRY

Another theory of mine is that there is **a** presence in this house. Like, maybe something **terrible** happened here, a long time ago—the house's **secret**, maybe. A murder, maybe. Or a poltergeist is **locked** in the walls. Maybe the house doesn't want any of us to get **away** because it's lonely, or malevolent. Maybe, **over the years**, it has become a sort of **living** house. A house brought alive by something evil—**a version of** a curse. Another theory to explain **the** unexplainable. I just want to know the **truth**.

Ω

Creeeeeak.

I am totally ignoring my brain.

Creeeeeeeak.

Nope.

Creeeeeeeak.

If I had a gun right now, I'd go upstairs and shoot Cath in the leg. That thought alone is enough to pull me from whatever half sleep I've been in. And that's when I realize that the creeping isn't coming from upstairs.

I wait.

Crrrrreeeeeeeeeeeak.

"Cath?" I call. "Are you out there?"

Has she finally come down? After almost two years?

Thump!

That came from above me.

"Auntie?" I whisper, hunching lower in my blankets. But the creaking is not my aunt. It is not the endless pacing in the attic. It's coming from the stairs. Like someone slowly walking up. Step by creaking step.

My heart goes from zero to a hundred in a second, and when I swallow, it's **LOUD.** *[GONNA RUN? GONNA HIDE?]*

And then I hear that sound again. The sound of a ball—only not rubber or plastic. It sounds heavy and warm, like flesh. A flesh ball. The creaking turns into a rolling sound, and then I hear the flesh ball *thump!* against something. Wood. The first step.

Another roll.

Thump!

Another roll.

Thump!

It's coming up the stairs.

KNOCK KNOCK KNOCK.

I suck back a scream and jump out of my bed, grabbing my comb as if that could somehow save me.

"Go away!" I yell.

There is a tiny shuffle, and then a sequence of knocks and scratches.

Scratch, scratch, knock.

— — •

ME.

I rush to the door and fling it open, pulling Nori, who still has her fist raised, inside. I slam the door behind me.

Nori signs: *Something woke me.*

[HE'S COMING.]

Roll.

Thump!

I grab her hand and rush out my door. Quick—*quick!* The flesh ball (if that's what it is) is getting closer. (Roll, *thump!*) I rush toward the staircase, but instead of going down, we run up. Up to the silent third floor, where I would never go unless I had to, and never with Nori.

Nori resists my tugging—she's terrified of this hall—but I pull harder and say, "Come on! We have to go up to go down!"

But she won't stop tugging, so I pick her up and run with her to the end of the dark corridor. I open the door to the wasp-husk room and run (the husks *CRUNCH* under my bare feet) to the end and take the dodgy back stairs down, down, down, until we are on the ground floor. I can't hear the flesh ball anymore, and that terrifies me.

And then I hear it. It rolls warmly (if sound can be warm) across the floor and *thump, thump, thumps!* down the stairs, faster and louder than before. We run to the basement, the only place left besides Python, and I lock the door behind me. I push Nori into the old cupboard in there and press my shaking fingers to her lips.

Keep quiet, I sign. *Not a peep!*

She is crying, but I shake my head. *Like a mouse, okay?*

She nods. A mouse. *Squeak!*

She couldn't make a sound if she tried, and right now I envy that. There is an old, tattered penguin doll wearing a knitted red scarf in the cupboard, so I pick it up and shove it into her arms, then I close the doors.

I crawl out of the shadows and back along the wall. At the foot of the stairs, I look up, toward the dull light coming from some-where else in the house. I closed the door. I did. I closed the door!

Auntie Cath.

We need you.

She is shut away in the attic. Walking, walking, pacing. *Creaking.*

She can't help us now.

The thing is getting closer. Not rolling now, but walking. My heart alarms like a panic bell, a siren shrilling silently inside me.

Trapped! We're trapped!

I hear something shuffling closer, on unsteady feet. Some-thing big. I can feel the presence.

I see the shadow. *His* shadow, stretching impossibly high along the wall.

I back away, return to Nori in the cupboard, and squeeze in beside her.

Like a mouse, she signs. I shut my eyes and nod my head.

Gowan—where are you?

We wait.

Ω

I dream of my mother.

There's something you've forgotten, sweetheart.

Stop it.

Did you think I would forget?

Shut up.

Well, I've got news for you.

Please...

I have a long memory.

...Mama...

The truth, my girl,

...go away.

is coming for you anyway.

Ω

I wake up alone in a cupboard with the vague notion that I had a dream. Then it comes back to me and I reach for Nori—

Who isn't there.

It's like the breath is knocked out of me. I mean to scream her name, but it comes out a pathetic gasp.

"Nori!"

I race up to her room, and find her fast asleep in her bed, her grotesque little mouth hanging open and the air saturated with her stale breath. I swallow and then go to shake her awake.

She rubs her eyes and squints up at me.

"Are you okay? When did you go back to bed?"

She frowns at me, and shakes her head.

"Nori, why didn't you stay in the cupboard?"

She sits up, still rubbing her eyes. *What cupboard?*

"We ran downstairs, remember? The basement? Hiding?"

Did you have a bad dream? she asks, and I can see she has no idea what I'm talking about.

"You never got up last night?"

No. I went to bed when you said, after I fell asleep by the fire, remember?

I do.

I shake my head and force a laugh. "Must have had a bad dream. Come on, up. I'll get some peanut paste and an apple, okay?"

She nods and watches me. I know that when I go, she'll be back to sleep in under a minute flat. I turn away, ready to forget this (crazy) nightmare, when I spot something under her bed.

A tattered penguin doll with a red knitted scarf around its neck.

I open my mouth to ask Nori about it, but she has already fallen asleep.

Ω

The nib of my pen flashes in the moonlight. Silence reigns, expectant.

There are twenty-nine candles left.

Four boxes of matches. *[BURN THE HOUSE DOWN.]*

Two gas lamps. A single jar of kerosene. *[TO THE GROUND.]*

Four batteries. One flashlight. *[WATCH IT BURN TO HELL.]*

I focus on my whisper note, looking for a core truth to these feelings, trying to ignore the tooth I am close to losing.

I sat in the library for a long time today, thinking about you. About what you said. I remember every single thing you said to me. "You're hiding in this dying place because you're a coward." The way your face fell—the way you gave up on me. "If you do nothing, you'll die here."

How could you say those things?

Why didn't I listen?

You were right. I am afraid. Afraid to leave this house. Afraid to find out what I have left behind in that world out there. In London. In my past. I can't even think about that. I can't face it. I was fourteen when I came here, and I dragged Nori with me. I dragged her through the rain and the mud.

La Baume is cursed. Haunted, even, maybe. I have too many theories to list. Though that might just be me going mad, like my mother always said I would. Except...I'm not mad. I know it. But I wish I was. Because then, all of this...all of this would make a kind of sense. And I don't think Cath is mad either. She stays in the attic because it's the farthest she can get from the trees.

Anyway. All this is to say that <u>you were</u> <u>right</u>. All along. But I don't want to be afraid, and I don't want to be trapped here. A voice in the night tells me that if I leave—if I leave… he'll—he'll… but it's just my own insecurities. My own fears that hold me hostage.

I miss my anger. Can't handle this fear.

I know you'll never come back. Who would? I'm going to burn this damn note anyway, so here it is:

I miss you.

I don't know when it happened. I don't know how I never saw myself falling off this platform I built for myself—a platform to keep me above the messy, noisy, painful world of emotions. I have a stone for a heart, but it is turning to clay. Softening. And you're to blame.

God, I hate you.

I like you.

I love you.

I hate that. I hate you. I do. You've ruined and broken me and I hate you forever you stupid, selfish, ignorant, happy shithead! I hate

you! I hate you for breaking my stone in half!
I hate you for leaving and I hate that you're
never going to come back and I am never
going to see you again.

I hate myself, too. For loving you. Love is a lie.
I will kill this heart, even if I die, too.
Silla.

I can't burn it. I hold it near the candle flame for a long time, but I can't make it ash and air. Instead, I leave the note in the garden, buried deep in the earth, and maybe it'll turn into a rock. I push the earth over the hole, letter inside. Poisoned earth, soft as ash, under my fingernails. I'm already infected. I know it. The green mold growing on my dress proves it. The way I'm falling apart proves it.

This should worry me, but doesn't. Nothing feels quite real anymore.

That's probably a bad sign.

Ω

In the morning, I discover a small pile of green pages on the kitchen doorstep, held down by a green apple. A green letter.

He came in the night.

I missed him again.

THE GREEN LETTER

STANDING ON THE OUTSIDE IS HARD, SILLA. AND YOU
DON'T MAKE IT EASY. YOU'RE DIFFICULT, ABRASIVE,
RUDE—AND I LOVE YOU. BUT, YOU'RE DIFFERENT. COLD.
HARD. I DON'T THINK I'M HELPING YOU.

I STAYED AWAY ONLY TO DO THAT.

DO YOU KNOW WHAT IT'S LIKE TO BE AN ORPHAN? NO
ONE EXCEPT AN ORPHAN COULD EXPLAIN. THE WHOLE
ABANDONMENT-ISSUE THING IS REAL. IT NEVER QUITE
LEAVES YOU.

LA BAUME WAS MY FIRST HOME. I GUESS YOU COULD
SAY THAT CATHERINE WAS MY FIRST "MOTHER." IT
MEANT A LOT TO ME, THIS PLACE. BUT NOW THERE'S
NOTHING. MY HOPE IS GONE. AND I DON'T THINK THAT
HELPS ANYTHING.

AND THEN THERE'S YOU.

YOU KEEP SENDING ME AWAY. BUT I WOULD KEEP
TRYING TO LET YOU KNOW THAT I LOVE YOU, THAT YOU
CAN TRUST ME, THAT I ONLY WANT THE BEST FOR YOU.
NO MATTER HOW LONG IT TOOK ME, I WOULD TRY.

BUT THERE'S ONLY SO MUCH DIRT A GUY CAN TAKE IN
THE FACE, SILLA.

I WANT TO HELP YOU. I WANT TO BE WITH YOU. I
WANT TO KISS YOUR LIPS AND SO MUCH MORE. THINGS
I COULDN'T EVER WRITE DOWN. I WANT YOU TO COME

WITH ME, FAR AWAY FROM HERE. I WANT YOU TO
BRING NORI. BREAK THE CHAINS. TRUST IN ME.

BUT YOU'RE TIED DOWN TO THAT MANOR. I SEE IT. I
FINALLY SEE IT. MAYBE I'M NOT ENOUGH. MAYBE I
NEVER WAS.

I'M LIKE SOME KIND OF SHADOW IN YOUR WORLD. ONLY
HALF-REAL. SOME KIND OF PROP. AND I'M HAPPY TO
BE YOUR SOMETIMES FRIEND, IF THAT'S ALL I CAN BE.
BUT I CAN'T WATCH YOU DESTROY YOURSELF—

IT'S NOT EASY TO WRITE THIS. I WISH I COULD SAY
EVERYTHING TO YOU.

I CAN'T DO IT, SILLA. I NEED MORE THAN THAT.

-G

14

see your shrink

The longer you wait
the closer he gets
so say your prayers
he never forgets.

Cath starts screaming on a Sunday night. The screaming pierces my head like a high frequency I can't tolerate, a ripping thing, and I press my fists into my ears. On and on, Cath screams. I can hear it through my flesh. It rattles my bones. *[GO AND CHECK ON HER.]*

I slide from my bed and check on Nori, but she is huddled under her blanket and hasn't stirred. I leave Cath alone. Whatever she's screaming about, I'm too much of a coward to find out.

Ω

GIGGLES

The girl, Silla, assumes Nori sleeps while she sits in the library reading my books. But while she leaves her little sister to dream sweet summer dreams, Nori is in the basement again, playing with a man made of shadows.

And in a house that doesn't speak, Nori begins to talk.

She stands in the corner.

And covers her eyes.

"...nine...ten...ready   or   not...here   I come..."

The Creeper Man is hiding, and Nori
giggles.

Ω

I heard it again, I *know* I did. A child's laughter. To be sure, I open the library door, which I had barricaded with a chair, and peer out. And listen.

There

    is

       only

          darkness.

Creak.

"Stop."

Creak...

"Stop it."

Creeeeaaaaakkkk.

"STOP IT!"

I slam the door closed and bar it again with the chair. I grip my head and huddle on the floor.

"Mama," I whisper. "I don't like this. Please make this stop. I don't want to be here."

Cath's screaming is the only reply.

Ω

15

all about the poison

Python striker, Python tree
please don't let the man get me
python striker, Python tree
let me sing this melody.

BROKEN BOOK ENTRY

I have another theory, and this one is worse.
Don't say it out loud, don't think it—don't
write it. That's what I tell myself. Would **you**
write down a mortal dread? Make it real? But I do
wonder about it and I have to write it to see if
it's true. To understand **why**. Closure, maybe? To
see if it sounds as ridiculous to **you** as it does to
me? I **never** thought of it before, but it makes
sense. I think my father might be in this house. I
think he might **have** been here for a long time. I

think that he—**the** granite beast—has been toying with me, punishing me with my fears. It's the only theory that makes sense. I mean: Curse? Or evil father? What's the **answer**?

Ω

The storm complains like a petulant child, worrying at the windows and the walls. I'm stowed safely in the library, while Nori is out there, being infected by this house. Being swallowed up, masticated like a piece of—

[SAY IT.]

Like a piece of meat.

I wander the library slowly, feeling fragile as brittle bones. My mind is heavy, though. My heart, too. Why won't he come?

The books lull me into calmness, if not a sense of security, and I find myself wandering the rows. I stalk along the ground floor, then take the spiraling side stairs up to the next level. I wander that floor, too.

A *thump* and a *crash* from above. I flinch, shoulders raised defensively.

A shadow moves along the edges of the far bookcases. It is distorted through the glass ceiling. I go up, my body tight as a guitar string, ready to snap.

It's on the third level that I spot him.

He's huddled like a ball of cloth by two corner bookcases, his head pillowed on *La Vita Nuova: The New Life*. He's shivering and twitching, lost in some terrible dream. He's knocked several books off the shelf to his left, his arm still raised, as if in defense or defiance.

Something inside me breaks to see him and I feel

irritation

exultation

rage

fear

confusion

~~joy~~

relief. I am so relieved to see him. I step closer, minding my feet on the floorboards, and then kneel down, quite close. His breathing is deep, but not steady. He is distressed, eyes flighty beneath the membranes of his eyelids. I want to wake him, to save him, but fascination stops me.

His breathing intensifies, his face twitching, and there is a fine sheen of sweat on his torso—which is bare. "Uhn…AH… No…*No!* No, please—NO!" And he wakes. He presses his fists to his eyes, teeth bared.

"Shit."

I feel bad for watching him, and want to sneak away. But I'm right beside him, and when he lifts his head and sees me, his surprise becomes brightness, and then caution in less than a split second.

"Silla…"

I have to bite down on my lip to keep myself from calling his name.

He left you, Daddy's voice says, the whisper floating beneath the crack in the door. *Don't forget that. He left you all alone.*

Gowan crawls to me and wraps his arms around my waist, clinging to me so tightly that I gasp with the closeness of it. I clench my fists at my sides, fighting my urge to hug his head closer, kiss the top of it, tell him I'm here to stay. Instead, I get to my feet.

"You left me," I say as he stands up too, his hands still on my hips, and his cheek twitches—the merest little flicker, but I know I've hit some kind of sore spot.

"I'm sorry," he says, and his voice trembles and for a moment I think he wants to hurt himself.

I recognize self-loathing.

"I'm sorry, Silla, I am sorry—"

"How long have you been here?"

He shakes his head like he wants to rid himself of the things inside it. "How did you find me?"

"I couldn't sleep. Tell me, Gowan. How long?"

"Since the night I left."

"You've been hiding out in my library for three weeks?"

I find myself trying not to laugh, and he smiles slowly. "I didn't want to leave. I just couldn't...."

There is a lot to say.

You stole my whisper note.

You left me a letter.

Green paper. Like the apple...

You left me apples.

To help or to torture?

Why did you leave?

I hate you for that.

I want to hate you for that.

I'm so happy to see you.

You came back.

"You never left."

He shakes his head. "Are you... are you okay?"

I don't think he's really asking me that. "I'm fine. I just... I couldn't sleep."

I know how I've changed. How I must look. So much hair has fallen out. I've lost five teeth, my nails are thin and brittle, and my skin feels too tight.

Cathy's creaking never reaches me in this room, but the

memory of it is enough to make me clench my teeth—the ones that are left. Gowan spots it.

"What?"

Creeeeaaaak.

Stop it.

"I...I hate this place."

Creeeeeeeeeak.

He doesn't ask me why I don't leave.

"Why don't we kill each other?" I don't know where the question has come from. But it feels important to ask.

I sit down, close to him, and wait.

"Silla, you can't be serious."

"I am. You kill me, I kill you. We'll do it at the same time."

He closes his eyes. "Stop it."

"I'll have to kill Nori first, of course. That would be difficult."

"Silla, stop—" He gets to his feet, stumbles, and steadies himself on the bookcase. I watch the muscles in his back move as he breathes.

"Don't say things like that to me ever again. Please."

I stand, putting a hand on the middle of his back. "I'm sorry." I'm tempted to kiss the back of his neck, taste his sweat.

I don't.

"You just left," I say quietly, as if this will explain my momentary weakness.

He turns to me slowly. "I promise," he says, voice low, "I *promise* I won't hurt you again, if I can help it. I promise you. You're...vital to me."

Vital. I don't even know what that means. Still, I nod and I even manage a smile.

Some people don't realize they are liars, even when they are.

"I saw some boxes in the basement," he says after a while. "We could see if they have any food. Tins or dry goods."

I glance down at the library door, firmly shut and locked. "I don't want to go out there...." I can't stop hearing that sound... that fleshy *thud!* and the way I felt chased....

"There's a secret passage. I could show you."

And he does.

It's hidden on the ground floor, between two of the last bookcases. A gap so small and dark I missed it for years. Gowan slips in and pulls me after him. Close...we are *so close.* He never lets go of my hand. We walk a few paces and then there is a *click* as Gowan opens a door. He takes me down three steps, and then we are facing a staircase. Concrete, all of it, heading into the dark.

I don't want to go, but he has my hand, so I follow him deeper. It goes on for a long time, this tiny, suffocating space, spiraling down until I feel sure we're just twisting ourselves into the earth like screws.

Then we are in the basement. No glamour. No tricks. No hidden locks or passwords.

The basement is just *there* in front of us. Huge and black and empty. And the windows, completely covered over with soil. Gowan doesn't say anything. I don't know if he sees. But him being here and me not being alone is enough of a reason to not bring it up. I want to protect this moment.

We don't find any food.

But we do find a stupid supply of wine. I grin and look at Gowan and he grins right back.

"Let's forget this whole damn thing," he says, offering his hand.

I take it, and we each grab two bottles of wine and run upstairs, cackling.

Ω

"Let's drink to the irony." Gowan raises his bottle in a toast. "No real food, plenty of alcohol. We could make passable college students yet."

The cork crumbles into the wine, and it doesn't taste particularly nice, but soon we are sprawled on the library floor in front of the fire, laughing and singing.

"...and her toe was sticking out of the slipper like this tiny little sausage!"

I can't contain my roar of laughter. One bottle of wine is gone. The embers burn low. The house cools and sighs.

"I've never had a boy over before. Overnight, I mean."

Gowan looks at me.

"It's kise to have numpany."

His eyes widen and we howl with laughter again until I've got tears streaming down my face and I can't talk. He's not doing much better.

"*Numpany!*"

I nudge him. "Shove off! You're nice *company,* okay?"

We laugh for a long time, until I've almost wet myself, and then Gowan's laughter dies suddenly and he sighs.

He takes a drink. "Unless I get through those trees in the garden...you may be stuck with me for a while."

"I...don't mind."

We talk for a while, back and forth, until the talking becomes a question game.

"Would you rather live alone or in a commune?"

"Alone. Easy." I think for a moment. "Would you rather have four hands or four feet?"

"Oh, come on," he says, laughing. "Four hands would totally win. Think of everything you could get done."

"Yeah, but you'd fracture your wrist bones if you tried to walk on them for very long."

He snorts. "I still vote hands. Okay…" He takes a drink from the bottle. "What is the craziest thing you've ever done?"

My turn to drink. I can feel the wine swimming in my head like floppy fizzy fish. "Once, when I first came here, I woke up on the roof. I used to sleepwalk really badly, so I guess I sleep-walked up there. Anyway, I woke up around midnight or so, and decided it was so beautiful, I just stayed there. Only in the morning, I was back in my bed. Craziest thing ever."

Gowan grins. "I remember."

"What?"

"Nori told me that one already."

I frown. "How?"

"She's a very good writer. Terrible speller. R-U-F-E I took to mean roof."

I laugh. "She's a nut, that one. Okay, well, then have this one: When I was four, my mother told me about La Baume. I was so obsessed with it that I spent six years trying to get her to draw me a picture of it. When she finally gave it to me, it became a sort of talisman of hope, and now I keep it hidden in my pocket at all times. To remind me what a goddamn idiot I was and still am."

Silence.

I fill it by drinking.

"You're not an idiot for wanting a better life."

I snort. "What the hell would you know about my life? It's stupid. *I'm* stupid."

"You should stop doing that."

"What?"

"Calling yourself stupid. You're not."

I shrug. "I guess I just got used to hearing it."

He's quiet for a while, and it begins to feel heavy. Then he asks, "Would you rather punch a toad or a slug?"

I feel a surge of affection. "Toad."

Back and forth, we play, until the room is spinning and I start laughing again, and then Gowan is laughing and we are rolling on the floor, howling, the night nothing but a backdrop to our forgetting. Forgetting the curse, forgetting this messed-up situation, forgetting that none of this can possibly be real.

I lean forward and the floor leans, too. "Did you know," I say, dangling the bottle between two long fingers, "that most artists and most scientists are technically insane?"

Gowan takes the bottle and I topple forward, landing on my forehead with a dull *bonk!*

"Is that a statistic of convenience?" he asks.

I manage to untangle myself from the floor and my own limbs and sit swaying. "Fact is fact. Insanity is common. And I am starting to think I might be insane."

"Define insane."

"It's a state of mind. Contrary to normal people. Unstable. Unusual. Seeing things that can't be real."

"Then, by definition, I could be insane, too."

I snort, and a little wine goes up my nose. I laugh until I'm rolling on the floor, and then I snort again.

By the time I've clawed my way back to sitting, using Gowan's shirt as a rope, he's grinning at me with his eyebrows up. His eyes say, *Oh, yeah?*

"You," I say, taking back the bottle and waving it at him, "are *not* insane."

The wine s s s s l l l o s h h h h e s s s s.

"How would you know?"

He means it a certain way, playfully maybe, but it comes out like: *You don't know me.*

It stops me, that. I've been telling him as much for weeks and he's never said it back. But it's true. I don't. Except, I do. I know how kind he is. I know he has anger, like me. I know he has a wound. I do know him.

My heart cries—**danger**. I buy time by drinking, and ridiculous hiccups ensue.

"I'd know crazy if I saw it." *I fear it.*

And he laughs. And I laugh. And we laugh and laugh together. Gowan's laughs turn into coughs, and when I go to take another sip from the bottle, I find it empty.

We giggle and open another bottle.

This is nice. So nice.

It feels almost normal. I've forgotten all about—

[DARK

      CREEPING

           TREES

                MOVING]

... well, almost.

"My turn," I say. "Would you rather kill yourself or kill someone else?"

His face changes, cheeks pale. It's like watching a car crash in slow motion, and I think: *Oh, no. What did I say?* For ages, I think he won't answer. Then, quietly, he says: "Myself."

He gets up, and I think he is going to leave, so I get up, too. This was too good to be true to begin with. But then he spins and grabs me and holds me firmly against his body and he is trembling and my arms are going around him and my heart is racing and I want him to *let go*

hold me forever

and then I have kissed him and I *am* kissing him and he is kissing me back. This first kiss. My first kiss ever. Something at the core of me, something that is hard and porous and dry, begins to fill in and soften and I feel my heart yelling: *DANGER! DANGER!* even louder, but I don't *care.* For this tiny moment, with the wine still swimming in my head and my inhibitions down, I don't care about anything else in the world.

I can't breathe, and he's not doing much better himself, and he is pulling me toward him and my whole body is one giant blush and I feel like I am going to pass out and I want to be here forever.

His hands explore me and mine explore him, and I don't want this to go further, but I do—

Gowan pulls away, steps back, clenching his fists at his sides and panting. His lips are flushed and red and I want to kiss him again—*always*—but he is shaking his head and saying, "I can't I can't I can't" over and over and I realize that he thinks this was one huge mistake and I am

mortified.

I fold my arms around my torso and look away from him, my heart still thudding in my ears, and when I look up again, he is staring at me with this blazing expression and I almost step toward him again. But he steps back. Steps away. Says, "Sorry... I can't do this," and then he leaves me all alone again and I feel the rage returning, but I don't want it anymore. I want him.

I am alone then, in a book-lined room of shadows.

Some time later, my father's voice floats down the stairs, meeting me where I can't escape a drunken nightmare.

SILLA DANIELS'S GUIDE TO NOT FALLING IN LOVE

1. Don't think about him.

2. Don't notice.

3. Remember the rejection.

4. Harden the stone.

5. Realize that something is wrong with you.

He finds me curled into the window seat, the curtains closed against the night.

"Silla?" He puts a hand on my shoulder. "I'm sorry."

My head is killing me, and I see no reason to answer.

And that's when he leans forward and puts his forehead on my arm. "Please, Silla... I'm so sorry. I wish... so many things."

His eyes are closed.

And his lips keep murmuring, "Sorry. So sorry."

And I hate seeing him like this. And I hate his stupid apologies.

So I take his head and hug it to me, and kiss the top of it. He smells like apples, but it doesn't make me sick this time. I breathe him in, and I tell him I'm sorry, too. But inside I'm thinking, *You left again. You left me again.*

"Silla..." he says, and I know what's coming.

I'll follow him anywhere.

Except... I *can't.*

"I can't," I say.

His jaw clenches as he gets to his feet. He turns away and I notice his hands are fists. Like rock. Like stone.

Stone-hearted girl.

This is it, now. He'll leave again. He'll go and leave me here, trapped by the trees and... and what?

"This isn't a haven, Presilla. It's a cage. Your aunt is crazy, in the attic. You have no food. Your garden is dead—why won't you come? Why won't you save yourself? Why won't you leave?"

"I have to stay. For Nori."

He takes my face in his hands. "Please. Come with me. Be with me."

"Gowan..." He doesn't understand. "It's Nori...."

He shakes his head, and his eyes are an overcast evening in winter.

"She would come."

"He'll get her."

And I need to tell him what I know—*know*—is true.

"If Nori goes into those trees, he'll get her. He wants her."

"Who?"

I take a deep breath. "The Creeper Man."

Ω

When I've explained everything to Gowan—all the illogical parts, like the moving trees (which he's seen for himself), the shape in the woods, Cath's story, the fact that I've *seen* the Creeper Man— he is pale. I'm not sure if it's because he believes me, or because he finally realizes I really am off my rocker. Just like I fear.

I don't mention my theory about my father being in the house because...because his presence in this house doesn't explain anything besides his voice. And, what, is he sitting in an endless hole just trying to scare me? He's a monster, sure. But he's not that patient.

Gowan doesn't say anything. But then he moves and I think: *He'll leave me now. He'll finally just go.*

Instead, he puts his head on my legs.

We stay like that for a long time, his head resting on my lap, my fingers curling into his hair.

"You asked me once if I loved anything," I whisper. This time of night, alone in this library, feels special. Our secret. Outside of time. Outside of reality.

"You said you loved your sister, and that was all."

"And there's a reason." I hesitate. Where do I even start? It might be a bit much to say that I find the world lacking. If that's true, I couldn't place the blame at the foot of the universe. I'd have to lay it squarely at my own feet.

Instead, I say, "My mother was a weak woman. She married a man who...should never have been a father. For anyone to be cursed with his genes would be punishment enough, without having to cohabit with him."

"Nori doesn't seem so bad," he jokes, smiling up at me.

"She got a lucky escape, unless you remember her teeth, her arm...."

His smile falters and dies. "You're perfect, Silla."

And you're a fool.

"My mother was like a leech. Needing someone to lock on to. She needed someone stronger than herself. But my father wasn't strong. He was weak. Weaker than her, even. I was born from weakness, and that's why I'm so flawed. And that's why I love my sister and nothing else. She's a victim of their dependency and cruelty. And I love her for it. But I love something else, too.... I love my anger. It's solid, pure. Anger doesn't lie. Anger allows me to carry on." I close my eyes. "It's all I have."

"Silla..."

"Don't say it again, please." I can't hear him tell me I'm perfect one more time.

"You can't take my opinions away."

"Even if they're stupid?"

He grins. "Even then." He goes very still, eyes taking me in. Eyes, to lips, back to my eyes. "Silla...I want—"

"Don't."

But he is going to. He leans in, and my treacherous body responds in kind. The gap between us, which seemed a gulf, is suddenly gone, and his lips are on mine, and his hand is on my cheek and I am losing myself to this kiss.

I fall asleep in his arms, and I think, *Maybe there is hope.*

My father's voice is cackling downstairs, calling me on my bull.

Ω

16

the mad always are

Four corners around my bed
four demons round my head
one to watch and one to prey,
two to eat my soul away.

Come, little darling, don't say a word
    I am trying to ignore
Papa's gonna buy you a mockingbird.
    his voice as it seeps
And if that mockingbird don't sing
    out of the black hole
Papa's gonna buy you a diamond ring.
    which has gotten bigger again.
    No one else can hear it. Only me. So I'm imagining it. It isn't real. But how perfectly the sound mimics his voice. How clear and ringing and deep the tones. I can believe, just for a moment, that my father—cruel, hard, and (horribly) beloved—is down there. Waiting for me.

    I find myself leaning over.

    Looking down.

    Wanting so badly to just—

                give in

                       —but I can't. I won't.

This isn't real. It's a hole, for crying out loud. The floor-boards have fallen away, that is all. So why does it seem like there may be a tangle of twisting roots, reaching to receive me, lurking down there in the pitch? I sometimes think I half see them.

I step away, which is very, very hard to do, and the hole seems to sigh with disappointment. I sigh, too.

And then I run into the dining room and begin to gather all the chairs. One by one, I place them around the edges of the tiny gulf, a barrier between the pull and me. I call Nori and tell her, while she stands looking solemnly at me, that the hole is a haz-ard and that she should go no farther than the chairs, not until Gowan has fixed it.

She nods that she understands, but I can see she doesn't. Not really. She thinks I am being overprotective and maybe just a little bit nutty, but at least I have an excuse.

You won't get me, I think.

Oh, Silla, darling, the hole laughs in Father's voice. *We'll just see about that.*

Ω

Along the hall, in Nori's bedroom, something is stirring in the darkness.

I assume that she's having a nightmare.

Though an infrequent occurrence, it has been known to happen, and I can always sense it. I lift my head from my pillow, holding my breath, and wait.

It's a muffled noise. A shuffling almost, punctuated with a little *bump!* here and there.

It is cold.

I don't want to get out of bed to check.

Instead, I wait.

As I suspected it would, the noise dies down, and the house is filled with absence.

Ω

About an hour later, it's the silence itself that wakes me. It's a heavy silence, and I startle so intensely that light spots of adrenaline prickle across my vision.

A terrible, horrible dread creeps up my legs and I suddenly regret not going to check on Nori sooner. It takes a moment for the paralysis to pass, but when it does, I hurry down the hall, ignoring the old paintings of madmen leering at me from the walls.

I stop just inside Nori's doorway.

I'm still.

I swallow.

Waiting.

Creep closer.

The sudden—and *certain*—sense that Nori will not merely be sleeping, but... something far, far worse, had come over me intensely upon waking. And now... it's all I can do to breathe.

The room is too still.

I stumble forward and lay a gentle hand on Nori's small head, and am racked with silent and intense sobbing—the kind of sobbing that jerks the soul from the deepest reaches of the body—when I find that the forehead is warm.

I was so sure.

So *absolutely* sure...

That I would find Nori in the bed, dead and cold.

The sobs pass after long, agonizing minutes, but the dread doesn't diminish.

It grows. And grows.

Until I am staring into the corners of the black room, waiting for some horror to rise up and engulf us whole.

And Nori sleeps on.

Ω

Cath has stopped screaming at night. And that is even worse.

I think the silence could deafen me.

There is no sound. None.

I go to the stairs that lead to the attic, making sure I keep to the middle of the hall—far enough away from the shadowy wallpaper. And then I make sure I am a pace or two away from the first step. I look up—so much darkness. But awareness, too.

"Cath?" I call in a half whisper. I don't know why, since Nori will sleep through thunder.

Creeeeeeak.

"Aunt?"

Creeeeeeeeak.

Silence.

"Tell me about him," I say, because I know she is right there, at the top of the stairs, two paces back like me, and waiting. "Tell me about the Creeper Man. Tell me now."

Aunt Cath walks. *Creak. Creak. Creak.* Cath sits down. A rocking chair. *Creeeeak, creak. Creeeak, creak.* Rocking back and forth. Freaking creepy. I look right, down the third-floor hall, and convince myself that the door to the husk room is *not* open. That there is *not* someone standing at the end of it.

"The Creeper Man, Aunt."

"He's already here." Her voices floats down the stairs like a moth, echoing and faint. She is at the back of the room.

"What does he want? Why has he come? Is he real? Or am I just as mad as you?"

Back and forth, back and forth. Creaking.

"He's here because of you."

"How? Why? *Speak clearly!*"

"He enjoys your fear. You deserve it."

"I didn't ask for this."

"But you deserve it all the same. Heart of stone, just like I told you before."

I could scream. "What did I ever do to you? What did I ever do to deserve this?"

"You're mad, my girl. The mad are always punished. Some of us even deserve it."

"Nori doesn't deserve this."

The creaking stops. Heavy footsteps across the floorboards. A sudden, leering white face out of the shadows, shaggy wheat-colored hair, wild around her face.

Cathy's eyes are wild for a moment, staring at me, but then they focus, unglazed, and she looks...sane. "Keep her away from him, Silla. He will hurt you through her. Protect her."

I blink and I shake my head, and this is all too hard. Crazy one moment, now lucid and terrified? I'm only seventeen. "I don't know how."

"You just have to reset. It will get worse before it gets better, my girl."

I slump against the banister. "I don't understand. I'm so tired."

Cath is fading away again, her last look one of pity. Sympathy. Understanding.

"The mad always are," she says.

Ω

WITHOUT WARNING

The hole grows larger without warning and without much sound.

I heard it in the night. S s s s p l i n t e r i n g.

Falling inward.

It should now be as big as the length of her spine. Silla will be sure, very soon, that the hole is definitely closer to sentient than not.

In the morning, I hear her put more chairs around the hole. Silly child. As if that could stop this!

$$\Omega$$

BOOK 4:
Meat Prison

DON'T STOP NOW, IF YOU REALLY SEEK

SILLA'S TRUTHS, WHICH MAY BE BLEAK

BUT IF YOU FEAR THE CREEPER MAN'S
GLANCE

BEST GO NOW; THIS IS YOUR LAST
CHANCE.

17

no. no, no, no

Sudden darkness, sudden calm
means the woods are close
don't you put up the alarm
you're the one he chose.

BROKEN BOOK ENTRY

His voice is calling me at night. It's like a **presence** I can't escape. The others **can't** hear him. Can't hear any of the **hurt**ful words he says to **me**. I wish I could argue back, deny the **tall** tales, heavy with lies **and thin** on truth. **He is** trying to torment me with his **poison** tongue. Shut **up**, shut up, shut up! I go down**stairs** to confront **the** thing but there is no form, only the endless **creaking** of the floorboards under my feet and his voice. It **is** torture. **Still** seems like the dark might be **endless**.

The same, every night. When I sleep, for however few minutes at a time, I dream.

La Baume is crumbling in my dreams. Sunken and warped. The red paint is peeling away, revealing a gross curling of rainbow colors beneath. Red, blue, green, pink, orange…it's a sick joke. And the house is choking underneath vines upon vines and roots upon roots. They rise out of dead ground to strangle the manor and I feel like *I'm* the one being choked. I feel like *I'm* the one who can't breathe.

As I watch, the vines grow, thicken, tighten, and La Baume begins to crack and sink, straining to remain, and I choke and I gasp and I can't breathe—

and I wake.

I still can't breathe.

I give up sleeping in my room for the night, and take to the second floor in the library, between the bookcases, where Gowan sleeps. We share a blanket and he kisses my forehead.

"I'm staying with you," he tells me. "Until you're ready to come."

I'm ready. So ready. But I never will. I can't lose Nori.

I curl into his arms, and for once, I sleep.

Ω

It wasn't a *boom*. Not even a *crash*. It was more like…a *creeeee-aaak* and I almost didn't notice it in my half sleep.

WRONG.

I open my eyes and see *nothing*. The room is a terrifying black. I'm about to panic about being blind when I spot the embers burning in the grill of the fireplace.

Oh, God.

I reach over to wake Gowan, but all I feel is the cold blanket beside me. And then I hear Nori banging on the wall upstairs, hysterical and alone. I can almost hear her terrified gasping, sense her tears. *[LET HER ROT, THE LITTLE PEST.]*

"Nori!" I spring up.

"Wait—what's going on?" Gowan says groggily from somewhere else in the library. Down a level—on one of the sofa chairs.

"I have to get to Nori!"

He's up in a second. "Damn. Silla, we need lights."

"There's a generator in the basement. But it doesn't work all the time. We stopped using it."

"Okay, I'll go down."

"No!"

"We need to check it, Silla."

"Okay, but let me come with you, then. I have to get to Nori first, though. There's a candle on the desk by the window." Even as I'm telling him this, I'm feeling my way down the spiral stairs. When I'm at the bottom, he already has the candle and is lighting it with the last embers.

I hug the blanket closer to me. It's so *cold*. And then I open the door, stepping gingerly forward, very much aware of the hole in the entrance hall and the glaringly loud *silence* of it. I bump into the armchair and adjust my trajectory. My heart thuds inside me. *[SCARED OF THE DARK, ARE WE?]* The flesh-ball thing could be right next to me. *He* could be right beside me, waiting to reach out.

But no. Gowan is here. He has a candle. There is enough light to see by, but it flickers and moves, making the shadows dance.

"Tell me where the flashlight is, and some candles, and then go to Nori."

But Nori is already coming to us.

Silla? Something's wrong with my room.

She is breathless and pale, and she takes my hand, holding it firmly.

"It's okay, bug. We've just run out of light." I pick her up, and sit her on my hip, even though she really is getting too big for this. I tell myself it's because she's scared, but I know that really it's because *I* am.

"Okay," Gowan says. "Now, quickly, candles—"

"Okay, but we don't have a flashlight. There are lanterns, though. Really old ones that will burn this miserable house down if we knock them over. I've gotten pretty good with them since being here."

Gowan makes a face. "Really?"

"Yeah, well, my aunt is a little eccentric, if you didn't notice. This house is old as hell itself."

"Better than nothing."

I grab his arm. "Gowan...this darkness...it's...could it..."

His eyes harden, and he storms to the window. He opens the curtains and I stagger backward.

Earth. We are buried in earth.

Gowan runs out of the room and upstairs to my room. I follow, Nori clinging to me like her life depends on it, and I'm starting to think it does.

The trees.

They have completely surrounded La Baume, not an inch of air between them.

The trees are here, rising over us.

And La Baume is sinking.

We are completely and utterly *trapped*.

Ω

It's the trees.

Silla says: This is...

Scary. I sign.

Silla says: ...insane.

I nod. We are at the front door, and the garden should be out there, but it's all dirt and trees! They are so close, like long wooden bricks. They took away all the light, all of it!

Gowan says: You're kidding me. You're actually f—ing kidding me.

Silla says: Watch it. (She looks at me.)

Gowan says: Sorry.

Silla says: This manor is—

Gowan says: Cursed. Or haunted. Or—

Silla says: Something. Yeah.

Gowan says: Bloody hell. (Silla squints at him and nods at me and then he nods back and then I nod, too.)

They talk for a long, long time, and I look at my friend, but he just smiles and steps back again, and I don't know why he didn't take my hand like before.

I put my arms around Silla.

This is a scary game.

Ω

Gowan gets the ax from the kitchen. It's partly rusted, so I'm not convinced of how much use it's going to be.

We run back up to my room.

"Stand back," he says.

We do.

He shatters my bedroom window and begins chopping and chopping and chopping and chopping until Nori tugs on my dress and signs, *Can we go away? Is there food?*

I nod, and we silently leave Gowan to it.

He's strong, Nori signs.

"Yeah," I agree. "But I don't think Gowan's strength is going to be enough."

Not him, she signs.

Ω

Gowan chops at the trees blocking the window all day.

"This doesn't happen," I hear him muttering when I pass.

The wood splinters and falls away, piece by painful piece.

"Tomorrow," Gowan says, dripping with sweat. "I'll break through tomorrow. And then we're getting the hell out of here."

"Okay," I tell him in a small voice. He doesn't need to tell me that this is all my fault. If I had just gone with him when I still could have, then we'd be long free. Instead of trapped in a cursed (?) house, waiting to die. Waiting to sink into the earth and be buried alive. Waiting for *him* to arrive and tear us to shreds.

He seems to read my thoughts in my face because he pulls me into a tight hug. I tense, but he doesn't let me go.

"There's blame to share," he whispers in my ear, softly, so Nori won't hear.

I pull away. "There really isn't."

I leave the two of them staring after me as I wander into the house.

$$\Omega$$

The next morning, the trees are full and whole again. It's like Gowan's ax never touched them at all. I am in the kitchen, trying to find something for Nori to eat, moving dishes around point-lessly, when I hear Gowan's furious cry somewhere above us.

I go to find Gowan. When he spots me, he walks over and wraps me in his arms, lips in my hair, heart pounding against me. He is shaking. I hug him back, clenching my eyes shut against his awful, impossible reality. The strangest sensation takes over. That he is clinging on to me because he is afraid. Not of being trapped, or of... *him*... But afraid of ME. Afraid *for* me.

"I don't know what to do," he says, but I have the strange feeling he means something else entirely. Maybe: I'm scared.

"I don't either," I say, and think: *We are going to die in here.*

He closes his eyes. "It's hopeless."

There's that word again.

Somewhere, out there, the trees are pushing even closer. If it's possible. And we are sinking.

And a thought strikes me with such a chill that I almost drop the dish in my hand.

If the trees are at La Baume's doorstep...

Then the Creeper Man is, too.

$$\Omega$$

The air is stale in here.

My imagination, I'm sure, since we haven't been trapped

long enough for me to be able to tell. But I feel like I'm breathing in Gowan's, Nori's, and Cath's soupy secondhand air. The rotting fruit full of worms doesn't help. Nori is so hungry, I caught her trying to eat it.

That's why I'm here, now. At the hole.

It's gotten so big that it has swallowed up the chairs I put around it for ~~my~~ Nori's protection. I let the plate tilt forward, slowly, so that the fruit slips off the plate in increments, leaving a trail of brown juice behind. A few worms linger, so I drop the plate, too.

I bend forward and listen. Intently.

I never hear an impact.

I stare down into the pit, straining to see *something*. And for a moment, the merest fraction of a minute, I think I see something writhing down there. Roots, maybe, twisting and bending around one another? Or were they vines? Hell, for all I know, they were arms, reaching out for me.

I certainly feel the pull. I think my future may just include an attic and a singular pacing path.

I will never tell Nori that.

I will never tell Gowan.

But it's getting to be a bit of a challenge to hold back.

That's right, his voice coos. *Daddy's little girl is coming home.*

We're trapped in this house, waiting to die. Why not...give in? Why the hell should I resist?

$$\Omega$$

Gowan is here all the time now and I'm happy. He's really nice.

But sometimes I get sleepy because my friend wants to play almost every night now. But I fall asleep during the day because Silla doesn't notice and we don't try reading anymore. But Auntie started screaming again one night while she walks up and down her high-up room, and now Silla walks up and down all night, too, and once I saw her pulling at her hair and it made me scared because she looked scary.

But Auntie screamed and screamed and then Silla screamed. But then Gowan came to sit with her and it got better after that because then only Auntie was screaming.

The only bad thing is that Silla shouts at me a lot and that's a bad thing. But my tummy is so sore that I have to put something in it sometimes and Silla doesn't like that.

I don't want to make Silla angry.

And I don't want to play with the man anymore.

I don't think he's really my friend at all.

But it's too late now.

Ω

Gowan is unusually quiet at our mockery of "dinner." It has been three days now. I think he is realizing how futile it is. The trees grow back each time he cuts them away. We talked about opening the kitchen door to dig a tunnel, but I pointed out that giving the earth entry might allow it to bury us alive. He had closed his eyes and covered his face with hands blistered and broken.

Maybe he is giving in to the HOPELESSNESS that pervades the air. I should feel satisfaction: *I told you,* a tiny voice whispers inside. Instead, I feel afraid. *Please don't lose hope, too. You are the only one with any vapors of it left.*

So now I am the one staring. Staring at the way even his hair seems limp. The slow movement of his hand as he runs his spoon listlessly through the watery soup. The candles burn low and no one speaks. Even Nori isn't eating.

"Please."

Nori looks up, but Gowan doesn't move. I hate the way the corners of his mouth fold down, the tiny wrinkles on either side of his mouth.

"Please," I say again. "Please, Gowan."

He looks at me then. But the light is gone from his face.

We are running out of fire.

I say it out loud, and he understands what I mean, because his face crumples and he shoves away his chair, leaving the room before I can see him cry.

Stunned, we sit in silence.

The candles burn low, and then die.

Ω

One night, I wake to find Nori gone. I wander out of the library, where we all sleep now, with one of the last candles, the light casting grotesque shadows along the high walls.

"Nori?"

The basement door is open, so I close it and hurry past.

"Nori?"

I hear something upstairs, a scuttling noise, and hesitate. Nori doesn't make sounds like that.

"Nori..."

And then I hear her footfalls, tiny *thump*s that I still recognize. I follow them upstairs, but they are above me still. I ascend to the third floor—the abandoned hallway. The door to the wasp room at the end is open, and my stomach lurches with some emotion. Fear? Apprehension?

I find her crouching in the center of the pile of husks.

"Nori, what are you *doing*?"

She turns to look over her shoulder, her eyes too big in her gaunt face. She has a handful of wasp husks, and she is chewing.

I bend over, the same feeling in my stomach intensifying. Not fear, not apprehension, but disgust.

The *C R U N C H I N G* sound as she chews seems to echo in my head.

"Nori, don't!" I scramble forward and open her mouth, scooping out the remains of decade-old dead insects from her tongue.

She bites down on my fingers and I swear, but I keep scooping.

"Spit it out! Spit it out now!"

She cries and tries to grab more of them but I lift her into my arms and I run. I run down the hall, my candle long-extinguished, and I dash into the library. I bolt the top of the door, where she can't reach, and I hug her tightly as she cries silently, her little fists beating on my chest. She wriggles to get free, and finally manages it, running to lie down with Gowan, who wraps her in his arms in his sleep.

She stares at me from his embrace, eyes accusing.

I hear the Creeper Man scuttling along the halls.

Ω

It's the smell that wakes me. A slow, noxious stench that first infiltrates my dream as a cauldron of bubbling witch's brew. Then it slowly penetrates and my mind wakes to escape it.

I cough.

Gag.

I stagger to my feet, retching. "What *is* that?"

Gowan enters the library, fully clothed, looking cleaner and more handsome than he has any right to in this filthy, rotting hovel.

"Smell it?"

"No."

He looks pale. Working too hard to get us out.

This is the day I begin hunting.

Ω

18

jesus, god

Wakey, wakey, rise and shine
mind your toe upon that vine
slinking in across your floor
oops! The woods are at your door!

BROKEN BOOK ENTRY

Listen to me. Listen very carefully. You're
trapped. Right now, you're trapped. You're stuck
to the bottom of someone's shoe. You're walking
around in **your** life, like your own little isola-
tion bubble, following their footprints, thinking:
This is it. This is me. This is MY SELF. This is
how it goes. **This** is how it works. These are the
rules. But here **is** the secret. You are free. You're
not one of those fools. There is no bubble except
the one they put you in. But it's made of soap, of

air—of nothing at all. **Only**, you're taught that it's indestructible—no **way** of getting through *that* barrier. And you can pop it with your little finger. **You** could pop it with your breath. You **could** *blow* on it, and it would fizzle away.

You are **free**.

You can do what you want.

When you want.

How you want.

On your time.

You can destroy **yourself**, kill yourself—

And then get up and walk away.

You are free. No **but**. No or. No either.

You are an indestructible machine.

You **are** magnificent.

You can steal; you can cheat.

And you can lie. Be **a liar**.

I am.

Ω

"If there was meat in the house, don't you think we'd have eaten it?" I yell. "Don't you think I'd have given it to Nori, instead of letting it *rot*?"

Gowan folds his arms. "Silla, what are you talking about?"

"Meat! This house reeks of rotting meat!"

He frowns. "This again?"

"Can't you smell that?" I retch, turning away. "It's disgusting! If there is meat in this house, I'm sure as hell going to find it."

I feel a tiny pressure on my hand—fingers encircling my wrist. She has no words, so I probably missed her sign—*Silla?*—and so I thought it was Gowan. I spin, rage beating through my veins in a pulsing, virulent rhythm of aggression, and I

slap her.

She is so small.

I remember when she was born, this tiny, wrinkly thing in my mother's arms. Squirming, and so...silent.

"I will protect you," I'd told her.

I was ten.

I was the biggest.

I was Big Sister.

I will protect you.

Ω

My mouth is open and my eyes are open and my palm is open. Stinging.

Nori has staggered, but she looks up at me, cupping her cheek, and she laughs, like this is a joke. A game.

My heart cracks

breaks

falls out of me.

Because that tiny, mute laugh is one of disbelief, forgiveness, alarm, shock

and then her eyes change, widen, fill up with water

she is crying

and I wish there was sound so that I could hear what I have done, but she is still trying to smile at me like, *It's okay, Silla, it's okay*, like I'm the one who is hurting, and I am staring at my hand and it is still burning and

I hit Nori. *[YOU ARE THE BIGGEST.]*

I hit my little sister. *[YOU ARE BIG SISTER.]*

Do you love anything? Anything at all? *I love my sister.* [HAHAHAHA!]

I will protect you. [LIAR.]

Gowan is as mute as Nori but I see something in his face that I recognize.

Rage.

I spin, nearly falling, and run away, leaving Nori and Gowan behind me. Leaving their shock and their goddamn silences and their eyes looking at me all the time and *seeing* me. Too deep. Too hard.

I am shaking.

What have I done?

Who am I?

The smell hits me again as I race past the hole.

Meat.

Meat.

Somehow, I let meat go to rot in this house while Nori gobbles up worm-infested fruit and wasp husks and tries to ignore the roaring in her stomach.

Meat.

Jesus, God.

How did I let precious food rot away to feed this damn house instead of *us*? How did I...*hit* my Nori?

"What's happening to me?" I whisper, but there is nothing except the creaking of Cath's pacing above me, and the creaking of the house around me, and the creaking of my heart inside me.

This house.

It's watching every mistake I make with glee.

"You're not going to win," I tell it, as though we are in some dangerous competition and it can actually hear me. "You hear that, you little bitch? I'm going to beat you."

But I'm beating myself all alone. I don't need any help.

Ω

I search for the smell all day.

Nori and Gowan are nowhere to be seen, and I'm glad. I can't face them. [HIT HER HARDER.] I can't look into his eyes and see judgment [YOU DON'T GIVE A DAMN] like that. I don't [DO] want to hurt them. I will never [ALWAYS] hurt them. [LIAR LIAR PANTS ON FIRE.]

"I will never hurt them," I whisper, hurrying on.

I end up in the basement, contemplating the wine racks.

And my palm, hot on her little cheek.

I don't want to think about what is happening to me. I don't want to think about what's happening to *us*. I don't want to think about the mold on our skin, our clothes, the walls. The rotting fruit and the maggots in the walls.

I don't want to have those intrusive thoughts

Rot

breaking into my mind

Decay

all the time

Stench

like flashes of lightning, *snap, snap, snap!*

I don't want to be here. I want to be a normal seventeen-year-old girl, worried about graduation and prom and boys (like Gowan) and getting my own car and going to university and "getting a life." Aren't I supposed to be freaking out over my eyelashes, the new tattoo, this hot band, my next outfit like those kids out there? Or shouldn't I be pondering my career, my path in life, the meaning behind everything for me, the future?

My head is a word cloud of turmoil, but all of it is silenced—frozen still—by what I see in the concrete of the basement floor.

A root.

A root has broken through the concrete, and is growing out of the floor.

Holy shit bastard shit.

I thought being trapped in La Baume with Python right outside was bad. But now it looks like not even solid stone will keep the trees away.

We're infested.

We're infected.

We can't win.

Ω

When I finally come out of my hiding place, I feel my way through the house quietly and tentatively, realizing with an ache inside that I miss them…my family. I miss Nori. I miss Cath. And I miss Gowan.

I find them by following the glow. It's a soft orange light, moving like the gentle pulse of a heartbeat, drawing me to it.

The library. They lit the fire.

I find them on the sheepskin rug in front of the grate, Nori lying against Gowan, the light of the flames dancing over their faces. In Nori, it has a softening effect, her eyes faraway and unseeing as she stares at the flames. In Gowan, the effect is one of hardness. The light sharpens his jaw and brow bone and sets a fire in his near-black eyes. His gaze is here, in the now, even as he watches the heat.

He senses me, standing still in the doorway, and turns. Ever so slightly.

I expect his jaw to clench, or his eyes to narrow, or his hand to tighten on Nori's shoulder, protective.

But he smiles, and the tension in his eyes vanishes. He's… *relieved.*

I hesitate, looking down at Nori, who, sensing the change in the room, sits up and turns to face me.

She doesn't need to say my name for me to know that she thought it.

She gets to her feet and hurries over to me, burying her head in my torso. Shame, joy, relief, guilt, heartache, and *love* wash through me, and I hold her head, bending over it and covering it with kisses.

"I'm sorry," I whisper. "I'm so sorry. I love you."

I say these words over and over, and they become a mantra. When the frenzy has died, and Nori steps away to look up into my face, she is crying and smiling.

I cup her cheeks and connect my eyes to hers. "You are the whole world to me," I tell her. "Did you know that?"

She sniffs and shakes her head. She really *didn't* know that.

"I love you more than anything." And then I close the walls and step away. "Now get out of here, you pest."

She grins and skips off, settling back down in front of the fire.

Gowan smiles at her, and then looks over at me.

"We were worried."

I shrug. "Why? Nowhere I could go."

I know it's not what he means, and he knows I know, but he lets it drop and I'm grateful. We leave Nori by the fire and go up to the second level.

"I found roots in the basement," I tell him, when we are out of Nori's earshot.

His mouth falls a little at that, but he tries to hide it behind a smile. "Oh."

"I should have listened to you. I should have taken Nori and gone while we could. With or without Cath."

I wait for him to tell me I'm right, that I was stupid to wait, to resist. Instead, he says, "I don't think that would have helped. I finally realize that running was never the right choice. We need to face this problem, whatever it is. And we have to face it here."

"The curse."

"If that's what it is."

"I think Cath knows what's going on. She has a long history with this house."

"Has she told you everything? About…the Creeper Man?"

I catch Nori's manic motioning with her good arm over the balcony. *No eyes*, Nori signs from below us, by the fire.

"No eyes," I say for her. "No. I don't think she has."

Gowan swallows. "Well. Then we've got to go and talk to her."

"I…" *No, no, no, no.* "I tried once. She didn't make a whole lot of sense."

"We have to try again. This is the last chance."

"I…"

Gowan takes my hands. "She's your aunt. You have to try."

It's not my aunt that terrifies me. It's those stairs.

$$\Omega$$

Silla is going to be very upset, but I know that I have to go. The Creeper Man is beside me, so tall he is like a mountain! I am scared, but I know nothing bad can happen, so I tell my tummy to stop shouting that I must <u>be afraid</u> and <u>run very far and hide, quick!</u>

The Creeper Man is my friend. He said there were still games to play.

I put my hand into his and we go away.

Bye, bye, Silla! See you soon!

$$\Omega$$

19

we made a man

There was an old lady
who lived all alone,
until her nieces
came all the way home.
nightly she prayed
he'd stay away,
but childhood demons,
come back to play.

A panel of wood, followed by another one, higher than the last.

Up. And up. Up again.

Framed by two leering walls of stone.

They're just stairs. I keep telling myself that. Steps. A path to follow. That's all.

"What is it?" Gowan whispers behind me.

What is it about these stairs that makes him lower his voice? Something about them reduces volume, and that can't be good.

I shake my head, unable to speak.

"We have to talk to her."

I put my hand on the banister, but my whole body is rigid with tension. The stairs seem a mile high—they might as well be a mountain. I start to hyperventilate.

"Sill..."

"I can't."

I can't breathe—I can't breathe! No—nononono I can't, I can't—don't make me—"You can. We have to."

He takes my hand, and the spell is broken. I move because he is with me.

Step

   by

      step.

On either side of us, the roots twist and dangle with the stairs and the walls, and when the door swings open, it is to an infestation. Roots have bent and twisted their way into the house, draped along the floor, the windows, the walls—huge, gnarly, strong. Cathy lies trapped in the middle.

She looks like a princess in a fairy tale gone wrong. Her hair, sun-kissed wheat, is splayed over the roots and vines that have her in a stranglehold, choking her body into a smaller shape than it should be. She should be crying out, but she is smiling, a glassy glint in her eyes.

"Silla," she says, tears in her words but not in her eyes. "Oh, my Silla. At last."

I fall to my knees with the shock of it. "Auntie Cath..."

"This is..." Cath tries to take a breath, nice and deep, but the roots are so big across her chest, slowly crushing, getting tighter. "...all your fault."

I choke on the blow. "How? How is this my fault? What did I do?"

"All...your...fault."

"I didn't bring the Creeper Man here. You did that, didn't you? When you were a girl. Tell me the truth!"

"He was our protector...but we were wrong." She gives a tiny squeak as the roots tighten.

"We have to get her out of there," Gowan tells me, and he

runs from the room. I hear his feet thudding down the steps and I hate that he's left me here alone.

"Tell me about the Creeper Man. Tell me what you and Mam did when you were girls. Please, Cath, please!"

"We…made a man. From clay and twine and shadow. We… made him in the woods. We summoned a p-protector."

"But he wasn't a protector, was he? *Was* he?"

The slightest shake of her head, and another tiny intake of breath. "Not a protector. A demon. A curse. Anne…"

"Anne? Who's Anne?"

"Sister. Died. In the woods. Not a protector. A"—another gasp for air—"tormentor."

"How is that *my* fault? If you summoned him when you were children, how could I be to blame?"

A tear squeezes out of her eye as the roots, once again, tighten, pulling her toward them like a monster with many arms drawing her into its chest. I hear her ribs crack, and she winces, coughs.

"Silla…it's going to happen soon. This is all for you."

Gowan's feet thunder toward us, and he has brought the ax. He doesn't even pause, just roars, the ax high, and then brings it down full-strength on the roots holding Cath's body.

She looks up at him with increasingly vacant eyes. "I know you," she wheezes. "Don't…I? But…different. Is…it…different…?"

"Yes," he says, and somehow that one word calms her.

"Good," she wheezes. "Oh, good."

She fades off and her gaze slides to the side.

Cath smiles at me suddenly then, as Gowan chops, and the roots pull her ever farther from us, tangling around her body like some twisted version of a Grimm fairy tale.

"Cathy!" I cry, reaching out for her.

Her fingers are almost gone now, but I can still see a sliver of her face.

"Oh, Silla," she whispers, and for the first time in years, she sounds like the aunt I came to when I was fourteen. "I'm so sorry."

And then she is gone.

Nothing but a curling mass of chipped-at roots remains.

Ω

There is no sign of Cath now, not even a hair tangled in the roots. I should be horrified to see them moving and bending like no root should do, but instead I am furious.

I spin on my heel and head for the stairs, the flame on my candle nearly going out with the force of my turn. Gowan grabs my free hand.

"Where are you going?"

"If my own family won't help me," I snap, "then I'll deal with the devil."

I rip my hand from his and rush down the stairs, heading for the entrance hall. To hell with this. To hell with this house, this curse, this nightmare.

I stand at the very edge of the hole, my hands balled into fists at my sides. "Tell me what's going on!" I yell into the depths. My voice travels into the space but doesn't return.

Eerie.

"Tell me what this is!" My father's voice is silent. "You son of a bitch!" I throw the lit candle into the hole and never hear it land. *Tell me!*

Gowan is behind me then, taking my shoulders. "Silla..."

It is very, very dark.

"You torture me night after night with your damn words and *now* you're silent?" I yell.

"Silla—"

"What?"

"Where's Nori?"

"What do you mean? She's—"

I turn, looking for her, but there is no light in the house now. The black is so complete that I dare not move my foot even an inch in case I stumble into the hole. I hear Gowan rustle beside me, and then he has a flame in his fist. A lighter.

I peer around for Nori. She's not with us. Something inside me makes a tiny *click*, like a piece of a wooden puzzle falling into place. And I feel sick.

Gowan's lighter goes out, and he flips it on again. He lights another candle—the one sitting in the sconce on the wall, and I'm grateful for the tiny orange bubble of light.

I walk to the kitchen, very calmly, but it is empty.

"Nori?"

We check the scullery and then I head for the stairs. The roots have spilled into the halls now and I don't want to think about being crushed alive by evil trees, but I can't help it. Gowan heads back toward the entrance hall and I turn for the stairs.

"Silla!"

His voice is alarm.

I run toward the hole, and see her. She's at the other end of the corridor, only now it's more like a tunnel of trees, impossibly long, and she is impossibly small—impossibly far away. And her hand is in the hand of a **TALL,** thin man with

no eyes

and

a **wide,wide**
mouth.
Vanishing
    down   *the woods*
       the   *also*   disappearing
        hall,   *is*   into
           that   the
                                eerie
                                indoor
                                    mist.

"Eleanor!"

I scream, rushing on, but the trees are growing and before I can even think, she is in that thing's arms, her own
around
his
neck
and he has carried her off into the depths of La Baume, which is now the thickest part of Python Wood.

I step forward—*get her back, get her back!*—right into the yawning black hole.

Ω

BOOK 5:
Rooted Fire

Three little girls
knelt by an alder
to summon a man
to be their protector.
the little girls found
their game hard to bear
when their protector turned
and gave them a scare!

20

kansas

Hold on tight
we're going for a ride
toward a light
on the other side!

BROKEN BOOK ENTRY

Okay, fine. **I'm** a little **afraid**. So? **I'm** even angry. But anger and fear aren't **going** to feed her. **To** clothe her. I could even argue that he's the one who might **kill** her. But relying on **someone**—anyone—is useless. I know that now. It's **one** of the many mistakes I've made. **Day** turns into night turns into day, and still I wait. Waiting is pointless. And it's too late to go now.

Ω

Memories come.

I am five, wearing a yellow skirt that I will love fiercely and keep until it becomes so short that Mam calls it obscene and burns it.

A straw doll at seven, which I pretend to love to please her.

A sunset on my eighth birthday when Father locked me out of the house.

Nori's birth when I am ten.

My pride.

My terror.

Ω

Some things pass with a storm, loud and vexing. Full of drama. They are delightfully, dramatically disruptive. They blunder past like shouts of thunder and shrieks of lightning, and are always a brilliant spectacle.

Other things whisper by.

So it is that Gowan saves me from the Stygian pit.

I wither in his arms, like a wilted flower. And I shudder.

"I lost her. I lost her."

Maybe he knows I am falling away from him, because he holds me firmly and kisses me fervently, trying to rouse me from the haze Nori's abduction has left me in.

He got her.

I shake my head, squeezing my eyes shut against the awful afterglow of that image. Nori, her hand in his, walking away with him.

She went with him.

It's over.

Everything is over.

All over.

All gone.

I lost her.

I close my eyes and lose myself.

$$\Omega$$

I wake to a new world.

My head aches, and as Gowan helps me up, I can't, at first, recall why I feel so scared.

"What happened?"

"You nearly walked into that hole. I pulled you back but you were freaking out a bit and you knocked your head."

I can feel the bump.

And then it comes back.

"Nori, oh God—"

"She's gone. He took her into the...woods."

"What do you mean into the woods—they were down the corridor, just there—"

I point and then freeze. Because the corridor is not a corridor. La Baume is utterly changed. The trees that were holding us under siege have now penetrated the walls entirely, growing in from I don't know where, twisting and tangling like those roots upstairs that stole Cathy away. They are growing through the house, out of the walls, through the floors, up to the ceiling, draped in thick moss.

We are invaded.

The entire manor is an eerie forest, too still to be real, fallen leaves landing on wooden floorboards and Persian rugs, trunks towering up into and through the ceilings, branches skimming paintings.

La Baume is laughing at me. But the laughter is silent, slow, and eerie. I am on the ground floor, facing the corridor that Nori vanished down. Only now it is a forest path, carpeted and surreal. I recognize the paintings that hang from the branches as those that were on the walls.

"This...isn't happening."

The floor—the wooden floorboards—are now draped with roots thicker than my arm. I take a step into this strange manor-wood and feel my breath catch. I turn to Gowan.

"This can't be...real."

Gowan stares into the trees. "I don't think we're exactly in Kansas anymore."

"I have to get Nori back. I have to.... He's got her."

For a moment, the world closes in—too overwhelming to live in—but then Gowan's hands are wrapped around mine and I know I can do this.

"I'm going to find her. Find the answer. This is some kind of family...thing. A debt, maybe. A curse. So, basically, it's all connected to Cath, to Nori. And me."

"Are you ready?"

I nod.

He lifts a hand and points down the corridor. Into the woodland path that stretches into...I don't know where.

"That way."

I have no choice. No more running. It is no longer an option. I've hidden in this damned house for too long, afraid of the trees and of...*him*. Well, now the trees are here, and he's got Nori, and hiding is not a choice. I am Silla Mae Daniels. I am sane. I am afraid.

I get to my feet.

And when I take my first step into the void, Gowan takes one beside me.

Ω

The house all but disappears into this eerie wood. It is too still to be any conventional forest, too creepily silent. There are no birds here. There is no breeze. No real life. Here and there, I spot a wall sconce protruding from one of the trunks and I know that I am in La Baume and maybe this is all just a messed-up delusion. Did I take some kind of drug—LSD maybe? Am I still back in London, hallucinating the hell out of my mind?

We walk for a long time, looking for signs, searching the carpet and bracken for footsteps, but there is nothing.

Ω

Cath is gone. And *still* I hear the creaking.

Only now, it's the boughs above us. The floorboards beneath us. My stomach even *creeeaaaks* as it growls. It's like I'm turning to wood along with everything else.

And the mold is still growing on me. And I still smell rotting meat.

"The smell," I say on the third day. "It's getting stronger."

He nods. "Yeah. I can smell it now." He glances over at me. "Wait. Sit down. You're practically falling over."

I shake my head.

"I want to ask you something. I've *wanted* to ask you something."

I'm so tired.

"Tell me about your mother."

I bite my tongue and sit down on the mossy, stinky carpet.

After a pause, Gowan sighs. "You always do that."

"What?"

"Whenever I mention your mother, your face changes. I know you lied to me before. I know that wasn't the whole story. What are you hiding, Silla? Why won't you talk to me?"

"Because you're...I don't know." *Too good.*

"You can't call me unimportant or a stranger or whatever line you have in your head. Not after everything we've been through."

I stare at him. "It's just the opposite.... You're just another thing to hurt me."

"What are you talking about?"

"Just leave me alone."

I struggle to my feet and walk away.

"No! No, I won't skulk off this time." He takes my shoulders into his hands. "You have to talk to me. You can't keep running away from me!"

"Why *not*?" I yell, my voice barely carrying beyond my face.

"Because I'm in here with you and I'm helping you and *I love you*!"

I try to shake him off with some violence. "Then so much the worse for you!"

He holds me tighter. "What happened to make you so cold? Cold as stone! Your heart is like a rock in there, drumming against your body and breaking everything inside!"

"Yes!" I shriek. "Yes, it is! I got that from my father, my wonderful, abusive father—happy now?"

"No, I'm not, because you're still hiding!" Gowan takes a breath. "All of this," he says, gesturing around us. "It's to do with you. Cath is gone. If she was to blame, then surely this would have stopped. It would be over, right?"

"Firstly," I snap, "what logic are you using here? Is this something you have prior experience with? Are you following the cursed-mansion-haunted-woods-child-stealing-creature hand-book?"

He gives me a pained expression.

"Second," I say, talking louder when it looks like he'll try to interrupt. "How do you know that Cath vanishing wouldn't just leave everything like this forever? How do you know that her"—death death **death**—"*disappearance* isn't part of the puzzle?"

His eyes burn me. "I don't. We don't know anything."

"Exactly." Our lips are close now. So close.

"But I do know this," he persists, his breath caressing my lips. "I know you're hiding something. You're carrying around a secret, Silla Daniels, and it's eating you alive."

His words stop me in my tracks. Suspicion pulses inside me. *Howdoesheknow? Howdoesheknow?*

It's **eating** *you alive.*

"What are you talking about?"

He leans even closer to me and the shadow of a thick branch falls over his face like a shroud. "I can see it in your face. It's like a weight pulling down your features. It's dragging you into the earth."

I snort. "Melodramatic much?"

He lets go of my shoulder and touches my cheek, and his words are soft. "Come off it, Silla. Let me help you."

"Gowan," I whisper, our lips touching ever so slightly. "Let me go."

"Silla, please," he breathes, closing his eyes. "Please don't do this to me."

"Let me go. Let me go, let me go—"

And he does. He lets me go, even though I can see in his face everything inside him is bursting to keep me. Love and hope are warring with despair, all on his beautiful face. He wants to help me, to love me, and to save me. I recall his words on those green pages; I hate what I'm doing to him. But he's an idiot because you can't save someone from herself.

"Stop trying!" I yell at him, as though he knows what I mean.

I walk some feet away from him and then collapse into a puddle because my legs can't hold me anymore and the weight on my shoulders is too heavy to carry much farther.

I'm just another rock on a forest floor.

"I can't," I say at last.

He stays still, breathing heavily. Waiting.

"It's too hard."

"Too hard to keep inside of you, Sill. It's going to break you if you don't let it go."

"My mother...my...she..." I pause. Wipe my face. "When we first got here, Nori had a broken collarbone and arm. It'd been healing for a few weeks, a month maybe, and..." I squeeze my eyes shut. *Can'tdothiswon'tdothis*—

I feel his hand on my fist, warm and sturdy.

"I told Cath it was a birth defect."

"So you left Nori's arm to heal askew."

"Yes. Her teeth, too. I...I left her to be a cripple with messed-up teeth and now I'm paying for it."

To prove it, I bite down on the loose tooth in the back of my mouth and spit it out, blood and drool on my chin.

Gowan swallows. "Why lie? Why protect your father?"

"I didn't want to, but telling the truth would have meant accepting the other truth. I was safe for the first time in forever, and I didn't want to leave. Didn't want to admit—"

I shake my head, and my body retches as my mind skims the edge of the truth.

He's still standing behind me, some way off. "Tell me," he says.

"When we first got here and Cath asked me what happened, I...I told her a story. But...I can't, Gowan. I can't."

"Tell it to me. Tell it to me like a story, just like you did to Cath."

Ω

A Story
Cause and Effect

Silla Daniels learns about cause and effect in school.

Cause: The blush of blue on Nori's cheek. The shock of red on her lips. The snap of her collarbone when the father pushed. Her silent cry.

Effect: A plan, over time. The stashed bag.

Cause: Nori's silent laugh, so full of sound. The sparkle in her eyes that, somehow, remains. The silent plea of the mother. *Go.* The teeth, broken and askew.

Effect: The attempted escape.

Nori is already awake when Silla removes their bag from its hiding place behind the loose boards in the wall. She watches, expectant, as Silla adds the good blanket to the bundle.

Ready?

Silla's hands seem worried, so Nori smiles. Nods. Everything is going to be okay.

Quiet as a mouse, Silla signs.

Squeak! Nori signs. Smiles.

Silla nods.

The sisters tiptoe into the living room on the balls of their feet, shoes in Silla's bag. *Like a bird,* Silla signs. *Like air. Sssssshhhhhhh.* Mam and Dad are sleeping in the middle of the floor again, a thin blanket tossed across his torso, hers draped close to his. Not too close. Just out of reach.

Silla hesitates a moment. If this goes wrong...if she fails...

One glance at Nori is enough to push her forward. The bruise, the cut lip, the way she holds her arm askew, shoulder raised. The terrible bend in her tiny collarbone, unnatural and awkward. So tiny—too tiny—to be so broken.

Silla moves, her hand wrapped around Nori's. They are traversing a minefield just as hazardous as the rumored ones out there in the war zone.

Step.

Stop. Listen.

Step.

Feel, stealth, shallow breath.

Five more steps.

Four.

Nori is being careful, even with her shoulder.

Three. Silla can see the door.

Two.

Something stirs.

One.

"What the bloody hell do you think you're doing?"

She slaps Silla.

"Your father would beat you blue if he knew you were running off to be with some boy."

Silla's cheek burns. It sings. "I'm going away from here. From *you*. And not for some boy."

Mam's contempt drips like acid from a mouth stretched with

age. She is grotesque, Silla suddenly realizes, because she was once beautiful. Beauty faded and embittered, marred by wounds so fierce that no scars remain, is the birthplace of the grotesque.

"I'm taking Nori."

"And where do you imagine you'll go? To *Cath*?" She dances a crazy singsong. "Crayyyy-zee Sil-la to crayyyy-zee Cath-ee."

"I should have taken her away a long time ago."

Mama moves very fast. Before Silla can blink, she has swooped down and lifted Nori into her arms.

"To hell with you, then," she whispers. "You're fourteen. You can take care of yourself. Two peas in a pod you and Cath will be. But you leave my baby here."

Nori's shoulder and collarbone bend at an awkward angle.

"Look at your daughter!" Silla hisses. "Look at what he did to her arm. She can't even use it properly! And you wouldn't even take her to the hospital. You're poison, both of you. And maybe Cath is crazy, and maybe I am, too, but if that's true, then you're to blame. You're crazy if I ever saw madness, Mama. I love you, but you're killing us!"

And then, there she is.

Silla's mother. The real mother. The mother who loves her. The mother who wants to save her.

Silla can see it in her eyes, which are shining with tears.

"Take her," Mam says, handing a pale Nori over. "Take her away. Now. Quickly—before he wakes. Before I forget, and change my mind! Go! *Go!*"

Silla turns and runs, grabbing the bags on the way out.

At the door she hear Mam's whisper.

"Take care of her like she was your own."

Silla and Nori run through the morning smog, directly for the train station.

Cause: An unlikely ally.

Effect: A successful escape.

Gowan is sitting beside me on the forest floor now, holding my hand. He lets the silence grow for a moment, and then reins it in.

"Okay. Now tell me the truth."

I open my mouth, and then I'm sobbing, shoulders heaving with each gasp. "Gowan, I—" The sobs take over.

"You can," he says, telling me a truth. "You can do it."

"I can't open this again—"

He kisses me on the cheek and whispers, "Slowly. Piece by little piece."

I suck in a breath, squeeze my eyes shut, and say it. "My mother...was carrying the getaway bag. She was coming with us. I was carrying Nori. We had to be quiet, more than quiet, or he'd wake up. We got as far as the living room, almost to the front door..."

"And then he woke."

"...yes..."

"And he was angry?"

"Drunk and angry, but different, too...He was out of control. Seeing us trying to leave him was enough to push him over. Mam confronted him. She told him, 'Stan, we're going.' And he grabbed her wrist. She threw me the bag, but before that she pulled free a hammer. One of Dad's hammers. She raised it and told him to let her go. But he wouldn't. She hit him on the head—over his eye, but she was small and frail—he grabbed the hammer from her and knocked her down. Nori was wedged in my arms, clinging to me. I just couldn't move. I just stood there and stared as my mother fell.

"Then Dad was on top of her, his hands...his hands around

her neck. He was choking her. And then I did move, I ran forward to try to help—but she gurgled, *'No!'* I saw what that cost her. I could see her eyes turning red—" I break off, retching, and the rest of my words are garbled together with my grief and my chokes and my sickness at myself, rushing from me in a tide. "He was killing her! She used her last breath to stop me from saving her, and her cry was so desperate. I looked her in the eyes and I saw her plea there: *Run*. She was telling me to take Nori and to run, and…

"…I did. I ran. I ran away while my father killed her, and now I have a part in her death. I'm the reason! If I hadn't told her I needed to take Nori away, she wouldn't be dead. I'm a killer. I killed her. I watched her die! I let her die! *I killed her!*"

Gowan is holding me now, rocking back and forth, stroking my hair. "No, no, you're not. You saved Nori. You honored your mother by doing that. I'm sorry, I'm so sorry."

It takes a long time for me to cry my grief into exhaustion. When I do, I'm empty.

"I'm just like him."

"Never," Gowan whispers, kissing my thin skin, what's left of my hair, my cracked lips.

"And now I've lost Nori, too."

"We're going to get her back."

"And then," I say, turning to him, "I'll lose you, too."

"Stop this. You're not going to lose any more people. Come on, let's get searching again. I'm sure we're going to find her, Sill. You have to believe it."

"Believe a lie?"

"Have hope."

I swallow. "I can believe a lie." *[YOU ARE A LIE.]*

And I trudge on.

Ω

21
young and stupid

Careful, my dear,
when you enter his lair
you may not hear
if he follows you there.

We walk in a straight line for a long time, but then the corridor breaks down and other paths fork off from it. We have to make a choice. I choose the one closest to straight and keep walking, looking through the branches for any sign of Nori's dress flashing past.

Something Cath said has been running around my head. I couldn't put my finger on it for the longest time, until...

"Nori's voice."

Gowan looks at me. "Huh?"

I stop. "Nori can talk. I...it was *her* voice."

"You lost me."

"I thought I was going nuts....I kept hearing a child's voice at night, echoing through the house. Giggling. I thought it was haunted. I thought there was a ghost or, you know...nutso Silla. But it was Nori. She's been talking and she never told me. Cath said I was missing things. She said I wasn't *listening*. She *knew*. She knew Nori was talking—probably to that *thing*...."

"Are you sure?"

"I think so. Like it matters. Cath was insane. And Nori's gone." *[YOU LET HER GO.]* "It was just something I realized. Something I had missed."

I keep walking.

Nori…talking. Nori, laughing! And I hadn't known. She hadn't told me.

The trees grow denser, and I don't know which way Nori and…that *thing* went. The forest, so like Python, yet so unlike Python, is the most peculiar place I have ever seen. Roots have twined themselves around the tapestries, which hang off-kilter from places that used to be walls and are now just more trees. The wall sconces flicker ominously, as though they are still, somehow, connected to our joke of a generator, except now they grow from trunks and branches.

"This is insane," I keep muttering. "This is not bloody *Alice in Wonderland.*"

"More like Alice in CreeperManland," Gowan mutters, and I can tell that this eerie stillness is getting to him, too.

"Nori!" I yell. "Nori! Answer me!"

She loves to hide. But she promised she wouldn't hide from me again. Still. She did walk off with that thing. She willfully went with it. Maybe he promised food. Maybe she thought he was her friend. Maybe he's some creepy pervert and I have lost her forever.

"Stop it."

I start, and look at Gowan. "What?"

"I can tell you're thinking the worst. Stop that. We're going to get her."

He raises a hand to touch my cheek and I can't help it, I instinctively draw away.

His hand freezes in midair. "What is it?"

"Don't fall in love with me," I whisper. "I'm..."

"Not ready?"

"I'm crazy."

He laughs. "Crazy? Silla, *that's* crazy."

"I don't know anymore! I mean—is any of this real? Are you? And if I *am* crazy, then you can't fall in love with me. It's too dangerous."

"Too late." He says it simply. "I love you."

Stop. Please, stop. "Shut up."

"I love you, Silla."

"You don't know anything. You don't even know me."

"And I will love you forever." He says it like I'm not really even meant to listen. Like I'm not really the one he's saying it for.

"How can you be so sure? How can you know that you'll love me forever?"

He smiles. "I do, Silla. I just know it. I will love you *forever.*"

He is so young. So naïve. There's no way he can promise me that. No one can, unless he is a fool. Did Dad say that to my mother? *I will love you forever?* God, what bullshit.

"I couldn't promise that. I just couldn't. I don't know who I'll be in ten, twenty—fifty years. So how could I promise for my future? I just can't tell. And neither can you."

He smiles again. "I just know I will."

I force a smile, but he is young and stupid and he has no idea what life is like. I know what it's like. I know that love is a weakness that gets under your skin and chips away at your rock until all that's left is a bleeding mess.

I don't have time for love.

I love Nori.

Look where that got me.

"Besides. I'm seeing this, too. I'm right here, with you, in this forest—*thing*. So either we're not crazy and this is really happening, or we're both totally bonkers."

I sit down, feeling the weight of the trees around me. "I don't know how to find her."

Gowan takes my hand. "We keep going. We keep searching."

"For how long? This is impossible. We've walked beyond the length of La Baume, and still..."

"I don't understand this either. But what else is there to do?"

"Something. Anything else. There has to be an answer. Maybe in the library. Something about this curse."

Gowan looks behind us. "I don't know if we could even find our way back."

"I have to try. I want to go back. Cathy is gone, fine. But her library is back there, full of answers."

"Half the books are in French—"

"I can't keep wandering this place like a maze! We could be getting farther away and that madman has Nori—*he has Nori*!"

Gowan gathers me into his arms. "Please, Silla. We have to keep going, keep trying."

I pull away from him and get to my feet again, leaning on one of the cursed trees. "Keep trying *what*? Walking in circles? There is a reason for all of this, and it's somewhere in Cathy's past, I know it!"

I'm running before he can stop me. I'm tired of talking. Tired of reasoning, of waiting. Nori is out there with a crazy man—a *thing*—and for all I know he could be doing anything to her. I'm going back to the library and I will rip every single book out of the bookcases if I have to. I will burn each of those volumes page by page if that's what it takes.

I run until I can't.

Until my lungs are bubbling and my legs are hissing with lactic acid.

I am lost.

And the library is nowhere. The house is one giant wood. A maze.

I am trapped.

I growl in frustration and then sit down in a heap.

"NORI!" My screams echo back.

Something has buoyancy, after all.

And then I hear a sound. Nori's tiny bell . . . tinkling through the trees.

Nori . . .

"Yes! Good girl! *Good girl!*"

I jump to my feet, listening, and then I follow the tendrils of sound deeper into the not-wood of La Baume.

Ω

22

between trees, a tinkle

Boys and girls
have their parts
but beware of
losing hearts.

I look behind me. The terrain is unfamiliar and uniform. Arched doorways have sprung up between trees in the distance—four at least that I can count—and I have no idea which leads back to the entrance hall.

I hold my breath and listen for my father's voice. Maybe he will guide me if I listen hard enough. Lead me back to that black pit of nothing. But he is silent once more.

"Useless," I mutter.

All of a sudden it is too much. I can't bear any more loss, any more suffering, and the hollow pain in my stomach has become so intense that I cough with the pain of it. I double over, breathing in deeply, but still the pain rises and expands.

Behind me, I hear Gowan's heavy footfalls.

"Silla!" he calls. "There you are. Don't do that again—please."

"I'm...sorry." I gag again, and feel another of my teeth loose in my mouth.

I begin to laugh. I am falling apart. This is suddenly hilarious and my laughter becomes raucous shrieks until the pain takes hold again and I'm gasping for air.

"You need to eat," Gowan says. "I've got one. One left."

An apple. In his pocket. Small. Tiny, actually. Perfectly green.

"No!"

"Silla—"

"What I *need* is to find my sister before this *thing* does something to her! She's my responsibility!"

He grabs me roughly, and I am so surprised that I forget my pain. And then he is hugging me, so tight that it almost hurts, and his whole body is vibrating—shaking. He is shaking like a leaf.

"Silla," he breathes. "Silla..."

I am so stunned that I stand there for a full three seconds before my own arms lift, seemingly of their own accord, and wrap themselves around him. He feels so warm and alive and *real* in my arms, and he smells like something sweet. Something I want to smell forever.

"You're going to destroy me," I whisper.

And then he is shaking even more, and I realize it's because he is crying. Not just crying, but the kind of bone-deep crying that only comes from grief. From the deepest sorrow. The kind of crying that tears deep down into the soul from some wound that time can never touch.

I let him cry, and we hold each other, and though I am bewildered, I *feel* his pain. I stroke his hair, and it is the most wonderful thing I have ever done. It feels so *right*.

"I'm sorry you're in pain," I whisper, before I can stop myself.

He pulls away from me, his eyes so dark they look black, rimmed with red that the tears have caused, staring at me with a look of wonder on his face, and I kiss him. I kiss him deeply, and it is so much better than the first, drunken kiss. It is so much more true and vital and worthy.

He kisses me and holds me tightly, pressing me into his body, firm against my own, and I grapple with his shirt as he grapples with mine. The light is fading, it will be dark soon, but I don't care because all I need, right now, is here.

My bare skin is a relief, even though I am exposed, and I am glad to be rid of the moldy dress, and then his arms are around me, naked and strong, and he is pulling me toward him and I want this.

It is a desperate meeting of mouths and bodies; we move together among the cursed trees—we are the only things moving. It is heat and breath and touch and dance—it is full of *life*. It gets faster near the end: a wave building inside me until Gowan cries out and holds me tighter, and we fall into each other like I never knew was possible.

I love you.

Treacherous mind. Treacherous heart.

Gowan clings to me, and he is still shaking. There are tears on his cheeks.

"I love you," he tells me again. "I'm so sorry."

He doesn't expect anything from me. I know it in the moment he falls asleep before I've had a chance to reply.

He loves me, without expecting anything from me in return.

"You're so stupid," I tell him, and then I hold his head, because I can't ignore what has happened, even though I'd like to try.

$$\Omega$$

It's brighter in the morning, which is weird, because there's no sun. There is no dawn and no daylight. There is no sky. I gather my green-speckled dress and slip it over my head, wincing with the coldness and the damp smell of the fabric, and then I turn to look at Gowan.

He is frowning in his sleep, and there are dark circles beneath his eyes. When did that happen? I bend down, curling my hand into a fist, and pretend to iron his forehead. Iron away his worries. Still asleep, he half smiles and the knot in his brow loosens. I grin, my lips traveling over his naked body.

Nice.

I reach for his shirt, intending to fold it neatly, when something occurs to me in the second before I touch it.

His shirt.

His trousers.

I lift both from where they have become tangled in roots that grew overnight. Both items are beautiful. Blue jeans and a green shirt. So new. So clean. So dry.

And not a dot of green mold anywhere on them.

I raise his shirt to my nose and inhale. The same sweet scent. No mildew, no rot. No damp—nothing.

I glance down at Gowan and realize that I have *never* seen mold growing on him the way I found it on Nori and me. I have never seen him looking less than perfect.

What is this? *[HE FOOLED YOU SO EASILY.]*

It can't be.... *[SILLY SILLA. HE'S BEEN SO CLOSE ALL THIS TIME.]*

Gowan can't be—*[THE CREEPER MAN THE CREEPER MAN THE CREEPER MAN!]*

I drop the clothes and back away, but the movement wakes him and he smiles up at me.

"G'morning," he says, sleepy-eyed and dopey-smiled.

I can't look at him. I can't stay. He's been lying.

He sees my thoughts on my face. "Silla?"

"Stay away."

He sits up, panic in his eyes. "Whoa, what's going on?"

"You never have any mold on you...."

"What?"

I swallow. *Calm.* But I back away from him. "Nori and I both had this green mold growing on us from the house. It's like it was infected and getting us sick, too. But you...you never did. You never look less than perfect."

"Silla..."

"The curse never touched you." Away. I back away.

"It's not what you think."

"Who are you? Why are you here?" *[LIAR. HE'S A LIAR.]*

"Silla, calm down."

"Tell the truth! Why did you come to La Baume that day?" *[RUN! RUN AWAY!]*

"I told you—"

"You told me you lived here once. But you're hiding something."

He hesitates.

"No lies! Tell me the truth!"

"Okay. Yes, I've not told you everything about myself, about...but I care about you. I love you."

"You're him. You're him...."

He looks scared now. "Silla—"

"Oh God. You *are*."

"Don't do this. Let me come with you. Let me help."

"Get away. Get away from me." *[YOU FOOL. YOU FOOL!]*

"Please, wait—"

I turn and I run, and though I can hear him scrambling up

and getting dressed, hear him calling my name, panic lacing his words, I can't stay.

I run faster.

I am a fool.

I am a fool alone.

Ω

23

fool, alone

Alone you must be
to find your reprieve
bet you can't wait
is it too late?

I run because I can't do anything else. The trees fly past, flashes of the fading wallpaper of this accursed La Baume winking at me in between, but I grit my teeth and push on.

How could I have been so blind? How could I have missed it? Not to have seen his link to this…this, whatever it is.

Gowan is the Creeper Man. He tricked me. All this time, he was just watching me. Gauging my reactions—torturing me.

Nori, Nori, Nori. It is a chant to the beat of my heart and I don't falter because Gowan could be behind me—*the Creeper Man* could be behind me. But then where is Nori? Where did he put Nori? *[YOU ARE BIG SISTER.]*

Her name floods my mind all at once. *[YOU LET HER GO.]* And I lose my footing and trip over crooked roots (or vines) and crash violently into the earth. Or is it a dusty hardwood floor? I don't know.

I lie there for a moment, defeated.

I am fading away into a half sleep, washed over with despair and unbearable hunger when I hear a lilting tinkling through the trees like a ribbon of sound.

Nori's bell.

"Good girl!" I whisper, scrambling to my feet. "Keep ringing it...."

And I follow the eerie tinkling between the trees, letting my ears lead me.

I'm coming, Nori. I'm coming.

I hear Gowan's cries echoing as they drift through the eerily still trees.

Ssssiiilllaa**a**.

Ssssiiilllaa**aa**!

Ω

I walk.

How can it have changed so fast? How can this be happening? I think back to every Japanese horror film I have ever seen. Am I dreaming? And I remember that particularly weird South Korean film, *Hansel and Gretel,* the way this mysterious door leads them into another place entirely. Is that what's happened here? *[LSD? WHAT IS REALITY?]*

I walk.

I feel as if the real world, the world where I lived, was normal 3-D and I was blissfully unaware of the dangers of reality. But now I'm somehow in a 63-D world and it's full of all these terrible things I can't understand. This is the ground-floor corridor of La Baume, but it is also Python Wood. But a really weird Python Wood because there is no noise. It is *silent*. And, also, none of the leaves are moving because there is no wind because *we are INSIDE*.

I walk.

"This is mad. Utterly mad. I am crazy. I have to be."

I walk.

"What if he's taken her to eat her or—" I shake my head. "Blah, blah, blah."

I walk.

Ω

I'm aware of everything. Each sound is an attack. A possible enemy. I flinch often, but don't laugh a breathless chuckle when I know no danger is present. Why, I wonder, have I become this bird, this mouse, this flea? When did *that* happen?

I hate myself.

The word slaps me, hard, out of nowhere.

hate

And I know, in the moment I think it, that it's true.

I hate myself.

Why?

Ω

24

obscurantism

Follow me here, follow me there,
Creeper Man comes to give you a scare
send him away, think you can?
foolish children call on Creeper Man.

BROKEN BOOK ENTRY

This one **time**, Dad gave us permission to make Halloween costumes. It was a total surprise because it was the first Halloween he'd ever allowed us to have. We had no **means** of buying costumes, of course, so we enlisted the help·of Mam. She had amazing sewing skills. I was a Jedi warrior, and Nori was Yoda. It was the best night of our lives, and **nothing** could top that. Nothing.

Ω

My feet no longer obey me. They drag and flop with every floundering step. Am I walking up the hill to La Baume in a storm, dragging Nori through the mud? Is it three years ago? Even my arms hang loose and numb, fingertips tingling with fading sensation. *[AM I DRAGGING NORI?]*

For the first time in a long time, I could cry. But my body has no water to spare, and the ache inside me explodes into a dry sob.

"Nori, I'm sorry."

All the times I wished she would stop with her ever-talking hands. I imagined tying them up behind her back... *[CUTTING THEM OFF.]* I was horrible. I would give anything to see them flopping about in excited animation. I would give anything to have her in my arms.

My fault. *Myfaultmyfaultmyfault.*

Ω

The thoughts break through again. Images mostly, in flashes. Painful.

I see the woods... the *manor* in front of me. Trees with moss hanging from branches. But then in a flash and a rumble of my stomach, they are full of maggots. I shake my head, even as I'm bending over to quell the horrible bone-deep pain in my gut, and the wood comes back into focus.

I stumble on.

Another flash, and the floor is rotten, organic mulch, moving and squelching beneath my feet. I gasp and cough as another bite of nausea and pain comes. When I fall to my knees, I land on the floorboards. Solid, hard.

"Stop it," I whisper.

But it comes again.

Maggots.

Worms.

Mulch.

Rot.

Slime. Mold. Decay. Bugs. Food. Stink. On and on.

"STOP!"

I spit out another tooth. Feel more of my hair dropping away.

Voices ring in my head—dozens of them, laughing, cackling, hysterical.

Stopstopstopstop oh stop please stop poor me boohoo hahahahahahaha!!!!!

I retch into the floorboards, the pain in my gut like a gaping hole filling up with bile and nothingness.

Notttthingnessssssss, cajole the voices. *Obscurantism…*

"You're not real," I mutter, covering my ears and squeezing shut my eyes. "You're nothing."

And they blink off, like someone turning down the volume on my mind's self-derision. I gasp, looking up tentatively, and there is a horrible

empty

silent
still
ness…

all around me.

Ω

La Baume has started crying. I find the first bit of water coming from a hole in the wall—the first wall I have seen in…how long? The wall is collapsing, soft around the hole, like cottage cheese, and it is spilling slimy maggots onto the floor in a puddle of putrescent-looking water.

I fall to my knees and I drink, my lips pursed and willing. The maggots wriggle and contort near my eyes but I shut them and keep drinking, swallowing whatever comes into my mouth.

I am going to die if I don't keep this down.

When my body begins to protest, my stomach to contract, I lean back and clench my jaw.

Keep it down. Keep it down.

I feel the maggots moving inside me.

I exert the last amount of will I have, but it's not enough. I am sick, my stomach purging more than I have to offer.

I roll onto my back, looking up at the ceiling (an interlocking tapestry of branches and waxy leaves), and I think only one thought.

I'm empty as a husk.

Ω

Hunger.

It's like a force of its own: a heavy, weighty feeling that you sort of forget about after a while, even though it's always with you. At first it's uncomfortable. A rumble, like stones, deep inside you. Then comes the choking, gagging nausea. Then come the daydreams. Roast ham. Gravy. Buttery potatoes. Peas soaked in butter and garlic. Then the imagining becomes torture. That food seems sickly. Disgusting. But it's infected your mind, so you can't stop.

GravySausageLimeTomatoBreadPeanutButterSquashRice Chicken—

So you cough and gag and you throw up nothing. Eventually

it fades into a dull, heavy ache. Your eyes droop. Your mouth bleeds dry. Your head pounds. Your tongue grows thick and heavy and you feel slow-headed and stupid. Clumsy.

Hunger.

It's always with you.

I try the words on my furry tongue. "It's...always... withoo..."

I remember the time Mam took me to the National Gallery of Art. It was before Nori, so maybe I was nine. Maybe ten. Was Mam pregnant? I can't remember. We went out for a "girls' day" together, and the museum was free, so it was the perfect choice.

I walked along the corridors, my hand in hers, and I could smell her vanilla oil, which she used like perfume, even though it was meant to be for potpourri, and I could hear the *click, click, click* of her heels.

This one particular section was all still life paintings. Huge pieces that stretched almost from the floor to the ceiling. To a seven-year-old, they looked enormous. Galaxy huge and impressive. And they were mostly food. I stared at these paintings in awe, thinking: *People painted food! Actual food that existed all those years ago. Right here in front of me!* Pears, apples, bread, cheese, meats—all of it laid out so neatly.

I remember wanting to pluck a giant pear from one of the bowls in the painting, imagining how it would taste and feel. Wondering how long it would take me to get through the whole thing. Thinking about how tiny I would be standing next to it. How I could eat myself a little corridor inside, live like James and his Giant Peach.

After that, I told Mam I was hungry. She found ten pounds in her pocket and we went to McDonald's and had a feast. I was sick for three days straight after that, but it was worth it. Mam kept saying it was all her fault, she should have fed me better, stopped me at McChicken Sandwich number two, but I kept grinning while I puked and told her it was the best day of my life.

Hunger. It stays with you.

It's like a disease that you can never shake.

Well, I suppose that's not strictly true.

If you're dead, there's not much use for hunger, is there? So all I have to do is die.

Ha.

$$\Omega$$

The pain passes slowly, and my stomach moves and complains inside me. When it is silent enough that I can move, I find that I am lying at the entrance to a dark, wet-smelling cave. I sense the depth within it the same way I sensed the depths of the hole. This is not a place I want to be.

Deep within the chasm, I hear dripping water—

and a tinkling bell.

"Don't go in there."

I gasp as I spin, hands raised to defend myself. Gowan's own hands are limp at his sides.

"Why the hell not?"

"Please, Silla, could you just trust me?"

"No."

He sighs. "I love my anger." He quotes my own words back at me, and I nod.

My anger is all I have now.

"And I'm going to find my sister, so you better stay out of my way, Creeper Man."

"You know I'm not him."

I raise my eyebrows—a monumental exertion of will. "Oh, really."

His lips are set in a grim line and he nods. "Let me come with you. You don't have to do everything alone."

I want to protest right away. I want to say, *No. No, I don't need your help. I don't need you.*

But I would be lying.

Instead, I turn back to the cave and walk carefully inside.

The light disappears.

Nothing much happens for a long time. The walls around us curve upward, and I have the impression of willingly walking down the gullet of some giant stone creature—a long granite snake, maybe. Not even that would surprise me now.

And all of a sudden, this seems irrationally funny.

And I laugh.

And I can't stop laughing.

My laughter becomes hysterical before I can contain it and I fall against the wall, clutching my sides.

"A—*snake*!" I manage, giggling.

Gowan looks at me like I have, finally, snapped. But he is grinning, too.

"I just... This is so messed up."

Gowan looks around him, at where we are, at where we've come from, and grins. "Yeah."

A tinkling echoes between us, cutting my laugh off like a diamond scalpel. Sharp and brutal. Quick and silent.

Gowan says, "Wait" at the same moment I rush off into the dark.

By the time he's reached me, bringing the flame of his lighter with him, I am standing stock-still. I don't understand what I am looking at.

Before me, on the floor, is a crumpled pile of cloth. Only, no—not cloth. *Clothes.*

"Silla, wait."

"What's..."

And then there is a light. Off to the right. I frown into it, leaning closer, trying to see the *something* beyond it.

"Silla."

The light is blinding. Like the sun decided to take a nap in front of my face. As it fades and my eyes blink through tears of pain and light spots, a kitchen table comes into focus.

It's *our* kitchen table.

La Baume. We're inside La Baume.

But it *can't* be. I'm about to turn around and ask Gowan if we made it back to the house, when I see the paint. Buckets of yellow paint, stacked on the cloth-covered table.

Yellow.

And then Cathy drifts into the room, paintbrush in hand. She is wearing a long yellow sundress, and she is smiling.

Ω

25

dare you

Grab some twine to twist and thread
some dirt plucked at night with dread
cloth to make his suit and tie
finish before dawn or else you'll die.

BROKEN BOOK ENTRY

My favorite food is vegetable pie. All **you** do is chop up as many different kinds of vegetables as you like, like potatoes and carrots. You could even **have** parsnip in there if you like. You chop them up fairly well, pop them **all** into a pastry base. Cover it with a pie crust, and pop into **the** oven for about forty-five minutes. This pie **answers** every question of hunger, I'm telling you. What's for dinner? Veggie pie. Hungry at midnight? Leftover veggie pie. I've made one **already**, so you'll need to make your own.

Ω

1980: *"Ring around the rosie, a pocket full of posies..."*

Catherine and Anne and Pamela skip in a circle, their hands joined. Cathy is wearing a blue dress. Anne is wearing red. Pammy is wearing yellow. Each has her hair in curls, as their mother prefers. Each a perfect flower.

"Ashes! Ashes! We all fall down!"

Cathy loves this part. The part where they all collapse. She doesn't understand what the rhyme means—none of them do—but she knows that the end (collapsing) is the best. For a moment, the sisters lie on the grass, staring up at the sapphire sky. In another hour they will be called inside, their adventure over for the day. Cathy closes her eyes, and feels the earth tilting as it does sometimes.

Then Anne is kicking her in the foot. "Let's go into the woods for a while!"

She tries not to get cross. Anne is always wanting more. Mother says she has too much spirit for her own good, and Cathy is beginning to see why.

Cathy leans up on her elbows. "We can't, Anne. It's getting dark."

"So? We'll be quick. Come on! I saw rabbits!"

"Imagine if we could catch one," Pammy says. "We could have it for supper."

Anne scrunches up her nose. "Ew."

"Nobody is going into the woods," Cath states, getting to her feet. She brushes grass from her dress and reties her bow. "Anyway, we should be going in right about now."

Anne rolls her eyes and Pammy giggles. "You spoil everything."

"Yeah, yeah."

"Anyway," Anne says, sniffing and lifting her chin. "I don't need you to have fun, and I don't need the woods. The woods can come to me. The protector will make sure of that."

"I think we're getting a bit old for the protector game."

"He's real," Anne says. "And maybe *you're* getting old. So old you can't even see him anymore."

"I see him!" Pammy declares.

"Neither of you sees him. We made him up."

Catherine hasn't got time for silly games anymore. Mother told her that she was growing up, and now she can see it is true. She does feel much older than both Anne and Pamela. Well, she *is* older, but now her age is accompanied by a feeling of superiority. She can see so much more than they can. They are still lost in a game about a make-believe man that they sewed from sackcloth one day in the woods.

I'm growing up, she thinks again, and smiles, closing her eyes and turning away so that her sisters don't see her pride. She envisions a future of long dresses—the kind Mother wears—dinner parties at the long table at La Baume in the grand hall, and long hours alone with all those books Papa won't let her touch. One day, it will all be hers, and she will know how to care for it. She has such dreams for La Baume and her life!

"Come on," she says again. "We have to get inside. Mother will be waiting."

She turns back to her sisters and finds that they are gone.

She clenches her teeth, watching their tiny figures rushing toward the forest boundary in the fading light.

They are leaving her behind more and more.

Well. She's moving forward without them.

What babies they are.

Ω

I'm somewhere else now.

It's quite dark in here. I can hardly see. In the corner of the room, a little girl sits bent over something. Her hands dance very well, quick movements, back and forth. She pauses now and then to check her work, and then bends low again over the thing in her hands.

I step closer, expecting the child to look up, but it seems I am a ghost in this place.

"Hello?" I call.

Nothing.

I look around, scanning the room for Gowan, and realize that I'm in La Baume again. The attic. The same room that Cath locked herself in for months and months. The same room where she was **eaten** alive by roots. As I think Cathy's name, the child looks up, as though startled by a sound.

"Hello?"

She leans forward into a shaft of moonlight cast through the tiny sole window to her left, and I see that this child is Cath. She looks about twelve years old, or maybe older. Her eyes are pink and swollen, her lips cracked and bloody.

"Cath...Auntie *Cath*."

The child frowns for a moment, and then shifts back into the shadows to continue her work.

I inch closer, aware of every step. I'm five feet away when I see what Cath is doing. In her hands: a limp and rather pathetic excuse for a doll. It is made of sacking cloth and strips of black material, long and thin with elongated limbs. It has no eyes, only a gaping mouth that has been roughly stitched closed again.

The sight of it sends a chill down my spine.

And when I realize what Cath is doing, I fall to my knees, dumbstruck.

"There," little Cath says, her voice breaking. "Now you can give her back."

Cath puts down her needle and takes up small sewing scissors instead. Carefully, she snips the black twine holding the doll's mouth shut, and it falls open in a manic grin like the jaw is weighted down with stones.

The lack of eyes disturbs me. *Look away.*

But then Cath speaks again.

"Anne...can you hear me, Anne?"

Silence.

"Anne, it's Catherine. It's Catherine, Anne, can't you hear me?"

Nothing.

"You took her," she whispers at the doll now. "You crept up and you took her away." A pause. "You're a Creeper Man. An ugly Creeper Man. You were never our protector."

I swallow.

"Come on, then!" Cath cries suddenly, throwing the doll into the moonlit strip of wood. She stands slowly, like a storm gathering the strength to surge.

"I dare you," she spits at last. "I *dare* you to come here."

The doll doesn't move, but it seems to me that it is observing the child. Considering her.

"Creeper Man, Creeper Man, I dare you to come. Creeper Man, Creeper Man, you are the one. Creeper Man, Creeper Man, bring me my Anne. Creeper Man, Creeper Man, I curse you, be damned!"

Cath-the-child is hissing the final words, her eyes leaking tears that she doesn't seem to notice.

I watch her fury with understanding. "You did this," I whisper. "Auntie Cath, *you* did this."

The image seems to freeze

and when I blink I am back in the cave and I finally, *finally* understand.

Ω

"He's a demon."

Gowan shakes his head. "What?"

"The Creeper Man. He's a child-stealing demon. I saw Cath summon him. She thought he was a protector, but she was wrong. She probably had no idea what she was doing, but she dared him to come. She rhymed, like a spell or something, and I got the weirdest feeling he could hear."

Gowan opens his mouth and then sighs into his fists. "Silla—"

"I *saw* it."

"Where?"

"In the cave. It's some kind of...I don't know. Portal. I just...I saw it. And this is his weird lair or something. It sounds insane, but somehow this is all real. He took Nori here into this—place—but we found a way in, too. I don't think he expected that. So we can save her."

"I don't know, Sill. This sounds too...out there."

His casual use of my name like that—*Sill*—sends a jolt of uncomfortable familiarity through me. And I hate him.

"Well, look around," I snap, gesturing. "Does any of this seem *normal* to you? You can either accept it and help me, or deny it and keep trying to find a rational and completely *useless* explanation. But I need your help."

He sighs, long and low, taking me in. "What can I do?"

"I need to find out as much as I can about this demon. Cath had a doll. She made it when she and Mam were little. I know she still has it. She wouldn't have thrown it away. It's a doll of him...the Creeper Man. I think that if I could destroy it, it might kill him. Maybe it's his vessel or something."

"So we have to find our way back to the house."

"Yeah."

Gowan glances around. There is no straight path anymore. "We could try..."

"We have to leave a trail. Like Hansel and Gretel. We'll find it eventually."

Gowan doesn't believe me, I can see that. But he follows me anyway.

We walk with purpose for the first time in...how long have we been here?

We walk straight, and reach the cave.

We walk in zigzags, and reach the cave.

We split up and walk in opposite directions. And end up facing each other.

I run up a rise in the floorboards, leaving Gowan at the bottom, and end up looking up at him. He runs away from me, and crashes into me from the other side.

And every

single

time

we end up at the mouth of the cave.

Ω

26

told you i was crazy

Round and round the halls we go
running from the shadows.
up and up and up we go,
when he gets you, he swallows!

1980: Catherine goes to check on Pamela and Anne as usual. Ever since Mama's passing, Catherine has taken the role of carer. She holds the position with pride, and takes it very seriously. Pammy is fast asleep, legs splayed, blankets in disarray on the floor, mouth open—as usual. Cath smiles.

Wild child.

One day, she is beginning to realize, Pamela Grey will break the hearts of many boys. Many men.

One day she will run away.

The last thought is unexpected. She pushes it away, but an icy chill has taken hold of her spine, like a cool hand, and won't let go.

She takes the blankets off the floor and covers Pammy up, then bends to kiss her hot cheek, and whispers, "Be careful, little nut."

When Catherine goes to check on Anne, she finds the bed

empty and the window open. Moonlight flickers into the room as the wind blows the curtains back and forth.

Dark, light, dark, light.

Flickerflickerflickerflicker.

"Anne?" Cath rushes into the room. *"Anne?"*

No, no, no . . .

She runs to the window and leans out, scanning the garden. Anne wouldn't be that stupid, surely. . . . Python Wood looms in the darkness and Catherine senses its grin. She wants to scream Anne's name into the night, but Papa would wake. It is her job to protect him from things like this. He needs to work so they can eat, and to work, he needs to sleep.

She swallows. *I'm going to have to go out there.*

She realizes this with a rising sense of dread. It is a cold, murky feeling inside her. She will have to go out there . . . at night. Out in Python Wood with the trees dancing in the wind with their long, leering shadows.

She has one leg out the window already when she hears it.

A sniffle from inside the room.

"Anne?"

Another one . . . and a soft whimper. It is coming from the wardrobe. She walks over to it slowly and opens the doors. Anne sits huddled at the bottom, wrapped in too many blankets to count, hugging her red-scarfed penguin doll tightly.

"Cathy?" Her voice is tiny in the expanse of the room.

"Anne! What are you doing in there?"

"I'm hiding. It's safer."

Catherine laughs, breathless in her relief. "Hiding! Hiding from what?"

Anne leans forward and peers around the room. "I can't . . ."

Cath climbs into the closet next to Anne and shuts the doors from the inside. The darkness is total, and Catherine is loath to admit that she does feel, somehow, safer. It is irrational.

"What are you hiding from, Anne?"

"The Creeper Man."

"Why would you hide from our protector? That's silly."

"But he's not our protector, Cathy. He's not. He's a bad man. He's all wrong."

"Don't say that. What would Pammy say?"

"Pammy already knows."

Catherine is stumped. A secret? Anne and Pamela never keep secrets from her.

That you know of, comes the horrible thought.

A terrible empty hollowness has opened up in her belly.

"Oh."

"We knew you wouldn't believe us," Anne says. Her voice is apologetic.

"I do. I do believe you."

Cath can hear the smile in Anne's next word. "Liar."

Ω

"What the *hell*?"

Gowan shakes his head. "I don't know."

"I think there's a reason we keep ending up here," I say, staring into the pitiless dark.

"I think so, too."

"It's like I'm supposed to go in and face whatever's in there."

Gowan nods. "I think that's the only choice."

"But it's full of lies."

"No. I don't think so. I think it's trying to show you something."

I stare at the cave with rising foreboding. "I'm not sure...."

"It's your choice, Silla."

"We keep ending up here. So...I think I have to try."

Gowan smiles. "I'm with you."

I am beyond what is impossible. I want Nori and I *did* hear her bell inside. No matter how dark or damp that cave is, no matter what I see, I have to go in. I have to find her.

I go.

Ω

This is a La Baume I've never seen. Sunlight streams through bright windows that shimmer like crystals, falling onto a table draped in a white tablecloth of the breakfast room. It is crisp, clean, and dry. The air smells floral, sunflowers sitting in a vase on the table. Next to the flowers are five large cans of yellow paint, one open, a tray and roller sitting to the side. Yellow paint, again.

A lovely voice floats across the room, as though carried on the sunbeams. It is warm, honeylike, and rich.

"Cold blows the wind tonight, my love, cold are the drops of rain...."

I follow the voice to the kitchen to find Auntie Cath, wearing another sundress, swaying in the kitchen while she peels and cuts apples into chunks.

"I only had but one true love, and in Greenwood he lies slain...."

Cath turns, an apple pie base in her hands, and begins to fill it with the apples she has cut. There is a smudge of yellow paint on her cheek, and she looks...*happy.*

"I do as much for my true love as any young girl may...."

She pops part of an apple into her mouth.

"*I'll sit and mourn all by his grave, for a twelve-month and a day.*"

"Auntie Cath?" I whisper, stepping closer.

"Oh, there you are, Silla darling!" Cath puts down her pie pan and sweeps me into a firm embrace. Unshed tears choke their way out of my chest and I shut my eyes, feeling her arms around me. So warm, so genuine. She smells like fresh bread and mowed grass and paint.

It is a good smell.

I hug her back, tightly.

This can't be real. This is La Baume, but when was it not rotten? When was it bright and clean and alive? When was Cath not crazy? When was the land not cursed? I almost can't remember.

I breathe this Cathy in, and something stirs on the edge of my memory. A ghost of a scene that I have almost lost in the Nothing my life has become.

Cathy, sitting on the edge of my bed. A book in her hands. Finishing a story. Then a soft kiss on my cheek as I fall asleep. Cathy stroking my hair, telling me I'm okay, loved, wanted. So safe, so warm.

When did I feel like that?

When was the world not cold, damp, and decayed?

Back in the kitchen, Cath pulls away. "I want you to get some more apples from the tree, okay?" She begins to cut strips of pastry to lattice over her pie.

Movement outside the window catches my attention. Nori is playing in the garden—a bright, living garden full of flowers and vegetable patches. The sun shines down from a cerulean sky. Nori's mouth is stained purple, her hands as well—hands that are picking all the mulberries off the bush and shoving them into her mouth with delight. I choke on a laugh, eyes bright.

Oh, Nori…

Gowan is beside me then, hands clasped in front of him.

"What's going on?" I ask him.

He just stares at me and says nothing.

I go into the garden, ready to eat mulberries—to try, in this bright version of my life—

But I am suddenly back in the cave. Dark, cold, echoing. Alone.

"Nori?" I call. It echoes back, and expands, growing in size and volume.

Nori? Nori? Nori? Nori? Nori? Nori?

Nori? Nori?

Nori?

Nori?

Nori?

The echoes then echo, distorting and bending around one another.

Nori? nOri? NoRi? NOrI? norI? Nori? nOri? NoRi? NOrI? norI? Nori? nORi? Nori? nOri? NoRi? NOrI? norI? nOri? NoRi? NOrI? norI? Nori? nOri? NoRi? NOrI? nORi?

"Stop it!"

Stopitstopitstopitstopitstopitstopitstopitstopitsto pitstopitstopitstopitstopitstopitstopitstopitstopitst opitstopitstopitstopitstopitstopitstopitstopitstop itstopitstopitstopitstopitstopitstopitstopitsto pitstopitstopitstopitstopitstopitst opitstopitstopitstopitstopitstopi tstopitstopitstopitstopitstopit stopitstopitstopitstopitstopi tstopitstopitstopitstopit stopitstopitstopitstopits topitstopitstopitstop itstopitstopitstopi tstopitstopitstopit

stopitstopitstopits
topitstopitstopitst
opitstopitstopitsto
pitstopitstopitsto
pitstopitstopitsto
pitstopitstopi
tstopitstopit
stopitstopits
topitstopitst
opitstopit!

I collapse onto my knees, pressing down on my ears. The noise is so loud it's going to burst my eardrums. It is dripping derision.

"LEAVE ME ALONE!"

It's like someone flips a switch. The world is mute.

When I lift my hand, I am in another place. It is dark in here, and closed in. Slanted wood panels all around me. A shuttered window, high up. It must be night because moonlight shoves in through the cracks, silvery white.

A little girl sits in the center of the room, head bowed low over something in her hands. Her hair is blocking her face, but I know her anyway.

It's Cath. Little Cath. Only older now. And the room is different. More cluttered. Less clean. Cobwebs hang from the corners of the attic and a thick layer of dust rests on all the surfaces she hasn't touched. Where she has, there are streaks.

I kneel in front of her, and she ignores me. Or maybe she can't see me. Her hands are nimble and quick as she sews the doll. A new doll? The same doll? It's an ugly thing, like the other, made of sackcloth, a black slash of a line for a mouth and no eyes. She seems to be repairing a tear in one of his long legs, but the thread isn't right....

I squint and peer closer. Mud. The thread is dipped in mud. Or clay. There is a little bowl of it beside her thigh.

"He'll come with the shadows," she sings, *"to take your fears away, he'll guide you like a father, he'll take away the pain."*

Something about the scene is terrible to watch, and I notice with revulsion that Cathy is wet. A putrid smell rises from her, and I realize that she has messed herself.

She's terrified.

And dirty—she's *filthy.*

And then I notice other things.

Her hands are shaking.

Her hair is oily.

Her spoiled dress is dry—she's been here awhile.

And no one has come looking for her.

And there are dolls everywhere…sackcloth dolls—the Creeper Man—*everywhere*. I stumble back, horrified. Dolls piled in the corners. Dolls nailed to the walls. Dolls dangling from the beams. Dolls scattered on the floor farther off into the shadows.

There are hundreds, all of them sightless and smiling.

"Oh my God."

"He'll take it back I know it, he'll take away this curse. He'll say he's sorry, truly. This can't get any worse—" She breaks off her thread with her teeth, leaving a muddy line across her face like an elongated grimace, then she lights a candle and places the pathetic effigy beside it.

And then she reaches into her basket and pulls free more straw, and another piece of sackcloth, and begins again.

"Three little girls knelt by an alder to summon a man to be their protector. The little girls found their game hard to bear when their protector turned and gave them a scare…."

I bend down until I am looking at this child and everything comes out. "You made me think it was me. You told me I was to blame. But *you* brought this curse down on us. On our family. And now he has Nori, too. And you were always insane. Weren't you?"

I realize that it no longer matters.

Cathy is gone.

Nori is gone.

And I don't have any answers.

"Stop this."

Gowan is beside me, standing in the shadows.

"Gowan?"

"Stop getting distracted."

"What?"

He grabs my arm and yanks me to my feet

              and I'm back in the cave.

He puts a gentle hand on my shoulder, like a warm blanket

              and I am facing the
cave opening.

Or is it the other way around—am I on the inside of the cave, looking out at the forest-manor? Standing before me is the tall, thin, blind man, and he is smiling—too wide to be natural.

I blink

        and he is a tree.

I blink

        and I'm back in the bright version of La Baume. A sharp pain in my cheek and now I'm in the woods. Gowan is standing over me, shaking me. "SILLA!"

The pain again.

He slapped me.

I don't know what's real anymore.

I look up at him. "I always told you I was crazy."

$$\Omega$$

27

—. — — —

Try to hold your stomach tight
till those feelings pass
close your eyes and think of light
the darkness doesn't last.

BROKEN BOOK ENTRY

There are **secrets** that I **have** forgotten. Like some kind of **power** that's inside me, eating away at me, **like** a cloud hanging over my head, haunting my **every** move. Like a **shadow**. And if I could rid myself of them **once** and for all, **I** would. Isn't it obvious? **Was** that not the point of this book? As though by putting them down I would make them less **alive**? Make them less real—or at least get them out of me. Out of my head. **But** it's pointless. All of it is. Because

now I've got nothing *but* those secrets. And **I'm** forgetting them. It's **just** ... it seems important. The garden is **dead**. The house is dead. And we are all nothings inside it.

Ω

"You have to eat. You *have* to."

I shake my head. Can't he see it's useless? My body won't allow it. "I can't."

He growls as he turns away, throwing out his hands in frustration. Then he whirls on me. *"Do you want to save yourself?"* he yells. "Stop getting distracted with things that don't matter!"

I open my mouth to reply, but it stretches wide and round, expanding into a dark chasm, and I am stepping through it, back into the dank cave. The Creeper Man's lair.

He's toying with me.

"Open your eyes," Gowan whispers.

The water, dripping somewhere in the distance, echoes louder than before. The cave is, if it's possible, even darker. Still. Too still.

A bundle of cloth lays ten paces away from me. I glance back at Gowan, but he is just watching me.

"Stop getting distracted," he whispers. "You have to face this."

I step forward, and though there is nothing to see but a bundle of—blanket? cloth? curtains?—my legs are weak and I stumble.

I

    fall

          to my knees when I realize. When I see. It's not a bundle of cloth.

"No," I choke.

NO.

My whole being shouts the word. Rejects the sight. Fights this reality.

"No...No. No. No." My hands are rigid like claws. "NO!"

It's a tiny, little, dried-out husk. A dehydrated thing that used to be a child.

It's Nori. Nori is lying on the floor of an impossible cave, deep along the corridor that is also Python Wood.

And she is dead.

More than dead.

She's a shriveled husk of a little girl, her mouth open and glaring, her eyes sunken and leathery.

I retch and retch, but there is no food and no vomit.

"No...no...no!"

My mind collapses.

Why? How can this happen? I just saw her running through the woods! I don't understand. This isn't happening. This isn't real. I won't believe it. Nori! How is this real? What's going on? NORI! NORI! NORI! I'm sorry—this can't be real I can't survive this—Idon'tunderstandthisisn'trealThisiswon'tbelieveit. Nori! How is this real? Whattrickthisisn'thappeningIcan'tIcan't Ican'tNoriNoriNoriNoriohNoriNoriNori...

I take all the pain, the anguish, the confusion, the *air* into my lungs, and I SCREAM.

Gowan is in front of me. I grab his shirt and I shake it. "Make it stop! Take it back!"

He takes my chin and he forces me to look at the thing that is Nori.

"I can't!" I scream. "I *can't!*"

Gowan's own cry does not block out my own; I hear him nonetheless. *"You have to remember!"*

But it is too late.

And I am falling.

Ω

BOOK 6:
Flaming Stone

The truth of the tale
reads between lines
what can you see
within those vines?
the manor is tall
the manor is wide
the Creeper Man is
the only divide.

Do you know what grief feels like?

Really feels like?

Like this.

28

do you see?

He knows when you slumber
because that's his domain
he feels your fearful blunder
in darkness he remains.

BROKEN BOOK ENTRY

The one thing I cling to now is the memory.
The **truth** in memory. Doesn't that mean
something? Like, a memory **will** hold the truth
even when everything else fails? While you **wait**
for something that may not happen? It's because of
that memory, that truth, that I'll wait **forever**.
Mam's voice. *Circling the loom, **dearie***, is also a
memory, and also the truth. Except she never called
me "dearie." Did she? Don't think about it. You'll
get all turned around. Who **does** my mother

think I am now? **That** is a question that might **scare** me if I think too hard about it. What does your memory do for **you**? What does your mother think of *you*?

Ω

1980: "Where is she, Pammy? Tell me, now!"

Pamela shakes her head, her lips quivering. They part and a stuttering of sound staggers out. "I—I—I—I—"

Catherine grabs her shoulders roughly. *"Pamela, where is Anne?"*

Her voice rings through the room and down the hall, louder than the storm outside. Papa left her in charge, and look what she has allowed to happen.

"Sh-she said s-something about the woods, about her biggest fear—"

"The woods? She went to the *woods*?"

"I think so!"

"Pamela, *why did you let her go*?"

"I'm sorry! I'm sorry!"

Pammy keeps screaming her *sorry*s but Catherine is already running down the stairs, out the front door, and into the storm.

Ω

It's bright. So bright that everything is white and painful.

I blink, blink, *blink*—slowly the light fades.

W h e r e   a m   I?

I know this ceiling. I know the crumbling paint and the cob-webs and the patterns in the dried drips. I'm in bed. In *my* bed.

Oh, I remember.

It's at least an hour before dawn, and I know they'll be sleep-ing downstairs. She will have placed a blanket over him and put him into the recovery position, draping herself over him for warmth or comfort. Maybe she wants to try to remember the man he used to be, long ago when she was a girl and his lies were dreams she still believed in.

I'm very quiet, because I'm not wearing my shoes. I hid them under my pillow for later, but forgot. I tiptoe over to Nori's bed and quietly rouse her—just enough to sign that she has to be *Quiet as a mouse.*

Squeak! she signs back, and then closes her eyes again.

I lift her onto my hip and her head lolls on my shoulder.

"Come on, bug," I whisper, and carry her downstairs.

I have to pass them to get to the door, but when I round the corner, I see Mam is awake. She is alone in the room, bent over her sewing, her aged hair falling in scratchy waves over her face.

"Mam? Where's Dad?"

She looks up at me and smiles. "There you are. We were wondering when you'd come looking."

"What do you..." My voice trails off as I take in what she is doing. My body grows cold and I hug Nori tighter to me.

Mam isn't sewing her dress. And she's not using cotton thread. It's her hair. She's sewing her hair into her leg.

"Mam! What are you *doing?*"

"War is coming, my girl." Her eyes are full of sympathy. "Something very hard is coming."

"I don't understand."

She keeps sewing, sewing, *sewing*. Her hands are bloody. It is slippery work.

"You'll have to be strong."

"Mam, stop this—"

"Cathy is crazy, after all," she says, smiling vacantly. "Just like you."

"I'm your *daughter*." I choke on the word. "Why don't you care about me?"

She looks up from her terrible work, and her eyes are shining with moisture and light. "Oh, Silla...How could you have forgotten?"

As I watch, her eyes change. They widen, then darken—the whites turning pink, then red, then vessels bursting as she stares at me. She is shaking—vibrating and swelling—as her eyes get darker and darker. Her mouth opens, and she mouths one word. *Go.*

"Mam?"

I am fourteen. Nori is in my arms, half-asleep. I am sneaking out of the house—running away to live with Auntie Cath, a woman we have never met, but have been told about. We are going to La Baume, a magical manor full of love and light. I am rescuing us from this house.

Dad is asleep on the floor. The room smells like vomit and whiskey and beer. There are cans littered all over the room. Mam stirs beside him, raising her head. She sees what I am doing. Sees the bag in my trembling hand.

She looks at me, right in the eye, and there is a profound connection, I think. Then she lowers her head slowly, careful not to wake the beast sleeping beside her, and I realize everything she is saying in that one motion.

It's okay. You can go. Leave me here with him. I forgive you.

I head for the door, but I forget about the cans and I kick

one. It spins over the carpet and hits the wall with a tinny sound, too loud. Far too loud.

Dad groans, moves, raises his head. Sees us.

Nori stirs.

"Where the bloody hell do you think you're going?" he says. His voice is loose gravel covered with phlegm.

I freeze, clutching Nori to me tightly. She lifts her head, but I push it back down onto my shoulder. "Go to sleep."

Dad gets to his feet, revealing his bruised but muscled torso. He was in a bar fight again. There is dried blood on the side of his head and his left eye is swelling shut. Mam scrambles up and puts her hand on his arm.

"Stan," she says, forcing a gentle smile. "Come back to bed."

His hand is so fast. It whips out to grab her arm and he squeezes. She cries out and bends as he twists. "Stan!"

"You're in on this?" His head snaps to me again. "Is it a boy? Running off to be with some goddamn teenage *runt*?"

I shake my head but it's useless. He's still drunk—I can hear it in his words. All I can think is, *Nori. Hide Nori. Protect Nori.* The last time he got like this, he broke Nori's arm and collarbone. She spent weeks in agony until finally it is almost set, crooked and useless.

Dad throws Mam away from him and a tiny *oof* escapes her. Then he rounds on me. I spin and put Nori down, standing in front of her.

"Daddy, please—"

I wince before the blow comes, knowing the look in his eyes. But it doesn't come. I open my eyes to a sight I have *never* seen. Mam is on top of him, on his back, hitting his head with her tiny fists, growling and yelling and pulling on his hair. He spins, trying to get her off, this pesky feline creature. Her head whips back and forth, but she doesn't stop hitting and tearing. She is wild.

"Leave my babies alone!"

But he is stronger.

And he is bigger.

I watch it almost in slow-motion, wanting to stop it. Wanting to change what is coming.

He flips her off, and she crashes onto the floor with a sound louder than should be possible. Her back has shattered one of the beer bottles. Then he is on top of her, his hands around her neck, pressing, squeezing, his eyes wild and manic.

"Stupid *bitch*!" he growls through his teeth.

I spin and pick up Nori in her blanket again, pressing her head against my shoulder so she can't see or hear. She is crying softly, shaking in my arms.

Mam writhes under Dad, clutching at his hands and yanking desperately, her legs kicking out uselessly from underneath him. But she is so small and weak, yet brave and strong, too. Her movements grow weaker, fainter, and then her eyes swivel sideways, and meet mine.

I am frozen—body lurching forward, then back to keep Nori safe, then forward to do—what?

I watch the grotesque changes in color. Pink, red, purple shattered with blood vessels. Her whole face is changing.

And then her lips move, and I see it. *"Help."*

This woman, who had seemed too weak and small and useless to me as I grew into a young woman, was strong. She had always been strong. The only one capable of holding us together for so long.

And I do nothing.

It seems to take forever, this moment. Something passes between us—infinite and universal. It is:

Help me.

I'm sorry.

I forgive you.
Save me.
Don't forget me.
Remember.
Remember.

And now I do. I was fourteen when my father killed my mother, and I took my little sister and I ran. I remember it all.

I stood.

I saw.

And I did—nothing.

She asked me for help...

and I did *nothing*.

I'm so sorry....

I'm so sorry *sorry sorry sorry useless coward useless sorry weak murderer killer coward weak sorry I'm sorry so sorry weak useless failure let you die never forgive hate myself useless weak coward stood there let it happen can't bear this I'm broken I broke you you're gone and broken and it's my fault because I left you there I left you there I left—*

you to die.

"Are you ready?" Gowan is beside me.

My voice is a moth in a hurricane. "Ready for what?" I hug Nori tighter for comfort, but the blanket is empty in my arms. "What's going on? Where's Nori?"

"You already know that. You'll need to go somewhere very dark if you want to find her again." The corners of his mouth fall, like he is trying not to cry for me. "Something very difficult is coming."

My mother's words on his lips.

What could be more difficult than this?

SILLA DANIELS'S GUIDE TO THE DEMON'S LAIR

1. Try not to look around.

2. But if you must, look carefully.

3. Watch out for tall, thin, creepy tree-men.

4. Try to keep hold of your sister.

5. If you lose your sister, follow the tinkling sounds.

6. If you happen upon a cave

7. DON'T GO INSIDE.

8. Should you choose to ignore this advice, you are a very stupid person.

9. You should probably go die now. You likely will by the end, anyway.

Everything is dark. I don't know where I am. I don't care.

My mind is full of cause and effect.

Cause: A man beats his wife and his children.

Effect: His children want to leave him.

Cause: A mother loves her children.

Effect: She dies to free them.

Cause: A girl runs away, leaving her mother to be choked to death.

Effect: A girl will hate herself forever.

Cause: Memories are suppressed so the girl can survive.

Effect: A girl grows a granite heart.

Cause: A child summons a child demon.

Effect: The next generation is haunted.

Cause: The sins of the mother

Effect: Are the sins of the daughter.

"Something very hard is coming," he says.
   The dark is so nice this time of day.

Ω

Did you know I can draw?

I could always draw, ever since I was a little kid.

It's my one talent, I guess. I used it to escape when Dad was bad or Mam was quiet.
I used to draw these huge colorful pictures of gardens and flowers.
I drew what I thought La Baume looked like,
and then I would add a tiny version of me in a window somewhere, pretending I was there.
Free.

What a joke.

Now all I use is black pen. It's all I've got. But even if it wasn't, it's all I'm inclined to use. Black ink. Because even though it's the most depressing thing to say, and even more depressing because it's true—I don't have any
colors left in me. They've all been turned to mud. Color is like hope, you see.

And I lost that a long time ago.

La Baume

Ω

Gowan crouches in the corner of the kitchen, counting shriveled, sprouting potatoes. He looks different somehow. Younger, maybe. Not as clean as usual. Cathy is standing nearby, her arms limp at her sides.

"Gowan, what's happening?"

He doesn't answer me. Doesn't even look up. Instead, he looks at Cathy.

"We need to get help," he says, standing up. "This can't go on."

This is La Baume. Another La Baume: Sunlight streaming into the kitchen, across the surfaces, warming the floor. The smell of flowers from a vase on the counter. That vase broke months ago.

Cathy stares at nothing, her mouth hanging open.

"*Catherine,*" Gowan snaps. "We. Need. Help."

She turns deadened eyes on him. "Why? We're all dead, anyway."

Gowan sighs, squeezes the bridge of his nose, and stalks into the garden.

And...

I'm in the garden. Some other me. I look...different. I look...fresh. Young. Maybe not *happy*, but closer to it than I am now. My hair is a bright, luminous chocolate brown; there are no shadows beneath my eyes. I seem to have all my teeth. No mold in sight.

And Nori!

I rush forward, unthinking, everything inside me roiling and shifting urgently. Nori is playing in the flower bed, oblivious to Gowan and the other me. She is smiling—no, *laughing*. Silent laughter I haven't seen in so long. My heart breaks with yearning.

I turn back to Gowan in time to see him smile at her—me—and take her—*my*—hands.

"I have to get help," he says. "This can't go on. People are leaving in droves. All this talk of another world war...I don't know what's true. But we have to act now or it'll be too late."

She nods, but her words are pleading. "You don't have to go...or...I could come with you."

"Stay here and take care of Nori. God knows Cathy won't." He pulls her close, embraces her. Whispers in her ear. "I love you, Silla Daniels."

"I love you," she whispers back, tears falling from her eyes like I've never cried. Genuine, simple tears. Not a storm, nor a crisis.

"I will love you forever," he says, and my heart drops because those are the words—*the* words—he spoke to me that night in the not-forest. He pulls back then, enough to kiss her. Their passion burns so bright I have to turn away.

And I see Gowan—my Gowan, dimmed, less, sad—watching from the gate. In his eyes, a quiet storm rages. He looks at me, and all I hear is

Do you see?

Ω

The garden sparkles in orange hues of sunset, the old wooden table draped with a pale cloth and sprinkled with bundles of dusty-pink roses from the garden. I smile at them, even though I wish Cath had just left them in the earth.

So pretty.

Cath made a cake and I take a slice from Gowan's offering hand.

"I like your nail polish," I tell Cath, noting how it matches the roses. Her smile is so wide that a jolt of pleasure jumps through me.

"Thank you, Silla dear."

But the smile doesn't reach her eyes.

"Shall we?" Gowan asks, indicating the garden.

I grin, and we walk off alone, away from the light of the kitchen.

"Did you see her nails?" I ask him when I sit down.

"Pink?"

I shake my head. "No...they were all messy, painted over her cuticles."

"I guess she had shaky hands."

"Gowan. There was some in her *hair*."

He shrugs. "Maybe she's tired."

"It's more than that. Something's wrong with her. Can't you see it?"

He glances back at Cath, who stands with Nori in the kitchen doorway, smiling at us.

"Maybe. I'm not sure." He smiles at me. "But tonight, you're all I care about, birthday girl. How about you eat your cake and make a wish?"

I lean closer to him. "What if my wish had already come true?"

He leans closer, too, kisses me tenderly. "Then wish for the impossible."

I eat the cake while he watches, and offer him the last piece. He opens his mouth and I pop it inside. He licks my fingers on the way out, eyes sparkling with mischief.

"Tease," he says.

I hand him the plate. "Another?"

He kisses me on the cheek and I giggle. "That's more like it."

When he comes back, there are three pieces on my plate. "Two more for you, one for me."

It's amazing cake. Moist and subtle, vanilla and raspberry. I am done with my third when Nori skips over. She puts down her plate and shows us what she is holding.

Something dangles from her fist, the one attached to the bad arm, so it shakes a little with the strain of lifting it up to show us. Her mouth is covered in pink icing. More pink.

Look, she signs, one-handed. *Look!*

The thing swings like a fatty bit of raw bacon covered in cake.

"What is that?" Gowan says, laughing with a frown.

Worms! She laughs and digs into her piece of cake for another, while she holds the first.

Everything s l o w s down around me.

Wrong. This is wrong.

Cath still stands in the kitchen doorway, the light pooling around her. She is laughing, tears running down her cheeks.

Gowan lets go of my hand, and the air seems to bite with cold.

"Give me that," Gowan says, his demeanor utterly changed. "No more cake."

Why? Nori signs. *I want it!*

"No more," he repeats, and gathers up my plate, too. He strides to the kitchen, gesturing at Cath and pointing at the plates.

She simply rolls off the wall, goes inside, and Gowan, agitated, follows her.

We don't see either of them all night.

It is the early hours of the morning when Gowan slides into bed next to me.

"You were right. Something is wrong with her."

Ω

The next day Cath goes up to the attic.

And never comes down.

Ω

1980: The woods are waterlogged, and Catherine has trouble finding her way. She screams for Anne as she runs, searching, but the trees all around her move and whisper, thrashing in the storm, and it is many hours later that she sees.

And the wood echoes with screams.

It was her job to be carer... to protect Anne. To protect them both. She was the eldest and the wisest. Anne tried to tell her about their protector, but Catherine, growing up fast, had not *quite* believed. At twelve, she fancied herself grown, and so her childhood faith in stories had started to fade.

And now look.

Anne is gone.

Shredded up on the forest floor.

And it is all her fault.

Ω

"You never came back. You left us that day. You went for help, but you never came back."

I *r e m e m b e r* him.

Gowan's face has fallen a lot since then. "That's not true."

Behind me, I can hear La Baume sighing and shifting and changing.

"You abandoned us." Nothing. There is nothing alive inside me right now. My heart died a long time ago. He left us. He left us all alone. He left me.

I don't wait for his reply. I just turn and drag myself back to the now root-infested manor, ready for the shadows to take me. Inside, the walls flake and peel away as I pass, which gives me intense satisfaction. Everything breaks down as I wander by; the roots bend and twist behind me, cutting him off, locking him out. And I know that it is *me* doing this to La Baume.

I am the infection.

I am the decay.

Ω

29

anne

Children are sponges, yes
we soak up everything!
including all your blackness, yes
we do it just by breathing.

BROKEN BOOK ENTRY

I miss someone. **I** wish I knew who. I feel
abandoned, which is silly. But I **can't** shake
this feeling that I'm never going to see this person
again. Nothing I **do** helps. Who do I miss?? I
tried to get Cathy to come down again last night,
but she just stared at me with **this** weird, empty
expression, and then after a while she started
screaming and tearing at her hair. I hurried to
leave because I didn't want Nori to hear and I
knew she'd stop if I left. But she started calling,

"Pammy! Pammy come back!" and I lost it. I ran from there as fast as I could and locked myself in my room. **Any**thing to get away. After a while, Nori knocked. She's looking worse. We curled up together in the huge closet and fell asleep. When I woke up it was morning, and it was **more** sleep than I'd had in ages. Need to find some food.

Ω

The other me steps out of the kitchen. She is following the sound that has plagued me for so long.

Creak.

Creak.

Creak.

Endless. Unendurable. Futile.

I follow her as she, frowning, searches.

"Nori? Auntie Cath?"

Her voice is so young! So innocent. Is this really me?

Eventually she finds the stairs leading to the attic. Cath, she knows, has not come down for at least two weeks; she has been leaving trays at the door. But maybe it's longer than two weeks now. It must be, since she went up there the day Gowan left.

Gowan...

The other me climbs the stairs slowly. "Cathy?"

I don't want to follow, but I do anyway. I need to remember this piece.

At the top of the stairs, she knocks on the door. She calls

Cath's name once more, tentatively, and then she walks in. She is probably worried about invading privacy, or seeing a weak moment, but that is gone the moment the door swings open, banging the wall on the other side.

I fall to my knees at the same moment the other me does. Our eyes are level with Cath's feet.

Creak

Her face

Creak

is a vicious

Creak

purple.

Creak

The rope

Creak

is cruelly

Creak

tight.

Creak

Her neck

Creak

is definitely

Creak

broken.

"C-C-Cathy..."

The other me screams, scrambles forward, tries to hoist Cath up. She jumps onto the window seat, where Cath placed a chair to jump from, and scrabbles to free the rope. All she does is make it tighter and break the skin at Cath's neck. There are

c r a c k s

as she tugs.

She falls off the chair, landing heavily on her hip. She is sobbing. On the wall, words: I CAN'T DO IT. And then: THE CREEPER MAN IS COMING.

A little bell tinkles behind us, and then we hear Nori's hurried footsteps. She is coming up the stairs—she must have heard the scream, the crash. Other me struggles to her feet, wipes her face furiously on her dress, and backs away, shaking her head in horror. She stares for one more moment, then closes the door on the scene and hurries to meet Nori farther down the stairs.

Behind her, the *creeeeeeeak*ing continues, and eventually slows to a stop.

Ω

I'm somewhere else. It's dark, yes, but so much more. Movement, wind, rain on my skin, fresh air all around, *sounds*. I see a shape moving quickly through the woods and I back away instinctively, falling over a log in the process. I land hard just as the figure pauses near me, hands on her knees, panting.

Cathy. The same age, or close, to when I saw her sewing that horrible doll.

She straightens, peering through her hair and the rain. *"Anne!"* she yells. "ANNE!"

That name again. When she runs off into Python, I follow. We run for a long time, but I don't seem to get tired. Cathy, though—she falls several times, covering herself in mud and cuts, and by the time we see the shape by a half-fallen tree—an alder tree—she has already been crying for a while.

Cathy pauses, and so do I, but I think I know what's coming, and I don't know how much more of this I can take. History really does repeat itself. Cathy moves over very slowly, her body taut like a stretched-out elastic band. She reaches the shape, and even I can't pretend it isn't what it is.

There is a torso. Of that I am sure. It has been shredded in parts, but I can make out the small rib cage, the almost-formation of small breasts. There is an arm, at least one, and I see two legs. I can't see the head, but there is a tangle of hair.

It is, without a doubt, the body of a small child. A girl in a black dress.

Oh. No. Not black. It's white. The black is...

Cathy stumbles, crashes in a staggering way to her knees, and then she throws up on the corpse before turning roughly away, trying to contain the vomit with her hands. It spews between her fingers and she gags, coughs, and cries.

When she turns back, her mouth is contorted and ugly. "Anne..."

I look at the legs, the arms, the hair, and the torso. Anne. The third sister.

"You did this," Cathy whispers, looking out into the woods. "You tricked her. You lured her, wooed her, then you crept up and killed her. You're a monster. A Creeper Man. You're the Creeper Man."

A legend born, right here.

I close my eyes for the aunt I never knew, for the pain I never realized Cath and my mother shared—for the darkness born that day. When I open them, we are inside, and Cathy is standing, drenched, in front of Pamela. My mother, but as a child. So strange.

"This is on you," Cathy says. She slaps my mother before I even see it coming.

Pamela cries out and grabs her cheek. Starts to cry.

"This is all your *fault*," Cath spits. "I will *never* forgive you."

"Cathy—"

"Don't talk to me again. You're a killer. You let her go out there alone while you hid in the closet, and he killed her. The Creeper Man killed her! It should have been you."

With that, she turns away, leaving my little mother sobbing behind her.

Oh, no. Is this what I am born of? Is this the pain that is passed on in my family?

We have no right to children if despair is all we bring with us.

Ω

30

s i n k i n g

Hush now, baby
don't mind the roar
that's just your tummy
asking for more.

BROKEN BOOK ENTRY

A man was in the woods today. **Nori** told me
that she spent a long time talking to him. His coat
was ripped and his face was blotchy with red sores,
but she said she wasn't afraid because he had a
friendly smile. She even took his hand to prove she
wasn't afraid and drank some of his water. She **is** a
stupid child sometimes. Do I teach her to be afraid,
as Mam would have me do? To feel fear when
something unfamiliar comes? Do I teach her to be
defensive, as Dad would? Is that the right thing to
do? Or do I bestow kindness, the way Cath might
tell her? I'm just glad he's **gone**.

Ω

I'm in the cave again. "You knew."

Gowan looks tired. So tired. "Yes."

"You weren't just here to fix the garden."

"No."

"You were in my past. I just didn't remember."

"Yes."

"Why didn't you tell me?"

"I couldn't. I *can't*."

"Why . . . where did you go? Why?"

"I came back."

"I don't remember."

"I know."

I close my eyes.

"Please," Gowan says. "Keep going."

I can't hold on anymore. I am so *tired*.

When I open my eyes, I'm standing on the lip of the hole in the entrance hall. Only there is no entrance hall now, the hole has taken over the entire space. A chasm at my feet.

I understand, my father's voice says. It is so warm. *I understand, my daughter, about being tired. Rest now. Come with me and you can rest your head.*

I sway. I want to. How easy it would be.

"Please, Silla . . ." Gowan whispers. "You're strong. You're so close."

I look at him. "Why are you here?"

I recognize that tension in his face. It's been there ever since he came to La Baume to "fix the garden." It's like he wants to say something to me, but he can't.

At last, he says, "To help you." His eyes fall, and I see his hopelessness. "To love you."

His words. His face. His voice. I remember him. I *remember* my love for him, and I feel a new love for him, one that grew all over again when I didn't know who he was.

And I fall into him. His arms come around me right away, and my lips meet his. *Perfect fit,* something inside me says. I kiss him and I hug him and I never want to let go. This feels urgent and desperate. Completely vital.

"Help me," I whisper.

"I'm trying," he says.

I allow him to lead me back through the Python manor, away from the hole—far away from it—but I can't stop my mind from thinking about everything I've seen. Especially...that...

My little Nori, reduced to *that*. It can't be real. It just... can't.

Ω

Not again. I can't take this anymore.

La Baume. The kitchen. I watch myself mash up peanuts, like I've done a million times before. The other me adds sugar and a little butter. She mixes it up, fiercely. I can see she is trying not to cry. When she's done, she turns, revealing Nori standing behind her, and hands the mess over.

I step forward without thinking. But something is wrong.

Nori eats the peanut butter slowly

something is wrong

and it looks

like the effort is gigantic.

She swallows it down and smiles at the other me

something is wrong

trying to reassure the other me—*I'm okay, Silla, I really am,* her eyes say—but then she vomits it all back up, curling over and heaving like her body won't take the food it is offered. So familiar. I know this feeling well.

And now I see it.

Nori is sick. She's very, very sick.

The other me says, "Don't worry," because Nori looks so ashamed of herself, but then Nori sits down very suddenly, looking dazed and thirsty, so the other me gathers her up and carries her upstairs.

I don't want to follow.

I follow.

I stay.

I watch.

It's like some sick kind of stop-motion film, sped up. I watch myself as the days pass, caring for Nori, who wastes away in her bed. She is so thin, so pale, so thirsty. The other me tries to feed her the peanuts, but Nori rejects it all. The other Silla wishes she had fresh apples. Gowan always brought the apples from the apple tree.

The other Silla wanders from the chair by the window, peering out into the woods, to the chair by the bed, sitting beside Nori and reading to her, feeding her, cleaning her, crying for her.

Day passes day passes day. She visits the window often, but the view doesn't change. No one comes.

One day, another long day of suffering, Silla finds a journal. It is old, so old, that it has calcified somehow, the cover turning hard as stone. It is cracked down the middle. She finds a pen, opens the broken book, and begins to write.

I peer over her shoulder.

They say I'm crazy, she writes.

Days, nights, days.

No Gowan. No sign.

Nori grows thinner, sicker, thinner. She stops taking water, too, after a little while. The other me looks better, but not much.

The food is gone now. Only one dried apple left, which she was hoping to avoid because it has some mold on the side.

I watch as Silla feeds it to Nori, instead of taking it herself, even though she *knows* Nori won't keep it down. But she must try. She has to try. I watch the slow painful bites, the excruciating swallows.

And then—

And then I am in the other Silla. I *am* her, and she is me, and there is ink on my fingers, which are curled around a broken book. I am so hungry. The pain is constant, inevitable, wholly distracting.

I try to feed Nori, but she is no longer awake or responding. Terror like a blinding flash hits me, and I check—she's breathing. Shallow. So shallow. I begin to cry, but there is no water in my body.

I try to say Nori's name, but there is not enough strength even for that.

I climb into the bed next to my sister, clutching her to me, and I fall asleep.

Please... I think. *Please, Gowan. We need you.*

Ω

When I wake, Nori is ice cold in the bed beside me.

Ω

"It gets bad after this." Gowan is standing in the shadows of the room.

"I know."

I stay in bed for a long time. The smells get pretty bad, but I won't let go of her, and it soon passes. There's something wet in the bed with us, but that passes, too. I can't...I can't do this....

And I'm out. Watching. Once more a spectator. The other Silla is in the bed, and I am standing at the foot of it.

I watch myself linger on, staring with yearning, desperate eyes at the window.

I watch myself write, sicken, suffer, and very slowly...die.

$$\Omega$$

"This is what happened," I say.

Gowan, beside me now, nods.

"This is how I died. How *we* died."

He nods again.

"I'm to blame."

He faces me, takes my shoulders. "No. You can't think that. It was so hard back then, all that talk of war, people running scared....People died. So many people died. Cath was weak and sick, and she went mad and killed herself. That's not your fault. Nori died from some kind of wasting sickness and that was *not your fault*." He pauses. "You couldn't have saved her, Silla." He pauses. "You starved to death, and, yes, that was your choice. But...you have to forgive yourself, Silla."

"I died," I whisper. "I'm...dead. I've been dead...this whole time?"

"Yes."

I look up at him. "Are you even my Gowan?"

"Yes."

"Are you...dead, too?"

He takes my hand. "Yes."

"And you've known I'm dead since the moment you came out of the woods...?"

"Yes."

I take a moment to process this information, but something is niggling at me, is wrong.

And then I see it.

"No."

All this…all this is happening inside the Creeper Man's lair—his cave. It's a trick! Oh, God. I nearly fell for it. He's trying to distract me from finding Nori. This is an illusion, a trap!

I push Gowan away from me, and I'm back in the forest. Before he can stop me, I *run*. I need to find his cave again. I need to find it and go in strong. I will find him and face him and I will *kill* him and save my sister.

Ω

I run for a long time chased by
>   *Creaking*

and
>   *The growl of my stomach*

and
>   *The retching of Nori throwing up*

and
>   *A symphony of suffering.*

And then he's there. The Creeper Man.

He is tall.

He is thin.

A dark outfit.

Like tree bark.

He has no hair.

No eyes.

No nose.

Only one

>   wide

mouth.

Which smiles.

Nori is crying for me somewhere. Gowan is watching from a distance away. I fill up with rage and hate, and I rush at the Creeper Man with a branch in my hand. I strike him, but he grins. I hit again and again and *again*, over and over, feeling my body weakening with every blow. I am so tired. I haven't eaten anything in so long. He's too strong for me. Always *grinning* with that wide mouth.

"Forgive yourself!" Gowan calls.

All around, vines and bushes curl out of the floorboards, berries, thick and black, pregnant with juice, growing up and up.

No. I won't give up. I will not eat.

I fight and I strike until finally there is nothing left. No strength. No energy. No will.

I collapse onto the forest floorboards, and I drop the branch.

There is a

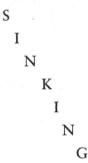

sensation, like falling, a fading noise distorting lower as it winds down—a slowing of the clock as darkness takes over—and I give in to it. It would be...so nice... to just...give in.

The last thing I hear is Gowan's cry.

"SILLA, NO!"

Ω

31

story

Pick a petal, he loves me
another, he loves me not,
kiss and tell that lady
all that was forgot.

I don't want to do this, but I have to. I've been planning it for months. Waiting for the perfect time. And that's now.

I rouse Nori. *Quiet as a mouse.*

Squeak!

I find the escape bag, and carry her through to the living room. He's drunk, asleep. She's got an arm slung over him. For warmth? Protection? To make sure he stays down?

His beer cans are scattered all over the floor, and his snores—

Wait.

What's happening?

This feels...familiar.

I glance behind me. "Gowan...?"

At first, nothing.

Then he steps through the shadows at the far side of the wall. He stares at me, his eyes full of tears, and smiles wider than I've ever seen.

"You remember," he chokes, grinning.

My eyes open, as though they had been closed, and I am lying on the forest-manor floor. And Nori is not.

"What just happened?"

Gowan helps me to my feet, and then folds me into his arms. His breath is hot on my neck.

"You almost reset," he murmurs, holding me tighter.

I pull away gently. "Reset?"

Everything feels so surreal. As eerily still as this horrible place has always been, only now there is no atmosphere. I get to my feet and look around. And he's there. The Creeper Man. Standing still as a statue, towering above me. I stumble back, but he doesn't move. Gowan's words: *Forgive yourself.* Cathy and Nori's words: *He's already here.*

I just stare at him.

All around me, the berries hang, oversized and plump and dark with juice. I want them. I don't. Every berry is matched and surrounded by at least three sharp thorns.

"I almost...reset."

I don't know why I do it.

Something inside me just melts like ice into water. I am tired of fighting. Tired of the sadness. Tired of the hunger. Tired of missing someone I didn't even know was gone. I have carried this load long enough. And I know what I am looking at. I finally know what I am looking at.

I reach through the thorns, flinching as they prick and tear at my arms, and I grab a handful of berries. The thorns let me go, curling away, setting me free. I step forward, up to the Creeper Man, and I offer him the berries. He raises one long hand and turns it palm upward. I let the berries drop.

I am crying.

I touch my face to make sure it's real. Water on my face, water in my heart, melting away the stone.

I am crying.

"I'm so sorry," I tell him, my tears still coming from a well of sadness deep inside me. "I forgive you."

He begins to peel away, like some awful wallpaper, like a suit he was wearing—a veneer—fading into a crumpled nothing at the feet of what was inside all along.

Me.

I stare at myself, holding the berries.

"You..." I whisper. "You're me. I was fighting...myself. This whole time, I was fighting myself?"

The me that was the Creeper Man all along collapses onto her knees and devours the berries, all the while sobbing. I cry with her. I watch myself laughing through my tears. The other Silla nods at me, and fades away, back into myself.

Gowan walks over to where she knelt and turns to smile at me.

"Why didn't you tell me?" I ask him.

"You wouldn't have believed. Not then. You'd have pulled away and I'd lose you forever."

I nod. "I...I feel—different." I feel whole. Full. Healed. I feel...like myself again. "This whole thing"—I gesture at the manor, the woods, the trees, where the Creeper Man used to be—"was all my doing, wasn't it? I was trapped...wasn't I?"

Gowan nods. "You've kept yourself locked in your own purgatory—one of your own making—since you died."

I see it. I see it all. The truth of everything. Like all the blank pieces I once turned into darkness and shadow are suddenly there, bright and urgent. "I turned myself into my own tormentor," I whisper. "And I used Cath's story to do it."

Gowan grins. "Not anymore."

There is so much to process...to take in. But I don't have time, because the trees begin to glow like lightbulbs. Pulsing like they each contain a heart of fire. The light grows, and grows, encompassing everything around it.

I am blinded by the light. Again.

When it fades, I am standing in front of La Baume. It is such a sad, old building. It is covered in vines—not the strange roots and vines of before, but real vines, still and old, tinged red with autumn. Spiderwebs hang from the gutters and windows and the house is utterly still under a gray autumn sky. Through the few gaps in the overgrowth, I spot red paint, peeling away, revealing blue, then green—so many colors.

La Baume is warped and sunken. Derelict and forgotten.

We are inside then, walking through the halls. All the furniture is covered up, dusty with time passing, lonely and sad.

"This is where I've been."

"Yes. This is what the manor has become," Gowan says. He is beside me. I can't tell if he was always or only just now. "You've been here for a long time."

He nods at a shelf along the wall in my bedroom. It is covered with seemingly endless copies of my broken book. The one with the omega symbol, and the gash in its cover.

"My journal…"

"That's how many times you've done this," he says.

I touch the row of them, unthinking, not really processing. "So many…"

"At least seventy-four."

"So many times…"

"This symbol wasn't in the real thing," Gowan observes, taking out one of the broken books. "Nor was this gash. You put them both here. Why?"

I close my eyes. Try to find the answer. "Omega…meaning the ultimate end. Death. I read up about eschatology in the library when I was...before. It means the end of everything. Omega—the end of it all. And the gash...I guess I was just...broken."

He nods. "I understand."

We walk to the kitchen and then I open the kitchen door. I'm expecting to be in La Baume's overgrown garden. Instead...

A garden bigger than any I have seen. So green, so lush, and flowers of all colors and sizes. Mountains in the distance promise snow, but down here...even the bees are happy.

And Nori...

She is playing and dancing with Cath—the Cath who used to be, the Cath lost so long ago—and I can't stop sobbing. I watch her, spilling over with gratitude. These tears are different, and I'm laughing.

"Nori," I say, the word choked by my happiness and relief.

Nori turns to me. "Silla!"

And her voice! Her voice is so clear and bright and *real*. She smiles at me, and then she turns away, and she and Cath dance toward the mountains.

"Wait—"

But she is going.

"Auntie Cath..."

But she is going, too.

"She had her own journey to go on," Gowan says, coming to sit beside me in the grass.

"But she was in the attic."

"In the beginning. Only you were in the attic by the end."

I pull at the grass and run it through my fingers.

"That doesn't make sense."

"A lot of what happened won't make sense, even though you're the one who created it all."

"I created that? The trees coming closer? The manor sinking, the Creeper Man torturing me at night? All of that?"

Gowan nods. "You had some pretty bad self-hate issues."

"And anger," I whisper. "I had rage. For everything. Myself. Nori. Cath." I hesitate. "You."

He nods. "I know. Especially me. And why not? I left you. I failed you."

I take his hand. "Tell me my story, Gowan. Tell me what I just went through." When he doesn't answer, I say, "I told you my story once. Please tell me this one." I hesitate. "I'm ready."

He laughs. "Oh, I know you are. I was just deciding if *I* was ready."

"Oh."

He closes his eyes, takes a breath, and—"It was 2013 when a fourteen-year-old girl called Silla Daniels fled from her London home, where she had witnessed her mother's murder at her father's hands, and came to live with her aunt Catherine in a manor house called La Baume."

I swallow. "She did, did she?"

"Absolutely. Now, things were beautiful at first, and Silla grew to care for a boy who lived there. He was the last of Catherine's orphans, the last of La Baume Orphanage. His name was Gowan, and he liked to take care of the garden." He grins, and I grin back. "Things were really good for three years, until Silla was seventeen. With rumors of another war, food shortages, disease rife, and her own personal demons, her aunt Catherine had a nervous breakdown. People started leaving the town. Silla and Gowan were alone, taking care of a little girl called Nori, who was Silla's sister. It was decided that Gowan needed to leave the manor and the town, to get some help from farther away. The world was a scary place, with talk of World War Three being around the corner, but Gowan knew that if he didn't go out in search of help, they would all die."

He pauses, and sighs.

"Go on," I say quietly.

"After Gowan had gone, the last bit of sanity that Aunt Catherine clung to snapped. She convinced herself she was being haunted by a menacing presence—the Creeper Man from her childhood—and she hanged herself. The Creeper Man was not a child-stealing demon," he says, with a glance at me, "he was a legend that two bereaved little girls invented to explain the terrible tragedy that befell their little sister, Anne, in Python Wood. Silla herself absorbed this legend and clung to the idea, as did her little sister, Nori.

"Having found Catherine's body, and wanting to protect Nori, Silla shut the attic door and forebade Nori to ever go in there. Silla was so traumatized by it that she developed an irrational (or so she thought) phobia of the attic stairs. A closed door might protect Nori from the sight, but not from the smell. The manor soon smelled of rotting flesh—"

"The meat! I could smell rotting meat! It was…my God. It was Cath?"

"Partly." He swallows.

"Go on."

"La Baume reeked of death. And then Nori got sick. She contracted something from a man she encountered in Python Wood. She helped wrap his head, which had a bloody gash, and she drank from his water, and then he moved on. Nori died, painfully, in Silla's arms some weeks later."

He pauses, I think because he can see me crying. Now that I've started, I don't think I can stop.

"Silla refused to leave Nori's side," he whispers. "And she

starved to death. When Silla woke, she was back in London, getting Nori ready for an escape. She came to La Baume, and everything went wrong, and she did not remember Gowan because he had left her, abandoned her, failed her—"

"Stop. Please, Gowan, stop."

I can't take any more. This story about torture, loss, hate, rage, suffering, death...

I don't want to know more. What good can it do now?

It takes a long time for me to recover enough to learn the rest.

"When Gowan returned with food and supplies, everyone in the house was dead and rotting," Gowan says emotionlessly.

I take his hand. "Oh, Gowan..."

"Rotting meat—" His voice breaks, and I see his jaw clench around his pain.

I stare at him with horror as I realize, and my voice is barely a breath. "Oh, God."

"Ever since then, Silla has been in her own personal purgatory, trapping Nori and Catherine along with her in that decaying house, each of them caged, together and alone in their pain. Catherine, unable to forget the madness, unable to forgive herself so long as Silla couldn't forgive her. Nori trapped because of her precious youth and her love for Silla, and Silla herself, trapped by her self-loathing, fear, guilt, and...rage.

"You were right when you said La Baume was cursed. It was cursed by you.

"You all repeated the terrible cycle of the last months of your lives in that house, over and over, exaggerating the worst elements of it, inserting clues but cutting off the truth—creating your own versions of hell, until this last time. When I came in."

"Why now? Why didn't you come before?"

"You died in 2016 when you were seventeen. I was only eighteen. I was…deeply affected by it, Silla. But I lived. I died an old man, alone in my chair, when I was ninety-two, in the year 2090. I could only come and find you when I was dead. Before all of this"—he gestures at the garden around us and the mountains in the distance—"I didn't believe there was anything more. I lived my whole life thinking you were just a photo on my coffee table. Just a fading memory. And then I found myself in Python Wood, staring at you tilling the soil, seeing Nori spot me, but not recognize me. I knew we were dead, I just…I didn't know what was going on at first. I kept having to leave to figure it out. I knew, though, that you had to free yourself. I could only try to convince you. And when that hole appeared…I knew that if you gave in to that, it would be over. Soul death."

"Soul death," I murmur, remembering how my father's voice tried to lure me in.

"I went from being an old man, barely able to walk, to the young man I was when I lost everything—when I lost you."

I stare at him, processing this news. "You…were an old man?" A deep and powerful affection settles comfortably inside me. "I wish I could have seen that."

"Oh, I was crotchety," he says, and grins. "By the end, all I did was sit in my chair and drink tea. Waiting."

"Waiting?"

He smiles sadly. "I was just waiting to die. Hoping there was something more after. Hoping I would be with you again."

I touch his face, trying to imagine it. "Ninety-two…" I pause. "I was in that place…living that hell…for seventy-four years?"

He nods, and I see it. I see in his eyes the life he has lived. The memory of him is similar but I can tell. It's in the eyes. His eyes, right now, are ancient eyes, full of scars and memories and hurts. Wisdom, experience, and age. He is him, but *more*.

And I kiss him.

Gowan. My Gowan.

"You were out there, living. The whole time. Did you marry a girl? Did you have a family? Did the war happen?"

His smile is sad, and I know the answers before he tells me.

"No family. There was no one after you. There was just an endless life. Empty. Long. Survival. And, yes. I'm sad to say that the war did come, as people said it would. It was a terrible time. Many died. It was senseless. I signed up to fight and I survived five years as a soldier. I was almost glad, at times, that you weren't there to suffer through it. I had no idea, of course, that you were trapped, suffering just as much as I was."

"We were together in that, then, I suppose."

He nods, and we stare out at the mountains. Nori and Cath are specks in the distance, shining under the sun.

"Such a waste," I whisper. Our lives, both gone before we could really be happy. "I need you to show me something."

He closes his eyes; he knows what I want. "I can't."

"I know it will be difficult. All of this has been...more than difficult. But...I have to see what happened when you found us."

Gowan's face is a waterfall in slow motion.

"But...why?"

"I need to face it. The...after."

"It was...a dark experience, Sill. The most difficult thing I have ever..." His calm is gone. "Please. Let yourself be free."

I smile. "I already am. But you're not. Show me this last piece. Let me free you from it."

The tension in his spirit is made suddenly and brilliantly visible. It hangs like a shadow—a heavy shadow, clinging to his shoulders and hanging down his back. A cloak of pain.

"Please...don't make me. Don't make me do this."

I gather him to me. "Please." It is a whisper. A word I said too often in my life. And in my purgatory. It is a plea. "Show me. I need this. And you do, too."

He doesn't answer, but the world around us shifts and changes.

Ω

A Story
Gowan Returns

The sun shines through windows that are no longer grown-over with seventy-four years of vines. The door bursts open. Silla watches as Gowan, so young, so *mortal*, bursts in, stumbling with the momentum.

"Sill?"
Breathless,
sigh...
the silence hits him.
"...Silla..."
He runs,
rushes,
up the stairs,
stumbling,
almost as though
"...please..."
he knows
"...no..."
what he is going
"—Silla—"
to find.

The room is dark, but he can *smell*...the rot. The death. The emptiness is horrifying.

He s

     t

       a

         g

           g

             e

               r

                 s

falls

to his knees.

"Silla—"

Chokes on her name.

Retches.

Vomits.

Screams.

"SILLA!"

He rushes

SillaSillaSillaSillaSilla—

to the bed

Nononononononononono—

falls upon her.

Gathers her into his arms, even though something is

                          dripping

                              from her hair.

He shakes her. Slaps her. Cries her name. Begs her to undo her demise.

Nori, so small, lies in the bed, still and gray. A husk, sunken eyes, not Nori anymore.

He hugs Silla for a long time, even though there are maggots and she is stiff and the smell...

He strokes her hair, his lips close to her ear. "Please. Silla."

He tenses, every sinew straining against the roaring pain of her loss. "I'm sorry—I'm sorry, I'm sorry…"

And he bares his teeth because there is nothing else he can do; the pain is ripping inside.

"I promise you," he says, whispering low, echoing words from long ago, "I will love you forever." His head falls onto her corpse. "Every night. I'll be saving you in my dreams *every night*."

And he sobs and he screams and the house listens and groans.

Ω

"Thank you."

Gowan is crying now, his hands pressed over his eyes. I gently remove them.

"You helped me to free myself. Helped me to forgive myself and dispel my guilt. Now you need to know that I forgive *you*."

"For letting you *die*?" He chokes and balls up his hands, shaking. The dark thing hanging on to him darkens. "For leaving you all alone?"

"For doing everything you could. *Twice*."

I kiss him, pushing my deepest hope and love and light into the kiss. "Now you have to forgive *yourself*."

He shakes his head, his eyes full of the wordless remorse that's been growing and eating at him for more than seven decades. "I…I can't, Silla. I was too late—I should have—"

"Please." I lean close to his ear. "*Forgive yourself*. I forgive you."

He sighs.

Gathers me into his arms.

All this time…

"Silla…I have you. After so long. I have you again."

"We have each other. Gowan...I don't feel it." I breathe into his neck.

"What?"

"Sadness. Guilt. Anger."

"What do you feel?"

I laugh. "I feel alive!"

Ω

epilogue

I am sobbing, if ghosts can sob, and we are clinging to each other and shaking with the wounds we have both suffered, apart and together. "I'm sorry," I say, over and over. "Oh, Gowan. I'm so sorry I couldn't wait for you. That you had to see—"

He kisses me—hundreds of kisses on my face, in my hair, on my forehead, on my lips. He is kissing my existence, holding my face like I'm the most beautiful miracle he has ever seen. And I'm not much better myself.

At last, he says, breathless, *"I . . . forgive myself."*

I laugh and we kiss, and the grass is there to meet us when we lie back under a beautiful sun. "Good, you stupid boy! Good!"

I sigh. "All that time, I was just walking around thinking, *This is my life*. How many other people are walking around in their own purgatory?"

"Probably more than I'd like to think about."

"And they don't even know it." Something occurs to me. "You know . . . Cath and Pamela, my mother, turned the Creeper Man into a villain after Anne was killed in the woods. I still don't know the story there, and I guess I never will now. But, it just occurred to me. When I made myself the Creeper Man . . . I made myself a murderer."

He touches my cheek. "Yes, dear Silla. That's what you thought you were."

"And the creaking was always her rope. And my hunger was..."

"You starved. You wouldn't leave Nori."

I sigh. "I thought...I thought I was anorexic or something. Or that the house had infected me somehow."

Gowan smiles, and there is no happiness in it now. "When in reality, you were infecting everything."

"But you came in," I whisper, and I lean my face into his hand and smile. "Into my hell. You rescued me."

"You rescued yourself."

"What happens now?"

"Now...we move on."

"I don't want to. I want another chance."

He looks at me, and I see the fear in his eyes.

"I didn't get enough time with you. Enough time with *life*. It was bad, Gowan. So much of it was so bad. And the good—with *you* and with Nori and with Cath, before...it didn't last long. I want more."

He squeezes my hand. "Anything is possible."

"We could go back and have another try, you know."

"We might end up continents away from each other."

"I would find you. I know it."

I kiss him and the rest of my painful past rushes away on the raging river of joy inside me.

"Meet you on earth," he whispers,

and we are gone.

Ω

Acknowledgments

Thank you first to my husband, who believed in this story even when I had my doubts, and who believed in my ability to pull it off.

To my mother, my endless source of pride and light, I love you more than I can ever express. You listened to all the terrible stories I came up with since the moment I could talk—thank you for never once putting me down. You protected a little girl's ego, and made all the difference.

To Proff. S, Proff. O'G, Ngosi, Andrew, Diane, and all the staff at Kings—forever thank you. My donor and hero, I will thank forever. This is because of you. I never forget. Never.

My wonderwomen—I mean, editors—Alvina Ling and Helen Thomas. Thank you for seeing my story, what I'm trying to do, where I'm trying to go, and for bringing it out of me to the absolute fullest. I am so grateful you ladies are with me on this amazing journey. I will always edit smiling, knowing you are there, too!

A special thank-you to Maggie Edkins for her beautiful and elegant design. She brought this little book visual life.

Polly Nolan and Sarah Davies of Greenhouse Literary Agency—my advocates and agents—I adore you both. Thank you for taking this little bud of a writer into your care and letting me grow and bloom.

To my in-laws, for being so happy to see *The Dead House*

out in the world, and for singing my praises. To my family for always showing love and support: Mel, Josephine, Billy, Ross, Rebecca, Annie, Jesse, and Jason. Special mention to Jose Manual, who has been on my mind through the writing and editing of this book. Wishing you full recovery and happiest of days with Loli and the family!

To Aunt Isabel, for allowing me to use the manor as inspiration in this book, even though I have yet to visit! I hope I do it proud.

A big thank-you to my twin, Stacey, who always inspires stories and good chatter, and is, forever, my little chop. Bigger thanks to Isabel Sterling and David Purse for always being there for me. You two are my shining stars.

To Patti, once again, for her honesty, truth, and banging sense of humor. To Ley Saulnier, Colleen Mulhall, Kimia Ahmadi, Natasha Ellis, and Jenn Faughnan, for always bringing smiles and support. I love you girls.

To Kat Ellis for the above and much more—kindred spirits happen seldom, but when they happen, they happen true. I will be your friend, yes, but also your biggest fan. You are the yin to my writerly yang.

To the bloggers who have supported *The Dead House* and my work as a whole, Luna's Little Library, Jim @yayeahyeah, and so many more, thank you endlessly. The UKYA community is amazing, and I am so glad to be a part of it.

Thank you to the authors whose works inspire me always: Juliet Marillier, Marcus Sedgwick, David Almond, Jacqueline Carey, Mark Z. Danielewski, Margaret Atwood, Courtney Summers, and more. Your words breed my own and ignite my imagination. THANK YOU.

To the authors I have met, who have welcomed me so

warmly: Michael Grant (who led me down this writerly path when I was a wee thing, along with his brilliant wife, Kath Applegate), Victoria Schwab (my little evil unicorn), Carrie Ryan (who holds all the world at her brilliant fingertips!), Renée Ahdieh (the most beautiful lady I have seen, maybe ever—and whose lipstick choices are brilliant), James Dashner (hands down the second-funniest, second-nicest man I have met—the first being my hubby, of course!), Shaun David Hutchinson (best guy ever to have a hug from! Plus awesome taste in tattoos), and all the other fabulous authors I met in Chicago.

To the Little, Brown and Orion teams: I love being in the family—you are all so brilliant and have supported me and my little books beyond anything I could have imagined.

To those who have read and loved *The Dead House*—thank you so much! You've made a timid little writer very proud and happy. I hope that you love Silla as much as you did Kaitlyn. I certainly do.

Thank you, always.

Dawn Kurtagich
February 2016
North Wales